THE
STARS
IN
APRIL

THE
STARS
IN
APRIL

PEGGY WIRGAU

illuminateYA
fiction

Illuminate YA Fiction is an imprint of LPCBooks
a division of Iron Stream Media
100 Missionary Ridge, Birmingham, AL 35242
ShopLPC.com

Cover design by Megan McCullough

Title: The Stars in April / Peggy Wirgau.
Description: First edition. / Alabama : IluminateYA, [2021] /
Summary: Based on a true story, a missionary's daughter, Ruth Becker,
must leave her home in India to save her baby brother and sail to America
aboard the RMS Titanic.
Identifiers: LCCN / ISBN /
Subjects: CYAC: Historical Fiction–Ruth Becker. / Historical Fiction–Titanic. /
Stars–Fiction. / Family problems–Fiction. / BISAC: Juvenile Fiction / Historical
Fiction / Family Issues / Country & Ethnic / Womens' Suffragette / Social Issues /
Disasters / Titanic /

Library of Congress Control Number: 2021931171

Kim Childress
Literary Agent: Kim Childress, Childress Ink LLC, Seeking Out and Sharing the
Best in Children's Literature

Product Developer: Kelly Anne White

ISBN-13: 978-1645263067
Ebook ISBN: 978-1-64526-308-1

PRAISE FOR *THE STARS IN APRIL*

A captivating, honest, lovingly told story of a young girl's courageous journey. If you only read one book about the *Titanic*, read this one!

~Francisco X. Stork
Award-winning author of *Marcelo in the Real World*,
The Memory of Light and *Illegal*

I feel as though I'm sitting in Ruth's apartment (in Santa Barbara) and she is sharing her life story with me. This could very easily be a non-fiction account… so very well written…one can hardly stop reading.

~Floyd Andrick
Titanic Historical Society member
Personal friend of Ruth Becker

Reading *The Stars in April* was a bit like listening to a beautiful piece of music, filled with crescendos, dips, and breathtaking, melodic moments. From the first lovely chapter to the last, this beautifully-written story draws you into Ruth's journey and compels you to keep reading, page after wonderful page. You will fall in love with the people she loves and experience both mischievous and tender moments alongside her. And then, as she faces the trauma of *Titanic's* fateful ending, you will link arms and heart with Ruth as the lessons she's learned throughout her journey give her the courage to face a new day with faith and determination. I loved every second of this amazing story. Highly recommended.

~Janice Thompson
Author of *Queen of the Waves*

Peggy Wirgau has eloquently captured the story of twelve-year-old Ruth's harrowing experience and tells it in an unforgettable way. Thanks to Peggy, Ruth Becker's memory continues to survive. I felt as if I were experiencing it [the story] along with Ruth.

~Yvonne Lehman
Author of *Hearts that Survive—A Novel of the Titanic*,
Why? Titanic Moments, and *Personal Titanic Moments*

A satisfying, well-written, fun-to-read book—though (of course) sad. The character of Ann, combined with Ruth's beautiful dream, offer a way to help younger children grappling with the *Titanic* disaster.

~**Julie Hedgepeth Williams**
Author of *A Rare Titanic Family*
Winner of the 2014 Ella Dickey Award for Books that Preserve History

I love how author Peggy Wirgau's goal is to share stories of lesser-known strong girls and women from history, like Ruth Becker, the feisty heroine in *The Stars in April*. Besides the beautiful, prose-like writing, this book offers a new take on the *Titanic* disaster through the eyes of a teen survivor who helped others—even after being separated from her family. Especially love the side-theme on suffragettes—so important. Highly recommend!

~**Karen Bokram**
Publisher, *Girls' Life Magazine*

Twelve-year-old Ruth struggles to live up to her mother's expectations as they leave their beloved missionary home in India and face the frightening unknown of a future in America in Peggy Wirgau's engrossing debut novel, *The Stars in April*. Putting the needs of others before her own desires and trusting that the life she has is enough, Ruth learns, is not for the faint of heart.

Based on the real life adventures of Ruth Becker, a second-class passenger aboard the ill-fated *Titanic*, *The Stars in April* is a colorful portrait of 1912 life and the tragedy aboard *Titanic* as seen through the eyes of a talented girl with hopes and dreams of her own. Wirgau's detailed historical research is spot-on in this compelling and heartwarming coming of age novel. I loved the exploration of stars and their constellations that connect Ruth with her absent father, and the informative guide to stargazing in the back of the book.

For lovers of *Titanic* stories, young history buffs, middle school and homeschool students *The Stars in April* is a must read.

~**Cathy Gohlke**
Award-winning author of *Promise Me This, William Henry is a Fine Name*, and *I Have Seen Him in the Watchfires*

The story is told with both fact and fiction marrying perfectly well together. The research was thorough and is brilliantly written. It is difficult to leave this novel out of your hands for long, as it is a constantly moving scene as we travel every step with Ruth ....

The Stars in April is a fitting title for this novel especially with so much star and constellation detail in Ruth's regular Sky Reports throughout the novel. The sky at night was such a constant in Ruth's travels, she felt it linked her to her "Papa" as they gazed on a shared sky from far differing locations.

A wonderful read throughout concluding in rescue of the Becker family. So sad there was such great loss of life in the freezing North Atlantic of April 1912.

~Vincent McMahon
Historian
Titanic Experience Cobh Ltd., Cobh, Ireland

Dedication

To Matt, Daniel, Lizzie, and Marco
And to Kim, who always believed

Acknowledgments

In April 2012, one hundred years after *Titanic* left on her maiden voyage, I learned of a twelve-year-old passenger aboard the ship by the name of Ruth Becker and what happened to her in Lifeboat 13. Her story begged to be told, and that was when the idea for *The Stars In April* began.

The journey of this idea to published novel has been much like Ruth's journey as she traveled all the way from India—a voyage filled with doubt, unexpected events, and rough, rolling seas. Yet, as Ruth discovers, I, too, have not been alone. Many have ridden the waves with me and have come alongside me in countless ways. Each of you play a part in this book.

I especially want to thank the following people:

The readers and fellow writers who saw the early versions and offered encouragement and suggestions, including Meline Scheidel, Mary Vee, Dawne and Elizabeth Webber, and members of American Christian Fiction Writers.

Faye Cramton, for your support, prayers, and for always letting me bend your ear, no matter where we traveled together. A shout out to Rose for tweaking lines with me at the PA Panera.

Brenda Price, Theresa Riviera, Sue Shea, and Lynn Turk for your tireless listening as I've ranted about the writing roller coaster and for keeping me stocked in peanut M&M's.

The entire Randazzo family for your encouragement and love—specifically Chris, Connie, and Maria, for hosting the Florida reading group and *Titanic* party.

Floyd Andrick—author, Ruth's friend, and Titanic Historical Society member—for graciously endorsing the novel and sharing more stories with me about Ruth, stories that have found their way into the book.

My critique partners, Deb Garland and Mary Hamilton, for your patient fine-tuning of many chapters, praying me through the years of waiting, and never losing faith in this story.

Tessa Hall, my editor at Illuminate, for believing in the story and working diligently to help me polish the manuscript to perfection, and for pulling all the pieces together to bring the book to fruition.

Illuminate's early manuscript readers for their enthusiasm and kind words.

A big thanks to the team at Iron Stream Media for your willingness to introduce Ruth to the world.

Kim Childress, whom I've known almost since the beginning and who served as my first editor, then as agent, and always my friend and sounding board. I can't begin to list all you've done on my behalf, with the highest level of integrity and love. We've prayed and cried and marveled at "coincidences," and you refused to let me quit. Thank you.

Kelly White, for your editing prowess and long hours of combing the manuscript for missing commas. So great that you have a *Titanic* birthday.

Jacque Alberta, for your thoughtful and insightful opinions throughout this entire process.

Kim's interns—Laurel Childress, Luca DeGraff, Alyshia Hull, Brayden Probst, Stephanie Stapert, and Stephanie Udell—for work on the manuscript and proposals, and special thanks to Laurel Childress for assistance with edits, cover art ideas, and creating the awesome map of Ruth's journey.

The talented team of Laura and Brennan Standel, for your fabulous work on the book trailer.

My husband, Matt; son, Daniel; daughter, Lizzie; and favorite son-in-law, Marco, for your unconditional love, encouragement, and never-ending willingness to listen. *And* for the plot ideas, chocolate, and champagne! I love you all.

And thanks be to God and my Savior, Jesus Christ, for bringing each of these dear ones into my life, and for this blessed opportunity to tell others the incredible story of Ruth Becker and her family.

Peggy Wirgau
March 2021

In Memory of

Ruth Becker and family
The passengers and crew of the RMS *Titanic*

The Journey of Ruth Becker

March-April 1912

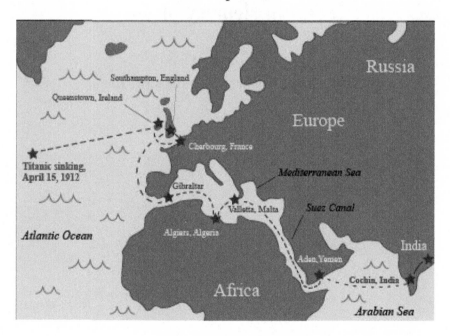

Illustration by Laurel Childress

CHAPTER ONE

Guntur, India
March 7, 1912
Morning

The train whistle gave one last piercing proclamation. *Ready or not, Ruth Becker, your journey begins now!*

Perched next to me on the edge of the middle seat, Marion laughed and covered her ears. I rubbed at the train's grimy window with my sleeve. Would Papa and Sajni still be waiting on the platform?

Wiping away tears, I spotted them outside just as they found my window. They waved, and Papa blew a kiss.

How can you let me go, Papa?

Mother scolded me from her seat on the aisle while Richard squirmed in her lap. "Ruth, you'll dirty your coat! Better take it off. It's much too hot."

Sajni, who stood beside Papa, tossed her thick black braid over a shoulder and wiped her own eyes, even as she smiled for me. As one of the oldest orphans under Papa's care, Sajni would share a rickshaw back to the orphanage with him.

I clutched the bag that held the quilt she'd given me in the station. For months, I'd watched her stitch together the work of art, not knowing I would soon be forced to leave India forever and Sajni would insist that the quilt go with me.

I should have been home, practicing my violin before school rather than sitting aboard a hot train bound for the coast. This was all Richard's fault. If he weren't sick, then we wouldn't be on our way to America. But how could I blame a two year old?

1

It was the Guntur doctors' fault for not knowing how to cure him, then talking Mother into dragging him to America. To her, that meant we all would go—except for Papa—and I had no choice.

The last of the passengers boarded the train. While I kept my gaze on Papa, I hoped the three seats that faced ours would remain empty. The last thing I wanted now was someone else bothering me.

We had no idea how long it would take for the mission board to find another director for the orphanage. I'd begged to stay with Papa, listing a dozen reasons, including the violin recital at the Spring Festival. How could he let me miss it, especially after my years of hard work? But all my begging and bargaining had done no good.

The attendant led a man and a boy down the aisle, stopping at our row. My heart sank. *There goes any chance of peace.*

Before our train pulled into the station, the pair had entertained the crowd on the platform by juggling mangoes. The boy now clambered over our knees with his dirty shoes, and I grabbed my string bag and bedroll off the seat that faced mine just before he plopped down.

"Pardon us, ladies," the man said, taking the middle seat next to the boy.

Mother squared her shoulders. She tucked her skirt in closer and glanced across the aisle at the last empty seats. Ten seconds later, an elderly couple claimed them. *Too late now.*

Freckles covered the boy's nose and cheeks, and he made a great deal of commotion for someone so skinny. I guessed him to be around twelve, like me. He stuffed his basket of mangoes, a cap, and a blanket under his seat.

The exit doors banged shut, trapping us in. With another blast from the whistle, we lurched forward. I held my breath, watching my world disappear.

This is it …

Mother and Marion leaned over me and waved to Papa and Sajni. Both of them walked alongside the train, calling out words I couldn't hear. Then our train picked up speed, they were gone, and I was left staring at the empty platform in the distance. When would

I see them again?

Mother was all business. "Let's settle in, girls. It's going to be a long, hot day."

The temperature soon rose in the full compartment. I pulled off my coat and rolled it into a ball, ignoring the boy's stares. Where was I supposed to put everything with my knees only inches from his?

Marion slapped her seat, making certain our brother knew she'd claimed it for eternity. "My seat, Richard."

The conductor came along the narrow aisle, punching tickets row by row. A little on the round side, he probably sat too much on trains. His handlebar mustache was overly waxed, and he reminded me of Mr. Liddle, my violin instructor. He took our tickets from Mother and punched them, letting the tiny paper dots fall to the floor.

Richard's cheeks were now red-hot. Mother removed his coat and unfastened his top shirt button. He let out a moan, a warning that a full-blown cry was not far behind.

While the conductor punched the jugglers' tickets, Mother turned to me. "Hand Richard's bag to me. It's too soon for his medicine, but perhaps he'll take some milk."

I found the sack stuffed with all the supplies my brother could possibly need for the two-day train ride to Cochin, give or take a few months.

Marion yanked off her coat. "Can I have my book, Sissy?"

"*May* I have my book."

Richard took his bottle as Mother fanned him, causing his wispy blond hair to wave in the breeze. She lowered her voice and glared at me. "You need to be patient."

How could she have said that today of all days, when all I wanted to do was turn around and go home?

The train charged through an open field. Marion occupied herself with an animal book, leaving me to stare out the window. Cotton and poppy fields blurred like an endless Impressionist painting.

I used my sleeve to wipe the perspiration from my forehead. The rhythmic swaying of the train car soothed me like a lullaby, and my eyelids soon grew heavy.

I led Sajni by the hand to the swings on the orphanage playground.
"Want to swing?"

She watched while I showed her what to do. "Nee peru yenty?"

What did she mean?

She pointed to me. "Nee peru yenty?"—she pointed to herself—
"Sajni." Then she pointed to me again. "Nee peru yenty?"

I understood. "I'm Ruth."

The train whistle blew, and I jerked awake.

"Who's Sajni?" the boy asked, in a thick British accent. "You said the name."

Mother and Richard dozed in the aisle seat, and Marion had fallen asleep with her head against Mother's arm. I scowled at the boy. "I was dreaming, that's all."

He opened his book as the juggler man snored beside him.

I found my journal and drew flowers in the margins as I recalled the dream. Instead of growing up with Sajni by my side, I was bound for the Indian coast against my will. But nobody cared.

I loosened my shirtwaist collar and pushed the sleeves past my elbows. India's heat had never bothered me—it was all I knew. But until now, I'd never ridden inside a jiggling steel cave stuffed with sweaty travelers.

Most of the passengers looked to be European. They read, fanned themselves, or dropped their heads back with eyes closed. The juggler man snored loud enough to drown out the train whistle, and—thank goodness—the boy kept his attention on his book. I didn't feel like socializing.

How were we supposed to have any privacy, let alone sleep in our seats that night as we all faced one another? I fiddled with the rusted window latch. With a couple of shoves, the window gave way a few inches. At least the hot air outside was more bearable than the stench of body odor.

"That's some breeze," the boy said.

His accent almost made English sound like a foreign language. He laid his open book in his lap. "What's your name?"

I knew few boys in Guntur and even fewer pushy ones. If I told him my name, maybe he'd leave me alone. "Ruth," I said, folding my arms and concentrating on the terraced rice fields that zipped by the window.

"I'm Michael Frank, and this is me dad." He jerked his thumb toward the snorer. "We're from Biggleswade. That's in England."

Mother cleared her throat, even though her eyes remained closed. I wasn't supposed to talk to strangers.

But what if I wanted to talk to someone? Who was I *supposed* to talk to? My little sister?

The train jolted to a stop at a small station, pulling my family out of slumber. A faded schedule hung at a crooked angle near the station door, next to a dirt-encrusted window. Did all trains and train stations have dirty windows?

I groaned and let my head hit the back of the seat. Here was my last chance to enjoy the Indian countryside, and I couldn't even see it clearly.

Several Englishmen stood on the platform in the hot sun, waiting to board. Their gray and brown suits blended with the dark building. How they could dress so formally in the heat of the day was a mystery to me. The loose tunics Indian men wore seemed much more practical.

A sour-faced man who carried a newspaper took the empty seat next to the snorer. He stuck an ivory-handled cane under his seat. Did he shoot the elephant himself? The train departed the station, and I turned away in disgust as he opened his paper.

Mother tilted her head back and closed her eyes. Richard fussed until he found a comfortable spot in the crook of her arm. Marion swung her legs up and down, nearly kicking the juggler, and turned a page in her book.

Michael Frank spoke again. "Goin' to the States?"

Marion jerked her head up and shouted, "We're goin' to America!"

"Are you from America?"

I glanced at Mother. She was already breathing deeply and had relaxed her grip on Richard. "No, I was born in India," I said. "But my parents are Americans."

"You're a Yank, then! I mean, American."

"Yes, I suppose." Why was he taking the conversation in that direction? I sure didn't feel American.

Next, he looked at Marion. "What's your name?"

She frowned and twisted her body toward me. Served him right.

"I'll tell you about us," he said, "then you can tell me about you."

Before I could respond, Michael Frank jumped right in. "Me and Dad, we're in a travelin' circus. We're acrobats—The Great Frank and Son." He flexed his wrist. "We spent a fortnight in Calcutta, and China before that."

Even if he could juggle, he didn't look like an acrobat to me. Not that I'd ever seen an acrobat, but he looked much too skinny, and certainly not old enough.

"Am I supposed to believe that?"

He raised his chin. "You can ask Dad when he wakes up."

If he was telling the truth, and two real-life circus performers were sitting across from us, I would definitely have to write to Sajni about it as soon as possible.

"All right," he said. "It's your turn."

Mother barely opened her eyes, then she shifted in her seat to ease Richard's head to her lap. Marion closed her book and lay back on Mother's arm. The elephant poacher had drifted off as well.

Mother wouldn't want me telling Michael Frank our business, but we had a long ride ahead. I inched closer. "My father is a missionary who runs an orphanage. I've lived in India all my life, but my brother is sick."

I cast a quick look at Richard. A drop of milk drooled from his mouth onto Mother's skirt. "We're going to the States because he needs a good doctor. We'll stay with my grandparents in Michigan until my father can join us."

Michael Frank's eyes widened. "You're not coming back?"

More of my home slipped past the window, and an ache filled my chest as I told my story. "No, we're not coming back."

His dad stirred for the first time since boarding the train. His eyes peeled halfway open, and he ran his hands over his face and through his wavy hair.

Michael elbowed him. "G'day, Dad."

The train zoomed into a tunnel, plunging us into sweltering darkness. Marion screamed and grabbed me. I dug my nails into the cloth seat cushion and counted the seconds. The tunnel amplified the *chooga-chooga-chooga* sound of the train. When we emerged from the inky blackness, I squinted to find the cord for the rattan window shade and lowered it to block the glaring sun. Dust from the shade floated to my lap.

Richard cried out, waking Mother.

She leaned toward me. "Take Marion to the washroom, please. I believe it's in the car behind us. Then we'll have our lunch."

"But how can I take her when the train's moving?"

"You never been on a train b'fore?" Michael's voice hinted at ridicule.

His dad spoke up. "Mind your manners, Son."

Mother blinked hard and pursed her lips like the knotted end of a rubber balloon. She stood, and with one quick move, she stepped into the aisle, motioning for Marion and me to go ... *now*.

Attempting to walk inside the moving train was no small feat. For a flash, I imagined I was a circus performer, balancing on a tightrope, until I stumbled into some seats. Marion lost her balance as well, and nearly tumbled across a woman's ample lap.

We found the tiny washroom one car back, and the two of us struggled to fit inside together. The sour smell made my eyes water. Marion held her nose.

But the soap was sudsy, and the jug of water meant for rinsing looked clear. Still, I wouldn't dare drink any water other than what we'd brought from home. I'd learned too much about the spread of cholera to take that chance.

We returned to find Michael's dad smiling and talking to Mother as she studied him over the rims of her spectacles. She had our lunches spread out on cloth napkins.

Marion clapped her hands. "Hurray! I'm so, so hungry." She squeezed between Mother's and Poacher Man's knees.

"Dad," Michael said. "This is Ruth."

"Very pleased to meet you, Ruth … uh, Miss Becker. We've just met your luvly mum and brother. I'm Robert Frank."

Mother gave an exaggerated inhale at the "luvly mum" remark.

My sister slurped water from her cup. "And this is Marion," I said.

"I'm four!"

At least she'd finally stopped holding up fingers to announce her age.

Mr. Frank pulled out a sack of food. He snagged a mango from the basket and peeled it with a pocketknife, sharing it with his son.

Michael noticed my stare. "When we're done juggling 'em, we eat 'em." He rubbed his short sleeve across his mango-stained face. "On the train to Guntur, we climbed the outside ladder and sat on top of the fruit car. Cooler up there, for sure."

Was that where their mangoes had come from? If only our train had a fruit car. I would've climbed out there too.

Our water was still fairly cold, thanks to its metal container. So were the cheese, our own sliced mangoes, and vegetable *dosas*. How was I going to manage in America without dosas?

Mother helped Richard eat a chunk of mango. "Tell me, Mr. Frank, what kind of work do you do besides juggle?"

He perched himself on the edge of his seat as though he'd been waiting for her question. "I work for a circus, Mrs. Becker. Michael and me are partners. We're an acrobatic duo—The Great Frank and Son."

Michael thrust out his chest. The expression on his face said, *See?*

"Oh my, circus acrobats?" Mother used her most polite voice. "How very … interesting. What about school, Michael?"

"I have a tutor sometimes, or Dad helps." He held up his book. "Plus, I read all the time and do sums on the road."

So their story was true, and I was riding a train with a skinny, freckly acrobat who juggled mangoes in his spare time. *Wait until*

Sajni hears this!

"Did you ever go to a real school?" I asked.

"When I was little, before I was big enough to work with Dad. B'fore me mum died." Michael looked down and bit into his sandwich.

"I'm sorry for your loss." Mother's tone was genuine.

"It's been four years," Mr. Frank said, "and we been on the road ever since."

I swallowed a juicy bite of mango. "Are you going home to England now?"

"Yeah, for eight weeks," Michael replied. "We're not on the doss. I mean, we aren't vagabonds. We're the only Brits in the circus, except for the elephant trainer and the tenters."

"While we're on our break," Mr. Frank said, "we'll work on our trapeze act. We practice with other blokes at a barn near our house."

"And tumblin', Dad." Michael turned to us. "I'm workin' on a triple back flip."

Mr. Frank nodded. "Then we'll pick up the circus in Germany and work a handful of cities in Europe."

I tried to picture this scrawny boy doing a triple back flip. Mother bit her lower lip, clearly having trouble understanding the Franks' strange life.

Poacher Man woke, coughed, and looked about. He adjusted his wrinkled gray suit and pulled out a handkerchief to mop his brow, then he mumbled something and felt around for his cane. He got to his feet and scanned the aisle in each direction. Mr. Frank pointed the man toward the washroom.

I glanced at the newspaper on the man's seat—*The Daily Telegraph*, an imported British paper. An advertisement for the RMS *Titanic* filled a quarter of its front page.

The day Mr. Liddle asked me to play in the festival, I felt as though all my dreams had come true. "Spring Song" by Mendelssohn was a difficult piece for violin, but Mr. Liddle had wiggled his index finger at me and said, "You are becoming quite an accomplished violinist, Miss Becker. One day, you may be ready for the Calcutta Orchestra."

That was before my parents had informed me about Richard, and Papa tried to make amends with tickets to America on White Star Line's newest luxury liner.

I stared at the ship in the newspaper advertisement. There would be no festival for me now. And no orchestra. Everything had changed.

March 7, 1912

Dear Sajni,

The jugglers at the station ended up sitting across from us on the train. They are actual circus acrobats! I must admit, if it weren't for The Great Frank and Son, I'm positive I'd jump off at the next station and walk back to Guntur.

Mother doesn't approve of them. Their clothes are worn, they both need haircuts, and they talk like their tongues are numb. But I'm getting used to their accent and I rather like it.

Michael is the boy's name. I didn't tell him much. When this journey ends, he'll just be another person I must leave behind. How I miss you and Papa already!

Selavu ... Your loving "sister,"

Ruth

CHAPTER TWO

Train to Cochin
March 7, 1912
Early evening

The train chugged into another station, and Poacher Man took his newspaper and left without a word, probably glad to escape Richard's constant fussing and Marion's squirming.

Mother handed Richard to me so she could take a washroom break. He protested, so I bounced him on my lap. Marion stood on her seat and grinned at the leathery-looking man in a turban who sat behind us.

"Sit down," I told her. "You know better."

Marion twisted around and fell against the seat back. "When we gonna get to Coochin?"

"It's Cochin. Tomorrow." *If I don't jump off or throw you out.*

I had to stop thinking that way—Marion wasn't the one who was responsible for ruining my life. When I had a bad thought at home, I would hum something, so I began to hum scales as I bounced Richard. *Do, Re, Mi, Fa, Sol, La* ... Why didn't Mother hurry?

Richard finally relaxed and grinned at me. His hair stuck out in every direction, the way mine did when it wasn't tied back in a ribbon. Michael and his dad played chess, balancing the board on the tops of their legs. Whenever it was Michael's turn, he flexed his right wrist. Maybe it helped him think.

Marion rocked left and right and bumped Richard's leg. He pushed her away and said, "No, Mimi." Marion's face lit up and she did it again.

Before I intervened, Mr. Frank spoke. "She can sit next to me, if she likes." He patted the empty seat beside him. "For a change of scenery."

Marion didn't wait for my permission. She scrambled over, smiling at the couple across the aisle. Mr. Frank winked at me before resuming his game. I immediately had a deep liking for this lanky man in worn, baggy trousers.

The train slowed to a crawl and stopped. Dusk settled on the fields, and I didn't see a station. "Why are we stopping?" I asked Michael.

He peered out the window along the side of the train. "We're in traffic. Three cows grazin' by the tracks."

Oh, to be a cow in India, seen as sacred. Cows never had to ride in stinky trains with crabby siblings.

Mother returned as the train started again. She scowled at Marion. "What are you doing in that seat? Come back over here this instant."

Michael's dad looked up. "It's hard for little ones to stay put for so long."

Mother glanced around, as if looking for an escape. Then she reached for Richard. "I'll give him his medicine. Then you'll have to come back to your seat, young lady."

"Checkmate." Michael knocked his dad's white king off the board with his black knight.

"Blimey!" Mr. Frank chuckled and dropped the chess pieces into a cloth sack. "Well, night's comin'. We better take our turns in the loo."

While they were gone, I yanked our bedrolls from underneath our seats. I unrolled mine first, spreading the thinner blanket over the worn train seat. Sajni's quilt was much too warm to use yet.

When they returned, Michael asked, "Goin' to nod off?"

"I don't know. I've never done this before."

"It's not so bad," he replied. "I pretend I'm on a ship, bound for undiscovered lands."

That was the last thing I wanted to pretend. I'd be doing it for real soon enough.

"Say," Michael went on, "are you sailin' from Cochin to England?"

Mother unwrapped Marion's bedroll. "Yes, we are."

"Any chance you'll be on the *City of Benares* day after tomorrow?"

"Yes." Mother's expression tightened. "That's our ship."

He beamed. "Ours too! There's a stroke o' luck now, isn't it?"

I didn't want to encourage him, but I had a hard time hiding a smile. *This could be interesting.* I'd assumed we'd be going our separate ways in Cochin. But with the Franks on our ship, I would know someone besides my family, and acrobats at that—even if Michael peppered me with questions during the entire voyage.

I rolled Sajni's quilt for a pillow and propped it against the hard window ledge. The heat inside the train hung overhead like a stinky, damp rag, and nothing we did made Richard happy for more than thirty seconds.

I could tell Mr. Frank's nerves were being plucked when he breathed a heavy sigh. "Want me to have a go at calmin' him down, Mrs. Becker?"

Mother refused. She wouldn't dream of handing her baby to anyone, least of all an acrobat. She held Richard in her lap, got his mouth open with one hand, and spooned in his medicine with the other. He coughed and sputtered a bit, but the job was done until the next day, same time.

Soon, a hush settled over everyone in the compartment for the night, and Mr. Frank began to snore. Marion, asleep at last, buried her head against my side. She then proceeded to shove her foot into Richard's belly, and he let loose a cry that would scare a herd of elephants. Mother jiggled him, kissed him, and shushed him. But nothing helped.

Mr. Frank continued to snore, undisturbed. Michael switched positions and lowered his cap over his face.

"Can't you do something?" I whispered to Mother.

She stood and bounced Richard in her arms, then she stepped into the aisle and headed toward the back of the car, Richard's cries trailing behind her and filling the compartment. *Wonderful.* Now everybody would wake up, thanks to my brother.

When they returned, she and Richard had both calmed down, to my surprise. As we chugged and clanged across India, I tried to allow the train noises to drown out thoughts of home, without success.

How many miles ago did Papa and I say good-bye?

He'd dried my tears with his handkerchief at the station and he gave it to me to keep. I drew it from my pocket now and held it to my face, breathing in his scent, then ran my finger across the embroidered initials, A.O.B. Was Papa asleep, or was he thinking about us?

It's a lonely feeling to be the only person awake in a full train. I should have been home, sound asleep in my quiet room, stretched out in my own non-jiggling bed.

I rolled up the shade and peered into the darkness. Sloping hills, studded with jagged rocks, now lay under the soft light cast by the high full moon. A few faint stars dotted the sky.

The train rounded a sharp curve, and a high-pitched rattle came from underneath the floor, sounding like a million marbles shaken in a jar. Outside the window, the land had disappeared. With my forehead pressed against the warm glass, all I could see was something glistening far below in the moonlight.

As the wavy outline of a river came into focus, every muscle in my body went rigid. The train was crossing a bridge—a very high and narrow bridge. My heart pounded. Why didn't Papa mention anything about towering bridges when I'd asked him what to expect?

I listened hard and held my breath, counting off the seconds. *One one-thousand, two one-thousand …* Were there crocodiles in this part of India?

It took seven painful seconds for the train to reach solid ground. I flopped back in my seat and looked again at the dark sky and handful of stars outside the train window. Was Papa on the veranda, seeing the same?

Some of my favorite times with Papa occurred at night when we'd studied the sky together. When I was small, he taught me how to find the constellations. And as I got older, we followed the stars and the planets, tracking their movements through the year. Eventually we began our Sky Report, recording our findings in a notebook.

Knowing Papa would continue the Sky Report, I felt connected to him, even though I was still mad at him. He'd told me we would see the same stars even though I was far from home, because I would still be in the northern latitudes, and that I might even see them more clearly than in Guntur, once we were aboard *City of Benares* and then on *Titanic*. When he would eventually come to us in Michigan, we could then compare our notes.

How long will it be, Papa?

~

Train to Cochin

March 7, 1912

Middle of the night

Sky Report: The few visible stars remain constant, ordered and beautiful, like music. Along with having to cross the high bridge, what else didn't Papa tell me about our journey?

This reminds me a little of Corvus, the Crow constellation, who was placed in the sky for lying to Apollos, as a warning to others who would dare lie. It's funny, but Corvus had lied to Apollos about why he was delayed in returning from his task, though of course Apollos knew the truth all along.

CHAPTER THREE

Train to Cochin
March 8, 1912
Early morning

"Sissy, wake-up time." Marion's face was three inches from mine, her curls dangling against my cheeks. I twisted away, remembering where I was and why, and buried my face in Sajni's quilt.

Marion jiggled my leg. "We're all awake."

As if on cue, the train whistle blasted, an industrial-grade rooster crowing at the break of day. I rubbed my eyes and blinked away the last shreds of sleep. Sunlight peeked through the grime of the window as butter-yellow fields swept past. Papa's wrinkled handkerchief lay in my lap. I stuffed it back into the pocket of my bunched-up coat.

A sweet scent made its way through the haze of waking up. I glanced over at Mr. Frank and Michael, who were sharing a large stuffed dosa pancake. My mouth watered.

Mother had already brushed and pinned her hair. "Good morning, Ruth. How did you sleep?"

I groaned, peeling damp hair off my face.

"Can you take me, Sissy?" Marion asked.

Michael Frank grinned at me between bites of his breakfast, and warmth flushed my cheeks.

It took a minute for me to straighten my chair-sculpted body. Marion and I managed to tolerate the jerking motions of the train as we made our way to the smelly washroom. Washing my face and brushing my teeth and hair made me feel a little better, even though the temperature in the train hadn't changed.

Back in our seats, I tucked away my tooth powder and brush. Mother had our breakfast ready. She handed a peach to me so I could share it with Marion, and we each received a roll filled with smoked pork.

My mouth was now a desert at high noon. "May I have a drink?"

Mother poked around inside the food sack. "We have three containers of water. That needs to last." She handed one to me.

"We have plenty, if you need more," Mr. Frank said.

"Thank you," Mother said. "I'm sure we'll manage if we're careful."

Michael finished eating and pulled his book from the crack between his seat and the window.

Mother tore a piece of bread from her sandwich and gave it to Richard. "What book are you reading, Michael?"

He held up *South Sea Tales* by Jack London.

"Didn't he write *The Call of the Wild*?" I asked. "I had to read that in school."

"Yeah, I read it too. This one's about island life and ships."

Mr. Frank stored their metal food container below his seat. "Michael likes anything to do with ships. Whenever we sail, he's merry as a grig."

"Is that so?" Mother said. "Then you must be looking forward to boarding *City of Benares*."

Michael bobbed his head. "Best way to see the world."

"I wanna see the City of Berries," Marion said.

"We read 'bout a new ship named *Titanic* that's goin' to start runs from Southampton to the States," Mr. Frank said. "Unsinkable they say, and grand as can be." He held his hands out as if framing a large picture.

"That's the ship we're taking to America," I said.

Both father and son's eyebrows shot up. "You lucky buggers!" Michael said. "I'd give anything to see that ship."

Mother gave a loud sigh and pulled her fan from her bag. She snapped it open and fanned her face with flicks of her wrist.

Mr. Frank patted Michael's knee. "What Michael means to say is that you're very lucky people—lucky indeed."

"Yes, well ..." Mother let her head sag against the seat back. "Ruth, pass me the water."

"I thought you said we had to save it."

She closed her eyes and fanned herself faster. "Water, please."

⁓

Only two weeks ago, the solution had seemed simple. As we all ate dinner on our veranda underneath the jasmine tree, I'd asked Papa to let me stay with him until Mother had returned from America with Richard and Marion.

"No, Ruth dear," he'd said. "We think God is telling us it's time to go home for good."

"But this is home!" As many times as I'd imagined traveling to foreign lands, I'd never considered moving to one.

Papa rested a hand on my shoulder. "Think of it as one of the Rudyard Kipling adventures. Only this time, it'll be real."

I shrugged his hand away. "It won't be an adventure, not without you! And why can't I stay?"

"Your mother needs your help." His voice was firm. "You must think of your brother. His needs take priority. And we cannot wait until after the festival." Then he turned to Mother. "I have a surprise, Nellie. I've purchased second-class tickets for all of you to New York on a new vessel. It's said to be the largest, most beautiful passenger ship in the entire world."

Were we supposed to jump to our feet and give him a hug? I almost ran to my room.

Marion kicked the underside of the table. "What's a passer ship?"

"A new ship?" Mother gripped the edge of the table.

"Everyone is talking about it." Papa grinned and focused on me. "What an opportunity, Ruth. Think of it!"

Mother lifted Richard's cup with a shaking hand. "Allen, do you mean to tell me we'll be on its maiden voyage?"

"It'll be a wonderful experience for the children, my dear. Aren't you delighted?"

She slammed the cup down, drops of milk splashing onto the tablecloth. "I should say not! I don't like the idea of being on a new ship." A warm breeze swept across the veranda, sending dozens of jasmine petals fluttering to the table.

I didn't want to ask my next question, as if I'd resigned myself to everything, because I hadn't. But I asked anyway. "What's the name of the ship?"

Papa reached into his vest pocket and pulled out several white cards. "Here are the tickets. You'll be sailing the tenth of April from Southampton, England, aboard the RMS *Titanic*."

~

Our train approached a large rice farm, where workers in the paddies stood to watch it pass. A small shrine, with a three-foot stone arch centered over a statue of Buddha, stood at the outskirts of the farm. Several chunks of stone had broken away from the arch, and weeds grew between the cracks.

Michael closed his book. "Finished! Want to have a walk, Ruth?"

"I wanna walk too." My sister stuck her lower lip out, making sure I noticed.

"Come on, then," Michael said.

Mother's eyes told me she didn't want us to go, but she was probably too tired to protest. "Take Marion's hand, and do be careful."

Michael led us toward the front of the train. A metal spittoon rested against the entrance where we'd boarded the day before, dried wads of chewing tobacco clinging along its edge. Thank goodness no one chewed in our car—Mother would've been mortified.

We passed through a doorway and into the next car full of passengers. Michael stopped short, and I nearly bumped into him.

Ahead of us, a woman screamed. A large man in the aisle shoved another man against the seats. "Give it back, thief!"

The man in his clutches shook his head, eyes bulging. "I—I don't know what you're talking about!"

"Oh, I think ya do." The larger man held his fist under the man's chin. "Give it back, or I'll give you somethin'!"

Passengers gasped. The woman cried, "Hubert, no! Stop!"

Michael pushed us back the way we came. "Let's find the conductor."

I tugged Marion's hand as we jostled through the doorway and past our seats. Mother was busy with Richard, and Mr. Frank was absent.

"Mama!" Marion shouted.

"Mercy's sake," Mother called after us. "What is the rush?"

In the car behind ours, Mr. Frank exited the washroom, blocking our path. He held up his hands. "Whoa! Where's the fire?"

Michael pointed toward the front of the train. "A bloke's mad as hops. It's a robbery or somethin'."

Passengers nearby turned to stare as Mr. Frank headed toward the front car.

Michael tried to stop him. "Dad, no! We gotta find the conductor."

Mr. Frank continued to stride forward. "Find him and send him up."

I held tight to Marion's hand and followed Michael to the next car. What would Mother think when Mr. Frank ran past her?

The conductor approached us from the back. "Is something the matter?"

Michael pulled him by the arm. "There's trouble in the front car, and me dad's there! You have to hurry!"

The conductor took charge. "Get back to your seats, all of you." He pushed us out of his way and hurried forward toward the danger. Michael broke into a slow run to keep up with him. We followed, but I did what the conductor ordered and returned to our seats. Marion pulled at my sleeve. "What happened, Sissy?"

"That is exactly what I would like to know." Mother's nostrils flared as she pulled us both in from the aisle.

I took a deep breath, hoping to sound casual. "There was a little commotion, and Mr. Frank went to help."

Mother wasn't satisfied. "Why did the conductor run after him? And Michael?"

I shrugged. "I—I'm not sure."

Several minutes later, Michael returned, his head lowered. He was followed by Mr. Frank who held a white cloth against his right eye. They slid into their seats as Mother scooped Richard to her lap from the vacant seat across from hers.

"Had a bit of a run-in, Mrs. Becker." Mr. Frank eased the cloth from his eye, revealing an ugly cut over a purple bulge.

Mother and I gasped, and Marion pushed her face into my arm to cover her eyes.

"The wife of the bloke that hit me lost a ring," Mr. Frank said, "and she suspected the chap next to them took it. When I showed up, her husband had already punched him in the jaw. I tried breaking them up, but I got a present instead. The man's off his onion, I'd say."

"Turns out the man never took the ring," Michael said. "The conductor found it on the floor. Now her husband is tied up and headin' for the Cochin jail."

Mother flinched. "You must see a doctor as soon as possible."

The elderly man across the aisle asked if Mr. Frank was all right. He assured him and the other silent observers that he was fine. When Michael went with him to the washroom to rinse out the cloth for his eye, Mother turned to me with a look of resolve. "Ruth," she said. "I want you to stay away from them."

"But it wasn't Mr. Frank's fault. Didn't you hear—"

She waved off my words. "I knew they'd be trouble the moment I saw them."

Arguing was useless. I was tired, sore, hungry, and I needed clean water and a good scrub. I leaned against the window and pretended to sleep, even when I heard Mr. Frank and Michael return.

I tried to think of a song to fit my mood. The old hymn "Farther Along" came to mind. Papa made fun of it because it was so sad, but the lyrics matched perfectly with how I felt. I closed my eyes and hummed the melody. *Tempted and tried, we're oft made to wonder, why it should be thus all the day long ...*

I desperately missed Papa—and Sajni. They would both have liked the Franks. I wiped a tear away before anyone could notice.

~

On the day I walked to the orphanage to tell Sajni I had to move halfway across the world, the pungent scent of curry had worked its way to the porch from the kitchen, where the bossy *bobajee* had cooked all day in the thick heat. The screen door stuck, as always. I entered the dark foyer, careful not to let the door slam behind me.

I went to Papa's office first. He rolled his worn leather chair away from the cluttered desk and rose to hug me. "How was school?" he asked.

I wouldn't hug him yet. I turned away and dropped my books in the chair that faced his desk. The only framed photograph on the wall caught my eye. All the Guntur missionary families had stood outside the hospital for the photographer, and Mother frowned at the camera, strands of hair escaping her tight bun.

"Mother wants to leave. She can't wait."

Papa stood beside me, facing the photograph. "She doesn't want us separated, and she isn't looking forward to the trip. But she's never grown used to India's heat."

"Or the reptiles," I said.

He raised an eyebrow. "Remember the time the snake charmer came to the door and said we had a python on our roof and offered to coax it down?"

"You paid him, and he took care of it, didn't he?" I couldn't help smiling at the memory.

"Except that python had a way of showing up on the roof every day for a while."

"And you felt sorry for the man and kept paying him to get it down. Mother was furious."

The front door to the orphanage opened and slammed shut, followed by boys laughing and running. Papa rubbed the back of his neck. "None of us want this, Ruth. But God will take care of us.

Meanwhile, try to have compassion for the needs of others."

Wasn't I doing that already?

I checked the wall clock. "I came to tell Sajni."

~⌒~

I snapped back to the present, every muscle in my body stiff, and stretched my arms, hands, and fingers. I never thought I'd be anxious for Cochin, but anyplace had to be better than this train.

My family was calm and quiet for a change. Michael and Mr. Frank were engrossed in another game of chess. I adjusted Sajni's quilt beneath my head, wanting to sleep away the rest of the horrid train ride, but strains of that day replayed in my mind.

~⌒~

Through the window of the sewing room door, I watched Sajni as she helped one of the younger girls with a sewing project.

When I entered, her face brightened. "Ruth! I did not know you were coming today." She hurried toward me in her long skirt and full white apron. Despite our two-year age difference, her small frame made her look no older than twelve.

Most of the girls called my name and held up quilt squares for me to admire. "Have you finished your quilt?" I asked Sajni, glad to have something to talk about besides the real reason I came.

"Almost." She led me to another table and unfolded a large silk rectangle. Each square reflected something symbolic to India, portrayed in bright colors against a black, silk background. I ran my fingers over the neatly stitched designs—a cobra, lotus flower, elephant, a Buddhist temple, a dancer, and the flag of British India. Then "our" square—silhouettes of Sajni and me. The last three squares weren't finished yet.

But my favorite part was the background, with its hundreds— *thousands!*—of tiny, white stars that Sajni had embroidered by hand. She waved her hand over the bare areas. "I am still thinking about these. You will stay for tea?"

If only I could pretend I came for tea. "No, but can we talk for a minute?"

She led me to a small storage closet. I examined the bare lightbulb mounted in the ceiling, the high shelves with labeled boxes, and the tile floor. I shifted from one foot to the other, but the explanation for my visit remained locked in my throat.

"Ruth, what is wrong?"

I swallowed hard. "My mother is taking us to America because of Richard. We're going to see doctors there." I swallowed again. "And we aren't coming back." There—it was said. A chill bolted through me.

Sajni stepped back against a shelf, rubbing her arms. She spoke a shade above a whisper. "And Reverend Becker?"

"He's staying for now, until he's replaced. I'm sorry."

Her voice was halting. "Everyone I love leaves me. First my parents, then my brother, and now ..." With a hand over her mouth, she ran from the storage closet just as the bell rang to announce tea.

I crossed the room, and Sajni turned toward me, eyes downcast. "I will pray for you and your family, Ruth." She brushed past me, grabbed her quilt from the table, and hurried down the main hall.

CHAPTER FOUR

Cochin, India
March 8, 1912
Evening

"Cochin! Cochin Station." The conductor paced down the aisle as our train rolled to a stop. "All passengers prepare to leave the train."

"Hurray!" Marion said. "We're in Coochin!"

The conductor paused at our seats. "How's the eye, sir?"

"Not bad." Mr. Frank kept it covered with the cloth. "How's the other bloke?"

"He had quite a cut on his chin. I'm sending him over to Dr. Barkley across the way. You better go as well."

Michael answered for his dad. "Yeah, we will."

In the fading light outside the window, I scanned the deep green hills at this edge of India. Where was the Arabian Sea?

Two families stood on the platform, searching faces in the train windows. Someone's journey had ended, and mine had only begun.

Mother fanned Richard who was asleep in her lap. "I don't know when I've ever felt so drained."

My legs were day-old mush, my back a warped board. I hung my coat through the handles of my bag, checking that Papa's handkerchief was deep in the pocket. I gathered my quilt and our belongings as my stomach growled.

Mother hoisted Richard over her shoulder, and we worked our way into the crowded aisle. I handed Marion a bedroll to carry, and she took it with only minor complaining. We shuffled toward the doorway where the conductor helped each of us down to the platform.

An unfamiliar scent entwined its way through the breeze. Was it the sea? And something else, like cinnamon. The early-evening sky was clear, yet it was too soon to see any stars.

Mother buttoned her jacket with a free hand. "We must see that our trunks are unloaded and sent to the shipping docks."

Mr. Frank and Michael followed us out of the train. "The conductor told us to wait here," Mr. Frank said. "All I want most is a bowl o' soup and a kip."

The conductor approached. "I'll take care of your trunks, Mrs. Becker." He held up a pen and scrap of paper. "How many do y' have?"

"Two," I answered for Mother. "A brown one and a hideous black one."

Her look told me my remark was unappreciated. "They're both tagged with our name."

"Don't forget about the brown one," I said.

Mother shifted a fidgeting Richard onto her opposite hip. "Please mark the brown trunk as the one we need in the cabin, and the black one to be stored aboard."

The conductor made a note, and he and the Franks walked toward the station doors. Michael turned and waved. I waved back, not caring what Mother thought.

We found the boarding house that Papa had told us about, as well as a restaurant at the end of the platform next to a twisted old banyan tree. A weather-beaten sign swung above the restaurant door.

"E-A-T." Marion spelled out the letters. "What's it say, Sissy?"

"Eat," I told her. Nothing like a direct approach.

As soon as we were seated inside, Mother ordered three bowls of chicken soup with rice and three cups of steamy, spicy-sweet chai. The waiter brought water so Mother could mix it with Richard's medicine.

Mother sipped her chai and removed the spectacles to rub her eyes. "I don't care what the boarding house is like, as long as there's a real bed."

"Will it jiggle like the train?" Marion asked. "I like jigglin.'"

"It better not," I answered.

The clear sky had darkened by the time we walked toward the boarding house. Diamond-white Venus stood above the horizon, exactly where Papa and I had found it so many evenings.

A middle-aged British couple ran the six-bedroom boarding house. Mrs. Potter led us to a small room in the back hall and left us an oil lamp. At home in Guntur, we had electricity that worked most of the time, so I wasn't accustomed to the dimmer light. But I was too tired to care.

The nearby washroom was a refreshing surprise—clean and cool, with fluffy white towels and a new bar of soap. Mother rinsed our underthings so they'd be fresh for the next day, and she laid them on the sill of an open window.

The four of us were soon ready to climb into the one bed that was meant for two people. I listened as the clock in the hall chimed eleven times. Within minutes, everyone was asleep—all except me.

I slipped out of bed and adjusted the lamplight to find my journal.

Cochin, India
March 8, 1912

Sky Report: Very clear, stars appearing early, Venus low in the west. Papa taught me that, long ago, many people thought Venus was actually two stars that they called the "morning star" or "evening star," because its orbit made it appear at different times. It's the brightest object in the sky, after the sun and moon. Ancient civilizations called Venus the Queen of the Sky.

But not even the brilliant appearance of the Queen can erase the ache in my heart for home, and the dread of all that lay ahead.

CHAPTER FIVE

Cochin, India
March 9, 1912
6:00 a.m.

We joined other passengers from our train at a long table in the boarding house for a hearty breakfast of eggs, potatoes, bacon, and thick buttered toast. I didn't tell Mother, but I was disappointed the Franks weren't among the guests. Maybe they'd found a kip, whatever that was, someplace else.

From our horse-drawn taxi to the harbor, I hung out the left side for a better view, shielding my eyes from the blinding rays. Then, just beyond a grove of almond trees, the Arabian Sea stretched to the horizon, shimmering like a polished turquoise floor.

Four steamships were anchored near the docks, all flying the Union Jack of Great Britain. Our taxi driver pointed out the SS *City of Benares*, our home for the next four weeks. With its tall masts and single large funnel, it dwarfed the small fishing boats on the rivers and channels near Guntur.

My knees shook, partly at the sight of the enormous ship, but mostly at the terrifying thought of crossing the sea and leaving India.

I turned to Mother. "Did you and Papa sail to India on a ship that big?"

"Yes, but I've heard they've made vast improvements since then. Many more people now travel back and forth between England and India." She tightened Richard's shoelaces and squinted at the ship. "I do hope it's comfortable."

I didn't have the slightest idea what *comfortable* meant aboard a ship. And I wished I didn't have to find out.

Overhead, dozens of seagulls called out to one another. The sun felt good on my face as I sniffed the air, thick with the smell of fish and wet wood.

The driver brought our open carriage to a stop. I held Richard in one arm, my coat and quilt in the other, and helped Marion step down. Mother paid the driver and carried our bags. The wind whipped our skirts as we trekked down the wide stone path toward the docks.

Marion pointed to a sign. "What's 'PO' mean?"

Mother read from the tickets in her hand. "It stands for Peninsular and Oriental Steam Navigation Company," she said. "That's a mouthful. No wonder it's called 'P&O' for short."

The dazzling sea reached to the ends of the earth. By nightfall, I would be floating in the middle of that massive body of water. My throat tightened like the knots on my string bag.

As we walked, my brother rubbed his open mouth on my shirtwaist and muttered a string of unintelligible words.

"Richard's drooling, Mother."

"Try not to complain, Ruth. It's unladylike." She stopped to get a better grip on our bags. "I was just thinking of when we went to the Bay of Bengal for your birthday."

I recalled the scratchy sand between my toes. It was my favorite birthday, especially because Papa had allowed Sajni to come too. "I haven't seen this much water since then. It looks ... deep."

Marion kicked a stone. "When do we get on the boat, Sissy?"

"As soon as we get there, probably. And it's a *ship*—too big to be a boat."

A man and woman up ahead pushed a little girl in a pram. "We need one of those," I said.

Mother dropped one of our bags. "Please don't point." She ran a handkerchief across her forehead. "It's too early to be so hot."

Don't complain, it's unladylike. I readjusted my hold on Richard. "Let's teach him to walk on the ship," I said.

"Your brother is sick." Mother's jaw was set. "He'll walk when he's ready."

With every ounce of determination I could drag from my heart, I took another step toward the *City of Benares*. I hummed a bit of "On the Road to Mandalay." The song spoke of palm trees, temple bells, and calling a British soldier back to India.

Come you back to Mandalay where the old flotilla lay, Can't ya hear their paddles chunkin' from Rangoon to Mandalay?

For my last minutes on Indian soil, it seemed fitting.

A crewman greeted us as we crossed the rickety gangplank. He wore black trousers, a white jacket, and a white cap with the P&O symbol on the front. "Tickets and names, please."

Mother presented our tickets. "Mrs. Allen Becker and children."

The man examined our tickets and made a check on his clipboard. He turned to another crewman wearing all black except for a white sailor's cap. "Show them to D-29."

Mother took Richard, and I rubbed some life back into my arms. The crewman took our bags and beckoned us to follow him across the deck. "Your cabin's down these stairs. You'll 'ave your luggage straightaway."

His accent reminded me of the Franks. Where were they, anyway?

We dodged chattering passengers and busy crew members. "Out of curiosity," Mother said, "how many passengers will be on this voyage?"

"We can hold four hundred," the crewman replied, "and I was told we're fully loaded."

"Do you happen to know if any Americans are on board?"

"Not to my knowledge, ma'am. Most are Brits comin' back from Bombay and other Indian cities."

A group of young women stood at the railing, laughing. They wore slim skirts well off the floor, airy-looking shirtwaists with sleeves that stopped at the elbows, and small straw hats. *Are these new styles?*

I felt like burning the old dress I wore, complete with its wrinkles and sweat from the train ride. Mother's pinched mouth showed her disapproval.

Marion smiled up at me. "This'll be fun, Sissy. Where do we eat?"

My sister, the optimist. "We'll find out later," I said.

We descended two sets of stairs and walked along a narrow passageway that was lit by bare electric bulbs every eight feet. The crewman pointed out the door to the washroom. "We call it the WC. Short for water closet." He unlocked the door to D-29.

"Here y' go, ma'am." He turned on a light inside and handed Mother the key. "Your steward should be 'round. If your trunk isn't here by the time we sail, let him know."

A lamp in the ceiling provided the only light in the cabin. One full-size bed, one smaller one, and a crib took up nearly all the space, except for a narrow dresser and washstand. A patterned rug partly covered the scuffed wood floor.

How would I survive in this cramped space? I dropped the bags and laid my coat and quilt on the bed. "This is so small and stuffy. And our trunk isn't even here yet."

"Is this one mine?" Marion patted the white coverlet on the smaller bed.

Mother set Richard in the crib and planted her hands on her hips. "Hmm. You and Ruth should take the bigger bed. I'll take the small one, and Richard will have the crib."

We spent a few minutes settling in and investigating the WC. Mother said she needed a rest, but I'd had enough of the tiny room and I wanted to be on deck for my departure from India.

Mother consented, but only if I would take my sister and brother. "Perhaps someone will bring our trunk while you're gone. Marion, don't let go of Ruth's hand."

In two minutes, we were back on deck, and I took a deep breath of the fresh air. It didn't take long to figure out there were two passenger classes—first class, and everybody else, like us.

First-class cabins took up the main deck where we'd boarded and part of the next deck down. Only first-class passengers could use the back half of the main deck. They also had their own dining room, one level down from the main deck. Second-class dining was next door.

A loud horn blast made us all jump. Richard covered his ears. A white-jacketed crewman spoke into a megaphone. "All ashore that's going ashore!"

I want to go ashore …

I led Marion to the railing and found a spot between two lifeboats that hung off the sides. I let Richard down so he could stand at the railing and hold onto the lowest rung, but I wrapped my arm around him to keep him steady.

A handful of visitors scurried across the gangplank and back onto the dock. Four crewmen pulled the plank away from the dock and onto the ship. Other crew members untied huge ropes from the dock, and the floor vibrated as the ship's steam engines roared to life.

Tears blurred my vision. *It's time.*

Marion hopped up and down, her hands on the railing. "Hurray! Here we go, Sissy! Wave bye-bye, Richard!"

I felt a tap on my right shoulder and whirled around.

Michael squinted in the sunlight. "Been lookin' for you."

I lifted Richard and glanced behind Michael. "Where's your dad?"

"He's playin' cards. The doc stitched his eye up last night. Said he'll have a scar, but no worries. He says we can sit with your family at supper."

What would Mother say? "I'll need to check." It was worth a try, anyway.

Loud grinding and swishing from the engines made the deck shake as the *City of Benares* began a slow turn toward the open sea. The other ships, the docks, and the people who watched from shore began to slip away.

I'm going, Papa …

Marion tugged on my arm. "I have to go, Sissy."

I turned to Michael. "I better take them down."

"See y' later, then."

With the ship now moving at a good clip, it wasn't as easy to cross the deck, especially while holding a toddler. Walking inside the train had been simpler. I swayed and nearly lost my balance. No doubt, the sure-footed acrobat behind me saw the whole thing.

Mother was up when we arrived back at D-29. "Our trunk is

here," she said. "Our cabin steward's name is Jack. He and another young man brought it just after you left." She gestured toward her bed. "And Jack returned with a tray of sandwiches."

I exhaled in relief at the sight of the open brown trunk wedged between the two beds. My violin case and some of my clothes lay on the bed I would share with Marion. I ran my hand across the case. "Thank goodness it's still in one piece."

Mother laid a small stack of Richard's clothes in the top dresser drawer. "You had all your clothes wrapped around it. I'm afraid most of them are quite wrinkled."

I dropped Richard in his crib and examined the sandwiches. "I'll manage. I can't wait to change into something clean."

My green dress was still in the trunk. I had it secured around my collection of miniature wooden birds that Papa had brought me from his trips to Bombay. The lumps in the dress told me the birds were still safe. No little hands were allowed to touch them.

Marion found her cloth doll in the trunk and climbed onto the bed.

"Shoes off, young lady," Mother said. "Then you and your brother should eat and take a rest."

"I would like to go back on deck, if that's all right," I said. "I'll put everything away later. This is the last I'll ever see of India."

Mother kept her back turned toward us as she unpacked. "That's fine, but I've seen all I want of India."

I flinched at her off-hand remark. Richard sat in the corner of his crib, holding his blanket, taking in the new surroundings but fighting to keep his eyes open.

I ate part of a chicken sandwich and quickly changed into a fresh white shirtwaist and dark blue skirt. Clean clothes and brushed hair always gave me a little energy. I tied my hair ribbon into a passable bow, grabbed my journal, and headed upstairs.

On deck, passengers roamed about or sat in wooden folding chairs that lined the outside walls. I claimed a spot along the railing so I could take in the jagged Indian coastline as it grew smaller by the minute. I reached out my hand as if to touch it. Would I ever return?

A burst of wind raked through my hair, loosening the ribbon. The ship rocked one way, then the other. A couple passed, and they both grabbed the railing to steady themselves. The man chuckled. "I guess we don't have our sea legs yet."

Where's Michael? I crossed to the other side of the deck by holding onto chairs and walls for support, wind gusts whipping my skirt.

Beneath the transparent skies, the blue-green sea with twists of indigo spread in every direction to the horizon. The *City of Benares* dipped toward the water, and I seized the railing. I didn't know what sea legs were, but I was sure I didn't have them either.

If only it were a simple sightseeing cruise, and we could return to Cochin and then to Guntur. Instead, I'd become a helpless leaf whisked along to the unknown by the wind, with nowhere to land.

I looked for our stairs and tried to retrace my steps—but things didn't look quite right. Why couldn't they have had signs or something, instead of just plain white walls and doors? *Maybe this way ...*

I spun around and bumped straight into a tall man dressed in a white jacket with three black stripes on each sleeve. He spoke with a crisp British accent. "Beg your pardon, miss. Are you in need of some assistance?"

The heat from the sun intensified. "I can't seem to find my way."

"Quite all right. It takes a bit of time. Do you know your cabin number?"

"Yes, it's D-29."

"Very good. Right this way."

We crossed to the opposite side. "Here are your stairs. Two flights down, then head toward the stern until you arrive at D-29."

The stern?

His mouth tipped upward at the corners, and he slowed his words down to a more understandable speed. "I see that a quick lesson in nautical terms is in order. The *stern* is the rear of the ship. The front is the *bow*. It's the direction the ship points while we're at sea."

"So, is the bow where the maidenhead would be?"

He seemed pleased at my question. "Very good. Now, you should also know port and starboard. If you're facing the bow, *port* is on your left and *starboard* is on your right."

I practiced, pointing as I recited the new terms. "Port is left, starboard, right. I think I have it."

"Excellent. May I ask your name?"

I cleared my throat and stood taller. "Ruth Becker."

"I'm Second Officer Clayton. Will there be anything else, Miss Becker?"

So, the men in white jackets are ship's officers. I smiled. "No, thank you."

"Good afternoon, then." I was almost positive he clicked his heels together.

I repeated Mr. Clayton's lesson in my head. *Bow is the front, stern is the back, starboard on the right, and port on the left.*

Now, if only I could convince Mother to have dinner with the Franks.

SS City of Benares, Arabian Sea
March 9, 1912

Sky Report: I must admit, I was excited to meet Officer Clayton today and learn something new about the ship. As a seafaring man, he must know the constellations too. The Argo Navis, the "ship constellation," was a gift from Athena to its Captain, Jason of the Argonauts, to search the seas for the Golden Fleece. The ship had a magical maidenhead with the power of speech, and it assisted Jason during his adventures.

I would never consider sailing the seas for a living, but I wish I had a magical ship now to show me the way.

CHAPTER SIX

SS City of Benares, Arabian Sea
March 9, 1912
5:30 p.m.

I maneuvered a brush through Marion's curls, maybe with a little too much force.

"Ouch!" She jerked away.

"Sit still." I yanked at a snarl. "I don't understand why we can't even sit at their table. You didn't see what happened on the train. Mr. Frank probably saved that man from something worse." *Mother's off her onion.*

She rummaged through the dresser drawers. "I don't wish to discuss it, Ruth. It just wouldn't be proper, and I've told you not to associate with that boy. You have plenty to keep you busy on this voyage. For one thing, you need to help me." She tossed a diaper and shirt for Richard on the bed, along with Marion's undergarments. "And practice your violin."

"That *boy's* name is Michael," I said under my breath. Practicing the violin was not an issue. I loved to practice, and I would, even though I was robbed of performing at the festival. But there would likely be no changing Mother's mind about Michael.

I only needed a ribbon for my hair to finish getting ready for dinner. My other one had blown away and was probably at the bottom of the sea by now. Not that it mattered much how I looked— we wouldn't be sitting with the Franks, and I didn't know anyone else. *My first meal at sea, and we'll be eating alone. I'm not even hungry.*

Mother had already filled the available drawers. To get half a drawer, I had to shove Marion's clothes to one side. Whatever didn't fit in the space, I stuffed back inside the trunk. I couldn't find my ribbons, so one of Marion's would have to do.

I led the way up one flight of stairs toward the dining room, where a steward greeted us. "Good evening, madam, children. You may sit anywhere you wish."

Mother scanned the large room. Most of the tables were occupied. "We'll take that small table by the wall, please."

He led us across the room, away from the windows that were draped in green. The ship rocked, and I steadied myself with the back of someone's chair. As we passed a table of eight, the group of diners erupted in laughter.

Michael and Mr. Frank, sitting at one end, laughed along with the group. Michael saw us and sent me a questioning look.

My mother doesn't like you, so we can't sit with you. I shrugged in what I hoped was an I-don't-know kind of way, and hurried Marion along before she saw him. *This is so awkward.*

At Mother's table of choice, the steward pulled out a chair for her that faced the large room. "Your dining steward will be with you shortly."

Marion slid into the seat next to Mother. "What can I get?"

I chose the seat across from Mother that faced the wall so I could keep my back toward Michael. Did he tell his dad we had arrived, and what did Mr. Frank think about us not speaking to them?

The steward brought a high chair, and Mother took a moment to settle Richard.

"The Franks saw us," I said.

Marion straightened and peered around. "Where?"

"Never mind." Mother plucked a small card from the center of the table and handed it to me. "Here's the menu. Tell your sister what we're having."

I skimmed the menu and dropped it between the salt and pepper shakers. "Chicken and potatoes."

The look Mother gave me could have chilled the spiciest curry.

She picked up the card and read it aloud.

I didn't care what we ate. The Franks were having fun at another table, and all around the dining room, passengers chatted and clinked their drinking glasses together. *This will be the longest four weeks of my life, guaranteed.*

Marion turned to the windows. "When do we get to ... Where we goin', before America?"

"We're going to England," I said. "To Southampton." So far away—it might as well have been the moon.

Another steward brought a pitcher of water and basket of warm rolls. His dark hair and complexion told me he was part Indian, but his features were European—a *chee-chee*, as a person of mixed descent was called in India.

"My name is Sayeed. I am your server this evening." His bright smile made me ache for Sajni. *I belong in Guntur. And how am I supposed to eat?*

As if confirming my thoughts, the whole dining room angled and swayed to the window-lined side of the ship. Was it starboard? Or port? Regardless, I was glad to be sitting. Mother gripped Richard's high chair until we leveled again.

Marion laughed. "It's like riding a pony."

"It's not at all like that," I said.

Marion helped herself to a roll and sniffed it. "What's Papa doin'?"

Mother buttered the roll for her. "Probably eating dinner, just like us."

I hope Papa is miserable. I heaved a good fed-up sigh and poured myself a glass of water from the pitcher. Mother scowled at me, so I poured a little for Richard in his baby cup and half a glass for Marion.

Richard pounded the high chair tray, while Mother fussed with tying his bib just so. Watching her, I wanted to explode. I filled her glass and set it down with a *bang* on the table. It splashed on my hand. I ignored her certain frown.

This was so out of character for me that even Marion gave me a funny look. I hummed a few bars from "Oh, You Beautiful Doll," a ragtime tune Mother despised.

Oh! you beautiful doll, you great, big beautiful doll ...

Sayeed brought steaming bowls on a round tray. "Vegetable barley soup. Take care, it is very hot."

"Excuse me, will this be our table for every meal?" I pronounced *every* like it hurt, which it did.

"You may stay at this table if you insist," Sayeed said, "but tomorrow you will be assigned a table with other passengers. You will see, with bigger tables, it offers more room. And it is more pleasant for all. It is a long voyage." He flashed a smile and sauntered away with the serving tray beneath his arm.

Mother stirred her soup. "It will be nice to have someone to talk with, I suppose."

Good. There would be several *someones*.

And I would find a way to see Michael.

~

When we returned to the cabin, Mother placed Richard in his crib and prepared his medicine, mixing it with water and a little sugar that Jack had provided.

At the sight of the medicine bottle, Richard hid his face in the crib mattress, but Mother got the job done with efficiency.

"There," she said. "Let's hope that lowers his fever enough to help him sleep."

Marion spun around, ricocheting off the sides of the beds and falling across the one she and I were to share. Mother took her to the WC, leaving Richard with me.

I couldn't think of sleep quite yet. Where could I find a private corner?

The passageway lights were on, and it was much quieter than our cabin. While Richard sulked in his crib, I retrieved my extra stationery from the trunk. It was a wonder Marion hadn't used it for drawing paper yet.

Mother and Marion returned. "Help her get undressed, Ruth. I'll take Richard and give him a good washing."

I'm nothing but a babysitter. Can't I go write a simple letter?

When they left, Marion grabbed my hand and made me twirl her around. "Sissy, are you so excited to sleep on the ship?"

"Not exactly. It's ... bouncy. Not like home."

"But bouncy's fun! What are we doin' tomorrow?"

I made her sit on Mother's bed. "I don't know. There's not very much to do."

Marion fell back on the white coverlet. "Yes, there is! Maybe we can see Michael."

"Maybe." I yanked off her shoes and stockings and unbuttoned the back of her dress.

Mother came back with Richard in her arms. "There's a line forming outside the WC, so you and I will need to wait."

"I'm not in a hurry. I was just about to go write a letter."

She grimaced. "If you must. Don't get in anyone's way, and don't be long."

Finished with Marion, I snapped up my stationery and pen. My violin case was propped against the wall. Before Mother could stop me, I nabbed it on my way out. Once in the passageway, I moved as far as I could from the WC line and found a good spot to sit beneath a lightbulb.

I wrote to Sajni about the brawl on the train, our night in Cochin, the *City of Benares*, and the gigantic Arabian Sea. I left out the part about Mother telling me to stay away from Michael. I stuffed the letter in an envelope and addressed it in care of the Lutheran Orphanage, Guntur, India, to mail at our first port.

Should I write to Papa, too? No, Mother could write him. *He should be here, or I should be home, so I don't have to write him a stupid letter.*

I flicked the latches on my violin case, lifted the lid, and ran my fingers along the strings. I longed to play, to soak in the music, to embrace the escape it could offer. I lifted the violin from its old case. Mr. Liddle gave the instrument to me when my secondhand violin could no longer be tuned properly.

He'd told me it had belonged to a former student who left it with him when he enlisted in the Indian Army. He'd said, "Miss Becker, music is a gift, and a good violin such as this deserves a musician who will bring out its best, who will use it to bring joy to others. I believe you are that musician."

Only two elderly women stood in line now, and I didn't think they'd mind a little music. Frankly, I didn't care if they did. I needed to play for myself, to feel the strings through the bow, and to hear the music that I hoped would soothe my soul.

～⌒～

The bed I shared with Marion shifted a foot across the floor. Wind howled from somewhere above us, while the whole cabin creaked. This was much worse than all the rocking we'd endured during the day, and I had never heard such winds.

If only I could see what was happening on the sea. Had a storm rolled in?

The ship groaned and shuddered like a rickety old wagon, yet no one stirred. Could I slip out of the room without waking anyone and trek down the passageway toward the stairs?

My hands found my dressing gown at the foot of the bed, and I tiptoed toward the soft light under the cabin door. My little toe caught the leg of the washstand—the worst pain ever. I clamped my eyes shut and bit my lip. As the pain subsided, I slipped out the door and shut it with a soft *click*.

I headed for the stairs, but every time the ship rolled, I fell against the wall, then the other wall, narrowly missing a few cabin doors. One door opened, and a man in nightclothes ran for the WC, his hand over his mouth. *Will I get seasick too?*

As my foot touched the first step that lead toward the upper deck, another door clicked down the passageway behind me.

"Ruth! What are you doing?"

I whirled around.

Mother pointed at her feet. "Come back here this instant!"

She waited until I zigzagged toward her in rhythm with the rocking ship. "Where do you think you're going at this time of night?"

"I only wanted to see why it's so rough."

She took my arm as we entered the cabin. "You are not to roam around the ship at night by yourself, do you understand? It's only wind. Now, get back to bed."

But how was I supposed to sleep on a vessel that acted like a see-saw? How could anyone else sleep, for that matter? With less than one night down, and so many more to go, I had to learn the trick to sleeping at sea.

Thirty minutes later, the wind still imitated a train whistle, and the ship rolled like Richard's toy boat. My thoughts swayed along with the ship, bringing me back to the night before I left Guntur.

Richard had fussed and cried all that day, keeping Mother hopping between missionaries stopping in and all our travel preparations. The willow bark extract used to lower his fever didn't work for more than an hour that day.

Marion stood in the dim hallway outside my parents' bedroom. "I can't fall asleep, Sissy. I'm too excited."

If she didn't stop interrupting me, I'd never finish packing. Plus, I didn't care to see any more of her that night, after what had happened earlier.

She padded into the room. "Can you tuck me in?"

I walked her back to the bedroom we shared. "No more getting up. Morning will be here before you know it."

She climbed in bed beneath the mosquito net and pulled my shirtwaist until our noses touched. "I'm sorry I broke Tessa." She gave me a wet kiss on my nose.

I broke her hold. "Mother told you not to help pack. Dishes can't go on top of a china doll."

Just that week, as we'd begun packing up our lives, Mother had given my only doll, Tessa Rose, to Marion without even asking. Tessa and I had shared a special bond. She had been a patient audience when I'd first begun violin lessons, before I could even hold the bow properly. She'd attended countless tea parties with Sajni and me and had listened to my whispered prayers at night.

I was partly at fault, I supposed, for what happened. Mother had told me to watch Marion, but I went outside to look for Teddy, our cat. Now Tessa's delicate pink face was crushed under a stack of dinner plates. I knew Marion was only trying to help. But by the time we reached America, would I have anything left?

I returned to packing, swallowing tears. I carefully folded my dark green dress around my birds. The tiniest one, a hummingbird, was my favorite. They needed to be safe, where nobody, especially Marion and Richard, could find them. I placed the dress in the huge brown trunk on the floor.

Long after the house was dark, I lay in my bed, cuddling Teddy for the last time and listening to the clock tick away the minutes of my last night in India.

CHAPTER SEVEN

SS City of Benares, Arabian Sea
March 10, 1912
7:00 a.m.

Mother scooped peaches onto Marion's plate at the buffet. "Ruth, for heaven's sake, cover your mouth."

I stifled another yawn and tried to focus on choosing sausage or bacon. I'd barely been able to sleep. And thanks to our alarm clock— or, more specifically, my brother—we all woke too soon. Now we were almost the first passengers in line for breakfast. The wind and seas had finally calmed, and the sun had never looked so large or made the air so warm. Open windows on either side of the dining room provided a welcome cross-breeze.

As we left, the head steward handed Mother a card. "Your table assignment for dinner, beginning this evening, Mrs. Becker."

"Becker, Table 18," Mother read. "I guess we'll find out tonight who will be joining us."

Marion swung my arm. "I'm guessing all girls."

I didn't care if they were a pack of hyenas, just as long as they weren't younger than five.

Mother insisted I spend the rest of the morning in the cabin reading to Marion and helping her with Richard. I felt sure I'd see Michael during the scheduled 11:30-1:00 lunch.

We arrived a little past noon, just as he and his dad were leaving the dining room. They both wore big smiles. "Mrs. Becker!" Mr. Frank said. "Enjoyin' the ship so far?"

Mother adopted her most subdued voice. "It's quite adequate,

Mr. Frank. How is your eye?"

He touched a finger to the ugly black stitches over his reddish-purple right eye. "Still tender, but the doc said no worries."

Mother shooed us along. "Good day, Mr. Frank, Michael."

I peered over my shoulder. Michael pointed his index finger up. *Is he signaling me?*

Later, when Marion and Richard finally settled for naps, Mother said she would try to nap as well. I was beyond bored with being cooped up in the cabin. "May I go on deck for a while?"

Mother laid her spectacles on the dresser and rubbed her forehead. "Yes, but I don't want to tell you again to stay away from that boy."

I took my journal and left. *You don't have to tell me again.* On deck, strong breezes toyed with my skirt and whipped strolling passengers' clothing. I faced the front of the ship—the bow. *Port side to the left.*

I made my way to the port bow, to the deck designated for those of us not in first class. Michael Frank stood at the railing, watching two crewmen set up deck chairs. His hair flew willy-nilly around his face. He turned and saw me. "You got my signal."

I wasn't going to say otherwise. "Of course."

He grinned. "How'd you sleep your first night on a ship?"

I'm not supposed to be talking to you. But Mother's napping, after all. "It'll take me a few nights, I think."

"When we get to the Suez, you won't even know we're movin'."

I brushed hair from my face. Why hadn't I paid better attention to my geography lessons? "What's the Suez?"

"You'll see." He grinned. "Did you get a table number for tonight?"

"Eighteen. What's yours?"

His mouth twisted sideways. "I forgot." He flexed his wrist and glanced at two ship's officers walking away toward the stern. "I need to go. See you." With a wave, Michael headed for the stairs. He sure didn't stay in one place for long.

It was too warm to sit in the sun and write in my journal. I wandered up and down the deck, stopping to eavesdrop on bits of conversations.

A gray-haired man clutched a straw hat to his chest. He turned to the man beside him. "Have you heard the Yanks added another state? They call it Arizona."

The other man tapped a headline in the newspaper he held. "They just added New Mexico, for God's sake! Americans—a bunch of cowboys and Indians. They're all rather balmy on the crumpet, I'd say."

I didn't really care about Arizona *or* New Mexico. But why were people in America called Indians when they had nothing to do with India?

Gentle waves lapped the horizon, where the endless sea met the sky. How far was I from India, and where was something I could look forward to reaching, something I could touch?

With no land in sight, the reality of my situation crept in again and clutched me by the throat. Sorrow swept over me, drenching me and pulling me under like a giant wave. *I'm lost! I'm in the middle of nowhere, with no plan and no future. No one cares, and I've been sent away.*

The sparkling sea became a muddled haze. I sank to a chair and covered my face, aware of the curious looks from passersby. I tried to fight off the sadness, but there, amid a crowd of onlookers, the tears won.

~

Passengers made their way to the dining room for dinner at 6:00 p.m. sharp. Even though the sun dipped below the horizon and the sea breezes blew nonstop, the temperature remained high. I wore the most lightweight dress I owned—a brown checkered one that had short sleeves. I had talked Mother into letting Marion and me wear our shorter cotton stockings in place of the usual long, dark ones that covered our knees.

The tables were now arranged differently, each bearing a number on a two-foot-tall stand. I searched for Table 18 and found it near the windows.

Three young women who were already seated stood as we arrived at the table. The tallest woman, a blonde, wore a blue shirtwaist with three-quarter sleeves and a calf-length skirt, like the ones I observed when we boarded. The pearls in her hair combs caught the late sunlight.

She extended her hand toward Mother. "Hello! I'm Natalie Haynes."

Mother grasped her hand briefly. "How do you do? I'm Nellie … Mrs. Allen Becker, and these are my children—Ruth, Marion, and Richard."

The redhead's hair was pinned high and poufed, with tendrils gracing her forehead—a perfect Gibson Girl style. I'd learned the term in school, when Miss Knauss told us about motion pictures and showed us photos of actresses.

"I'm Elizabeth Cooper," the young woman said, her smile as wide as the dining room.

The shortest of the three looked a bit older than the others. "I'm Millie St. Ives. It's lovely to meet you." She wore a simple shirtwaist and skirt like Mother's, but with a cameo brooch pinned to her lacey, sailor-style collar. Like Marion, she had tight, dark curls that looked like they had a mind of their own, pinned on top of her head in an unruly bun.

We took seats across the table from them. The women told us they were British, which I had surmised from their accents. "We're in University together," Natalie said. "We took a term off to go on holiday in India."

Elizabeth laughed. "Yes, Natalie's quite the world traveler. Millie and I enjoy it, but we have bigger plans than searching the planet for *love.*"

Natalie gave Elizabeth's arm a light swat. "That is not my intent, and you know it." She faced Mother. "I major in English literature. My parents simply believe I should see the world a bit before marrying or finding employment. And they've provided this excursion with my chums, for which I'm most grateful."

Mother straightened her posture. She seemed shocked to learn how different Natalie's lifestyle was from hers. "How very fortunate you are. And what are your plans, Miss Cooper?"

"Please, call me Elizabeth. I'm also an English literature major, and I want to teach school as soon as I graduate next spring." She flashed that smile again, blushing. "A husband would be nice, but I'm in no hurry."

"That sounds like a good plan," Mother said politely. "And you, Millie? May I call you Millie?"

"Of course, I prefer it," she said. "I'm studying the sciences. I want to be a doctor. I'm also quite active in a cause back home in Britain—the right of women to vote—although I don't believe in starting riots, as some of the suffragettes do."

An activist and a future doctor? These women were fascinating! I liked Millie straight off. But what would she think of a female lead violinist? Millie also held Marion's attention, probably due to those crazy curls.

"That's certainly a cause I'll need to think more about," Mother said. "My husband tells me American women are taking it up as well."

The steward brought water, a basket of hot rolls, and the butter dish. "I will serve your food as soon as the other seats at the table are filled," he said.

Natalie leaned forward. "May I ask, Mrs. Becker, what brings you and your children to the *City of Benares*?"

Mother's shoulders relaxed. "It's a long story. You see, my husband and I were missionaries—"

"Pardon us, ladies. May we join you?"

Marion looked up and squealed in delight. The Great Frank and Son stood beside her chair, wearing matching waistcoats, white shirts, and gentlemanly grins. Michael held up their table assignment card for us all to see. It read: Frank, Table 18.

SS City of Benares, Arabian Sea
March 10, 1912

Sky Report: Tonight, stars by the millions shine against the blackest, clearest skies. Next to the last quarter moon, the Big Dipper inside the Great Bear is showing off its brilliance. I imagine how the sailors of long ago must have felt, navigating by the stars, following their lead, and searching for somewhere to land.

What direction are the stars leading me, when I only wish to be led home to India?

CHAPTER EIGHT

SS City of Benares, Arabian Sea
March 12, 1912

For the third evening in a row, my family sat together at Table 18 with The Great Frank and Son and the trio of college women. While we waited for our first course, Captain Drummond passed from table to table, greeting passengers. In his neatly pressed white uniform, the stocky man with the built-in frown had the same air as all the ship captains I'd read about in books—a man in charge, born with the sea in his blood, and one who was not to be crossed.

Mr. Frank gathered tableware to demonstrate an acrobatic act he and Michael often performed in the circus. A butter knife, representing a tightrope, rested across the bottom of two upside-down teacups.

He reached for the pepper shaker—

"Here I am ..."

—then the saltshaker—

"And 'ere's Michael."

He held one shaker at each end of the knife. "We start 'cross the rope, walking toward each other, like this. When we meet in the middle, Michael's supposed to get on me shoulders." He held the salt over the pepper. "But that's when the monkey escaped from the other ring."

Marion's eyes were about to pop like loose marbles. "A monkey?"

Michael withdrew a chess pawn from his trouser pocket, sliding it across the tablecloth and under the butter knife. "Here comes the monkey. The audience was laughing and pointing. I couldn't see the monkey, but I knew somethin' was wrong. I lost me balance and fell." His dad laid the saltshaker on its side under the knife.

I was entranced. "What happened then? Were you hurt?"

Marion stared at the makeshift circus. "What about the monkey?"

"I broke me wrist." Michael held up his right arm, flexing the wrist like he so often did. "But I jumped to my feet and chased that monkey out o' the tent. I got a standing ovation."

"Simply amazing," Millie said. "Are you really able to get on your father's shoulders from a tightrope?" Her curls were a bit tamer than usual. I'd overheard her tell Mother she'd used Elizabeth's hair pomade.

Michael grinned. "It's not all that hard, unless somethin' monkeys it up."

We all laughed, except Mother, who smiled with tight lips. At least she hadn't requested another table assignment. She looked as if she enjoyed the women's company, and once in a while, she even acted as if she might be warming up to the Franks.

Rushab, our steward, brought a tureen of onion soup and filled our bowls. He gave a smaller bowl to Mother for Richard.

Marion pulled on my sleeve. "What spoon do I use?"

I pointed to the first one on her left. "Start from the outside, remember?"

Mr. Frank turned to Marion. "We had to learn the proper spoons on our first voyage with the circus."

Michael waved his outside spoon. "It's silly to have all these different spoons. A spoon's a spoon, when the soup smells this good."

I dipped a cracker into my soup. "They must have so many dishes to wash, with all these different courses and plates for everything."

"Wait 'til you're on the *Titanic*," Michael said. "I bet there'll be more, even in steerage."

The women let out a collective sound of awe. "How exciting," Natalie said. She looked stunning in a pale-lavender dress. "We've heard about the *Titanic*!"

Not exciting for me, thank you very much. I reached for another cracker. "What's steerage?"

"Same as third class," Michael answered. "It's for the poor people. Oh, sorry, you won't be in steerage, will you?"

I glanced at Mother, but she stared into her teacup.

"My father said he wanted us to be comfortable, so he splurged on second-class tickets for us," I said.

Mother fired her annoyed look in my direction. "Really, Ruth."

"It doesn't matter what class anyone is traveling in," Natalie said. "It's simply a matter of ticket prices."

"Not in the eyes o' some of the shipping companies," Mr. Frank said. "Or some of the passengers. The *City of Benares* only has two classes, but Michael and me travel steerage most of the time. Let's just say, steerage folk don't get quite the same treatment as first class."

Rushab brought our dinners. With a flourish, he lifted the domed lid off the large round tray. "Roast beef, ladies and gentlemen."

The aroma was from heaven. "I haven't eaten roast beef in ages," I said.

"What a nice surprise," Mother said. "Beef is *never* available in India."

"I don't understand. Why not?" Millie asked.

Natalie smiled in agreement. "The British rule India, and we love our beef."

"It's against Hindu beliefs," Mother explained. "They view cattle as holy."

"It certainly smells *divine*," Elizabeth said, smiling at her own joke.

The ship must have had a British chef. Did Rushab mind serving it to us?

"My husband and I were in steerage on our way to India many years ago." Mother placed bits of meat and crackers on the high chair tray for Richard. "I only remember being unable to sleep due to the waves."

I poked my fork into a mysterious vegetable. "Why didn't you warn me about that?" My words came out sharper than I intended. Everyone at the table went silent.

Mother's eyes narrowed. "I … I thought it wouldn't bother you."

I set down my fork. "I wake up every time the ship rolls."

Natalie coughed away the awkward moment. "How long were you in India, Mrs. Becker?"

"Since '98. My husband accepted the mission post in Guntur, so we left the States for India soon after we married. He was made assistant director of the orphanage, even though he'd never worked in an orphanage before."

"That must have been quite an adjustment," Natalie said.

"Yes, in so many ways." Mother smoothed the tablecloth. "Two years later, when Ruth was born, he was given the director's position. He loves his work. But because of Richard's health issues, we're going home."

Richard squeezed meat and crackers together in his fists and dropped them onto the floor. "Richard!" Mother bent over to pick them up.

"Allow me, Mrs. Becker." Mr. Frank dropped to his knees and scooped up the crumbs.

Rushab appeared with a small broom and pan. "I will clean. Please, sit."

Mother tried to feed Richard a small piece of meat, but he pushed her hand away.

"He's interested in everything but food," Mr. Frank said.

Michael looked at me. "I haven't seen him eat anything since the train."

Richard wriggled and jiggled, trying to release himself from his chair like a novice Houdini.

"Ruth," Millie said, "tell us something about yourself. What do you like to do?"

Not many adults had ever asked me about myself. I swallowed a bite of roast beef, considering how to answer. "I play violin," I finally said.

"That's fantastic!" Millie seemed genuinely interested. "How long have you played?"

"Since I was seven."

Natalie's eyes widened. "So young!"

"How wonderful to have a musician in the family, Mrs. Becker," Millie said.

"Yes, Ruth plays quite well," Mother said.

"I want to play in an orchestra someday, but—" *Oh, I shouldn't have said anything. They'll never understand.* I changed the subject. "I wonder what the first-class dining room is like."

Millie offered me an understanding glance. "We've heard it's lovely." She moved one of Marion's stray curls into place.

"I'm perfectly content here," Mother said. "The food is very good. And besides, we don't have the clothes or jewels or hats for first class."

Mr. Frank took a roll from the breadbasket. "Being a missionary is a callin' from God, Mrs. Becker. What's it like to work with orphans in India?"

She studied him for a moment, and her eyes softened. "My husband's policy is to simply love them and teach them they are valuable to God. My role is at home with our own children, but I support what he does."

You never liked any of the orphans, other than Sajni. I hummed a random tune under my breath.

"Are they ever adopted?" Natalie asked.

"A few of the youngest ones are," Mother said. "Most are educated at the orphanage and are able to leave and support themselves when they're old enough."

Sajni would never be adopted, not at fourteen. If she had been, we wouldn't have been friends for so long. She'd leave the orphanage someday, but not before Papa made sure she had a job and a good place to live.

A terrible thought made me drop my fork and splash gravy on my dress. *What will happen when Papa leaves?* Would the next orphanage director help Sajni or kick her out into the streets?

"Do you think you'll miss missionary life?" Elizabeth asked Mother.

Mother straightened her spectacles. "I'll miss the people, but I have to think of my family now. It's not an easy life. Missionaries aren't as welcome as you may think."

I carelessly dabbed at the gravy on my dress with my bunched-up napkin. Then I wiped harder, rubbing the stain. It almost matched the brown checks.

Michael turned to his dad. "What shall we do tomorrow?"

Mr. Frank glanced from Michael to me. "You're not busy?"

I held my breath. *Please don't let on that you know Michael has seen me outside this room.* But Mother was engrossed in something that Natalie was saying and didn't hear him.

"I thought we could do somethin' together," Michael said to his dad. "Or will you be playing cards again?"

Mother heard that time and looked down her nose at Mr. Frank.

He reached for his water glass. "What would y' like to do?"

"Maybe play some games on the port side, where all the single blokes spend time. They have checkers, shuffleboard, and silly races."

Mother turned to Elizabeth. "And do the women take over the other side?"

"Yes, on the starboard bow. It's mostly single ladies, but you should come!"

"I don't care much for games," Mother replied. "Besides, I'm always with Richard."

Michael laid his spoon in his empty soup bowl. "The ladies had a race today. They had to run 'cross the deck with an egg in a spoon. The winners won prizes."

Mr. Frank rubbed his chin. "I wonder if we could juggle those eggs, eh, Michael?"

S.S. City of Benares, Arabian Sea
March 12, 1912

Dear Sajni,

Still no land in sight, but I'm trying not to think about it. Tonight, we'll finally reach Aden, our first port. Then we'll enter the Red Sea. Mr. Frank told me the ship will rock less then. Maybe I'll sleep easier.

The women at our table tell us stories about college and their families, and about motion pictures they've seen. Natalie showed me a photograph of a famous actor, Charlie Chaplin, in a copy of Vogue magazine. If a movie theater ever opens in Guntur, you should ask Papa if you can go.

Natalie and Elizabeth wear the most up-to-date styles, and I'm learning about fashions from them. I heard them discussing the miseries of corsets. I'm never going to wear one. Millie has more outside interests. She'd make an excellent doctor, but she says some medical schools still don't allow women.

Natalie is the world traveler. She's even been to Australia! You know, I suppose when I finally reach America, I'll be somewhat of a world traveler myself.

The quilt is the happiest thing I own, with the best memories. It has the slightest scent of curry. Did you sew some in for me?

Before Papa leaves for Michigan, promise me you'll ask him about what you are to do when you leave the orphanage. Maybe he can help you find a home and a good job before he goes.

Your loving "sister,"
Ruth

CHAPTER NINE

SS City of Benares, Yemen
March 13, 1912

Our ship entered the Gulf of Aden and docked in South Yemen at the historic port of Aden, just long enough to receive a load of coal and for us passengers to post our letters at the gangplank. From there, a man tossed the bag of mail onto the back of a large camel-drawn wagon.

While the *City of Benares* pulled away to head for the Red Sea, The Great Frank and Son prepared to entertain passengers with their juggling routine on the main deck. Mother surprised me when she said she wanted to watch, so we stood in the shade of a hatchway. Millie and her friends joined us.

"Ladies and gents," Michael began, lifting his arms in the air. "Welcome to the SS *City of Benares* traveling circus, courtesy of The Great Frank and Son!"

Passengers smiled and clapped politely. Someone played a lively tune on an accordion. Mr. Frank had asked Rushab for a few unbreakable kitchen items, which were stacked nearby on a deck chair. He and Michael began juggling oranges, then they added pomegranates, and without stopping, they juggled two roll baskets and a metal tray. They shouted to each other and joked with the onlookers the entire time.

Michael caught the last item and turned to the audience. "Now, please give us your kind attention, as The Great Frank and Son will attempt to perform a most daring feat never before seen this side o' London."

"Take a step back, folks," Mr. Frank said. "For your safety."

Passengers turned to one another with questioning looks as they stepped back.

"What are they doing, Miss Millie?" Marion asked.

"Let's wait and see," Millie said.

Mr. Frank reached inside a small basket and tossed something white and round to Michael. He quickly grabbed another, tossing, catching, and repeating.

Natalie brought her hands to her cheeks. "They're juggling eggs!"

Uh-oh. Any second, and they might be scrambled.

"Wow!" Marion shouted. Mother bit her lower lip. Richard clapped, and the tempo of the music increased.

As The Great Frank and Son kept eight or nine eggs in the air, the impressed crowd gave their approval with a round of applause and whistles. The Franks shone with a contented happiness that everyone seemed to sense.

Two days later, Michael and I hung our arms over the midship railing as the *City of Benares* poked along the narrow Suez Canal. I studied the murky water below. "This is going to take forever."

"Because it's a hundred miles long and narrow," Michael said. "It's still an awful lot better than going all the way 'round Africa like people used to do." He shielded his eyes. "The other way was to take a ship from England to Egypt, then eighty miles on a camel across the desert, then hop another ship bound for India."

For a boy who didn't go to a real school, he knew quite a bit. "A camel ride sounds fun," I said. "I'm more than ready to see some ports and get off the ship for a while."

Encyclopedia Boy continued. "On the way from England to India, some ships let people off t' see the pyramids. They catch up to the ship after it's through the Canal."

I smiled, imagining the possibility. "If I ever return, I'm doing that and skipping this part. We'll never get to England at this rate."

Michael and I crossed from starboard to port, but there wasn't much to see on that shore, only more white sand and a small fishing village. Boats tied to the docks bobbed in the water as our ship created a ripple. The buildings beyond were little more than old shanties, holding each other up until the next strong wind.

A thin, sunburned man knelt on a rooftop and hammered at something. He stopped to rake sweat-drenched hair from his forehead and watch our ship pass.

"I was going to practice my triple back flip on deck," Michael said, "but it's way too hot."

The deck games had been canceled due to the heat. A steward approached with a tray of sweating glasses. "Ice water, children?"

Michael downed half his water in a single swig. "Did y' get all your letters mailed in Aden?"

"Yes, but I wish we could've gone ashore." I took a swallow, then I held the ice-cold glass to my forehead. "I sent two to my friend, Sajni, and a short one to my teacher."

"Letters shouldn't take long from there—maybe a fortnight at most," he said. "Is Sajni a good mate?"

I nodded. "We're this close." I crossed my middle and index fingers. "I don't know how I'm going to stand being away from her. Papa found her wandering the streets when I was four and she was six. Her parents had died, and her older brother ran away and left her. So Papa took her in at the orphanage."

"You're lucky, y' know, to have a good friend like that."

"She didn't speak any English when we met. She ended up teaching me some Telugu, and I helped her learn English." I laughed. "Now she speaks it better than I do."

Michael kicked at the lowest rung on the railing. "You can speak Telugu? Teach me something!"

I ran through words I might teach him. "How about this— *nemaskaaram* means 'hello,' and *selavu* means 'good-bye.'"

We laughed as he made several attempts, but the words became tangled on his tongue.

"I just wrote in my journal about one of my happiest moments with Sajni." As soon as I told him, I regretted it. How much did I want to tell this circus boy?

"Well," Michael said. "Are you going to tell me?"

I wiped my forehead with my sleeve. It didn't really matter what he knew—nothing was going to change. "Before we left Guntur, I was selected to play a violin solo for the Spring Festival. That day, Sajni walked me home after my violin lesson and I told her the news. We both jumped up and down and laughed and screamed the entire way to my house."

I didn't share with him how she erased my fears with her few, simple words.

"What if I make mistakes?"

Sajni stopped me cold and put her hands on my shoulders. "Ruth Becker, stop that talk this minute! You have talent, and Mr. Liddle would not have chosen you otherwise."

Michael let out a whistle. "Your parents must've been proud," he said.

"Actually, I didn't get to tell them when I got home."

Because when we arrived at the bungalow, Papa's white shoes were on our doorstep. I couldn't imagine why he was home so early in the day.

Sajni hugged me and waved good-bye. But she couldn't hide her look of concern as she started on the path to the orphanage, her skirt skimming the dirt.

"So, why didn't you tell 'em?" Michael asked.

"Richard was sick, and my parents were busy with the doctors." I didn't say how I had raced inside the bungalow, not bothering to unbuckle my boots, to find Mother standing over the sofa and fanning a fiery-red Richard, while two doctors examined him. Papa had hurried me out of the room with a false, shaky smile on his face.

"At the sound of Richard's moaning, I forgot to tell Papa my news. Later, when I finally told them, they were both thrilled, even Mother. But we had to leave India before the festival."

Michael shook his head. "That's awful."

We headed toward the stern as far as we could before we reached the area for first class. I was desperate to change the subject. "Do you have friends at home? Or in the circus?"

"Not at home anymore. A few chaps in the circus, but nobody close. It's all right. Me and Dad got each other. Tell me more about India."

"What do you want to know?"

He held out his hands. "Did you have servants?"

I grinned. "No. Some of the British have them, but not missionaries. But we had a *dhobi wallah* once in a while. He's a man who comes and washes clothes."

"Blimey!" He scratched his freckled nose, as if trying to imagine such an oddity. "How about a funny story?"

I glanced at the water below. What would a circus performer think is funny? My life was so ordinary. "I'm thinking ... We had monkeys too. Want to hear about them?"

"Monkeys not in a circus?"

Monkeys are usually born in the wild, Circus Boy. "They would show up once in awhile, at the worst times. One day, Mother invited some missionary ladies for tea. She worked all day, getting everything ready and making little sandwiches and cakes. It was a perfect day, so she set the table on our veranda with her best tablecloth and dishes. Right before the women were to arrive, she took the food to the table and went in to get something. When she returned, there was a monkey in every chair, each of them eating the food."

Michael threw back his head and howled with laughter. "Your poor mum!"

"She screamed and chased them off. I had the task of making replacement sandwiches while she cleaned up the mess. I don't think those women ever knew what happened."

We left our empty glasses on a table near the railing and ambled toward the bow. Men dozed or read books or newspapers in the deck chairs.

"Fellows don't mind a little sun on their faces," Michael said. "It doesn't bother me, even if it gives me more of these ghastly freckles. But women think sun on their face is the end o' the world."

"Ladies don't want to ruin their skin," I said. "In India, the British wear pith helmets to guard against the sun. Even the women wear them." I turned to face the rays. "I love the sun. And the heat doesn't usually bother me. I guess I'm used to it."

We continued toward the bow. "Do you miss your mother?" I asked.

"Sure," he said matter-of-factly. "She made the best bangers n' mash in all of England," he said. "I got me freckles from her, 'cept she was prettier."

"I tried bangers and mash once, at the home of some British missionaries." The dish was mostly sausage and potatoes, but onions and plenty of butter and gravy had made them delicious.

"She was an acrobat too." Michael held his arms high and walked along the line where two planks in the floor came together, as if it were a tightrope. "That's how she and Dad met, but Mum gave up acrobatics when I was born."

A fishing boat bobbed alongside us. We waved to the two old fishermen, and they waved back with their straw hats.

I propped my chin in my hands, elbows on the railing. "I could never be an acrobat."

"It's not for everybody. I'm lucky, 'cause a lot of boys back home are working in factories and coal mines."

"That's horrible! My father read about a six-year-old boy who lost his ear to frostbite in a Chicago factory."

He shrugged, as if that were nothing. "Families need money. Factories are not the nicest of places, though."

He looked lost in a memory for a moment. What else had the eyes of Michael Frank seen on his journeys?

"Dad and me—we don't have much, but we stick together." He shoved his hands in his pockets and poked a finger at me out of a hole in the bottom of one. "And what do you hope to be, Miss Ruth Becker?"

I blew out a long breath, thinking of our new college friends and their future plans. "I'm not sure. My violin teacher said I had a chance to be in the Calcutta Orchestra one day. I don't know what'll happen now."

SS City of Benares, Suez Canal
March 15, 1912

Sky Report: Warm and clear, many stars tonight. Best view of Leo this year, right over our heads. The Great Bear, Ursa Major, and Little Bear, Ursa Minor, containing the Dippers, appear so much brighter and larger than in Guntur.

Before the Civil War in America, the slaves called the Big Dipper a Drinking Gourd. When they wanted to escape slavery and flee to the northern states, they did so with the help of people along the Underground Railroad. They made up a song about following the Drinking Gourd to the north, because it was the path to freedom.

I'm not running in fear as they were, but I worry about my future. Watching the Dippers tonight in such a strange part of the world gives me a sense of the longing they surely carried in their hearts.

CHAPTER TEN

*SS City of Benares, Suez Canal
March 16, 1912*

The next day, I met Michael again near the port bow. Mother had finally relented and gave me permission to spend an hour or so with him while Marion and Richard napped.

I blew hair off my hot forehead. *It's Papa's fault I'm inching through this canal, baking like a sweet pepper under the Egyptian sun.*

Michael's eyebrows puckered. "What's Richard's problem exactly?"

I pulled my sleeves away from my sticky arms. "He runs high fevers. Sometimes he gets seizures. He vomits now and then, and he doesn't eat much. That's why he's pale and so small for his age. The doctors gave him medicines, but they don't work very well."

Michael stared at the cloudy waters of the canal lapping against the hull of the ship. "Do you think the Yank doctors will know what to do?"

I shrugged. "We hope so."

Then Michael turned, eyes bright. "But you must be excited about living in the States, right? And seeing your grandparents?"

How could a boy who had barely left his father's side possibly understand? "No, I'm not. And I've never met them."

We rambled further toward the bow until we reached a shady alcove. Michael slouched against a spiral iron staircase. I peered up to see where it led, but I couldn't tell. A heavy chain hanging across the stairs barred the way. A "Crew Only" sign dangled from it.

I leaned against the bulkhead. "What else do you do in the circus, besides swing on trapeze bars and chase monkeys?"

Michael grinned, as if he knew a secret. With a tilt of his head, he eyed the stairway, then glanced toward the bow and the stern. In one quick move, he unhooked the chain at the bottom of the winding staircase. "Come on. I'll show you."

"What are you doing?" I checked the deck both ways. "You can't go up there!"

He appeared to have a burst of energy. "A chain's just an invitation to an acrobat."

I looked around again but didn't see anyone. *If Mother found out …*

"You're not scared of heights, are you?" he asked with an accusing voice.

I wasn't about to say yes. With another quick glance at port and starboard, I trailed after him, trying to keep my shoes from clacking on the steps.

The stairs ended at a small, flat area that extended over the uppermost, first class deck. Thick ropes lay in neat, round piles. Larger cables and ropes led to the central mast and more rigging.

I hunched on the white painted deck next to Michael, trying to make myself as small as possible. "We shouldn't be up here," I whispered.

Michael tugged on a horizontal rope that extended from the floor to the mast. "No one can see us."

"We'll get in trouble."

Michael removed his shoes.

"Are you crazy?"

Of course he was. Michael crouched next to me, eyeing the rope like a young cheetah preparing to catch his lunch.

I tried to keep my voice low. "Are you going to try walking on that rope?"

"Not gonna *try*—gonna do it."

"I knew it, you are crazy!" I whispered.

Directly below us, two ladies twirled their umbrellas as they ambled toward the bow. A crewman approached them and tipped his cap.

I hissed at Michael. "You can't do this."

"Watch me." He stood and poked the thick rope with his toes, then he placed his left foot on the rope, adjusted his body into position, and took a step up, balancing himself.

I could barely breathe. "That's wonderful," I whispered. "You can come down now."

But instead of hopping off, Michael placed his right foot on the rope in front of the left. He teetered, steadied himself, and took another step. A flock of seagulls circled overhead, surely curious to see what this crazy boy would do.

Any second, someone would see him, and we would be thrown in the brig or wherever they threw passengers who broke the rules.

He continued to walk the rope, now almost past the floor and out over the deck—a good sixteen feet below. How would he turn around? The two ladies strolled by again, heading toward the stern, their laughter floating on the air.

My heart hammered. "I'm very impressed. Now, please, please stop before someone comes."

With a soft thud, Michael hopped off the rope to the floor, mere inches from the edge.

I exhaled and clambered to my feet. "Okay, can we go now?"

"Not so fast. It's your turn."

My stomach sank to my toes. "Oh, no. You're not getting me near that rope. We shouldn't even be up here."

He reached out a hand. "C'mon, Ruth. Just try standin' on it for a bit."

"You won't make me walk on it?" *What am I saying?*

"Promise. Take off your shoes."

With blood coursing in my ears, I unlaced my boot-like shoes down past my ankles. My fingers wouldn't cooperate. Why had I let Mother talk me out of wearing my easy ones? I pulled them off and smoothed my stockings, as if that would do any good.

Michael moved to the cleat on the floor where the rope was knotted. "Take my hand."

Sweat dripped down my back. "I'm only going to stand on it, and then we're leaving, right?"

"Yeah, that's all you *should* do the first time."

"First, last, and only time."

Maybe I could manage to stand on it for a second, if he showed me how. I took a step closer to the rope, and Michael caught my clammy hand.

Now my heart pounded for a different reason. I'd never held a boy's hand, other than Richard's and Papa's, if those even counted.

Stooping down, Michael grabbed the rope with his other hand. "Place your right foot here, at an angle. Get your balance, and boost yerself up when you're ready."

I concentrated on doing exactly what he said. In that moment, my highest goal in life was to balance on a four-inch-thick rope for two seconds.

As soon as I stood, I wobbled right and left, but Michael supported me with a quick hand at my waist, until I was somewhat balanced. Gritting my teeth, I straightened my body. My toes felt miles away.

"Don't look down. Look straight ahead."

I lifted my gaze an inch at a time. From my perch, the shining white *City of Benares* spread out before me, and the Egyptian shores that had looked so dull before now made the skin on my arms tingle.

One finger at a time, I released my death grip on his hand. With my feet more or less steady, I spread my arms.

"How do ya feel?"

I took one tiny breath, trying to ignore my shaky legs. "Invincible."

A shadow passed below us on the deck, followed by a holler. "Hey! What's going on up there?"

The next thing I knew, I lost my balance and fell, sprawled on top of Michael. Heavy footsteps bounded up the iron stairs. I scrambled off Michael and looked up into the angry eyes of Second Officer Clayton.

"Miss Becker!" He took hold of both our wrists and pulled us to our feet. To Michael, he said, "Who are you, and what are you doing up here?"

"Michael Frank, sir. I was just showing Ruth somethin'. I'm sorry, sir."

I was about to object when Mr. Clayton cut me off. "Passengers are not allowed up here."

"Yes, sir." Michael hung his head. "Terribly sorry, sir."

I couldn't let Michael take all the blame, but Mr. Clayton pulled us toward the stairs, rapid-firing his words. "We're going to have a little *chat*, you two. This is a restricted area, not safe for children. Did you think that chain across the stairs was for decoration?"

We grabbed our shoes, and Mr. Clayton led us down the stairs in our stocking feet into the alcove, away from strolling passengers.

He set our backs against the wall and faced us. "Tell me what you were doing," he said, folding his arms, nostrils flaring.

My throat went dry. "We're so sorry, Mr. Clayton. We were only exploring a bit."

"It was all my idea, sir." Michael flexed his wrist. "Me dad and me, we're in the circus, you see, and—"

"The circus?" Officer Clayton faced me. "Is that why you were up on that rope? Performing a little balancing act?"

I tried to steady my voice. "I said I would try it only for a second."

Mr. Clayton paced in front of us. "I must report this infraction to Captain Drummond. He will want to inform your parents."

I swallowed. The prospect of facing Mother scared me more than a confrontation with the captain, or even stepping up on that rope. My heart nearly galloped out of my chest.

Will Michael and I have to walk the plank? Which would be worse—the plank itself or Mother's tongue-lashing?

⁓

Mr. Clayton let me go, assuring me that we'd talk later. What did he mean by that?

While Mother bathed and rested that afternoon, I forced myself to practice violin and babysit, but I could hardly concentrate on doing either very well.

My knees twitched at dinner that evening, and I didn't have much of an appetite. A somber Michael and Mr. Frank strode in late. Instead of his usual chattiness, Michael barely lifted his eyes. He took his seat across from me at the end of the table.

"I'm sorry we're late," Mr. Frank said. I'd never seen him act so serious, and his scar appeared darker. "We had a problem, but it's taken care of. How is everyone?"

With that, the strange moment passed as the adults made small talk. Natalie kept Richard amused with a finger game, and Millie and Elizabeth played charades with Marion.

If Mother noticed anything unusual, she diverted it with trite observations about the weather. "I'm so grateful the canal is almost behind us. I'm looking forward to some cooler breezes from the Mediterranean."

Mr. Frank looked over the dinner menu card. "So are we, Mrs. Becker."

While Rushab took dinner requests, I cleared my throat until Michael looked up at me. I mouthed my words, *What happened?*

He drummed his fingers on the table and checked to see if his dad was listening. "I have something for you," he whispered.

He and I didn't talk at all during the meal. I could barely eat my chicken Italiano, even though the sauce was cheesy and spiced just right. Michael didn't exactly clean his plate either.

"My, you two are quiet this evening," Elizabeth remarked. "You look tired, Michael."

He avoided eye contact with her. "I'm all right."

His dad moved his chair back from the table. "He's had a long day. We'll be going to our cabin now. G'night."

"What about dessert?" Marion asked.

Mr. Frank sighed. "Y' can eat mine for me, Marion. Let's go, Son."

Michael stood and brushed his napkin off the side of the table.

We both reached for it. Under the table, he shoved a folded piece of paper into my hand. I pulled it into my lap as he left the dining room with his dad.

I needed a distraction. I couldn't let Mother get suspicious. "Could we walk on the deck together when we're finished with dessert?"

Natalie cut Richard's carrots so Mother could eat. "That would be lovely!"

"I suppose," Mother said. "Richard could use some air, and so could I, even if it is still ninety degrees."

Every second-class passenger seemed to have the same idea. From the bow of the ship, we watched the pink-orange fireball sink into the ocean, foretelling another sweltering day tomorrow.

"We're halfway to England," an elderly gentleman nearby said to his acquaintance.

That's all? Guntur seemed years behind us. The world was so much bigger than I had imagined.

Millie and Natalie twirled Marion in a circle until she was dizzy. They all moved to the railing to view the sandy Egyptian shoreline, which was not nearly as interesting as seen from my vantage point that afternoon.

Taking advantage of their good moods, I dashed around a corner, descended steps to the next deck, and found a bench where I could read Michael's note.

Dear Ruth,

Mr. Clayton took me to Captain Drummond. I told him it was my fault for what happened. The captain sent for Dad, and I had to tell him everything, but I left you out. Dad said I had to stay in the cabin for the rest of the voyage, but Captain D said I should be allowed out for meals, so Dad decided three days in the cabin will do. Please forgive me for all this trouble.

Michael

His penmanship was nicer than mine. I reread the letter and slumped back against the wall. Would Michael have received a lighter sentence if Mr. Frank knew I was involved? But thanks to Michael, Mr. Frank didn't know I'd even been there.

Was I off the hook?

But Mr. Clayton may have still wanted to talk to me. Should I have tried to find him before he hunted me down or told Mother? I shuddered. What if he was filling her in right that minute about her wayward, irresponsible, rope-balancing daughter?

I dashed up the steps and searched for my family. They weren't where I left them. I searched among all the groups of passengers. Maybe Mother had been summoned to the bridge.

"Sissy!"

Marion and Richard sat with Mother and our friends at two small café tables. Mother tilted her chin down. "Where did you go?"

I managed a smile, pretending all was well. "Only to the water closet."

She shushed me. "No need to make an announcement of it, Ruth."

The sun had nearly set, and the Suez reflected the still-fiery sky. The ship continued to move at a sloth's pace through the canal. If not for the ramshackle buildings floating by in slow motion, I wouldn't have thought we were moving at all.

"We decided to get ice cream," Millie said. "It's complimentary tonight."

"And it's free," Marion added. She wiggled in her chair.

I took the seat saved for me. A steward brought six small dishes of vanilla ice cream with butterscotch sauce, each topped with a cherry. Mother shared hers with Richard, but he pushed it away. When an officer walked by, I became deeply interested in stirring my ice cream. Thank goodness, he wasn't Mr. Clayton.

My ice cream was already melting into a butterscotch soup. "Do you think the ship will go back to rolling around when we're in the Mediterranean?"

"Some, but it won't be like the Arabian Sea," Natalie said, licking her spoon. "It should be mostly smooth until we reach the Atlantic."

Millie helped Marion clean ice cream off her chin. "I don't think we mentioned that we've been sleeping outside on deck. It's ever so much cooler."

71

"You sleep out here?" I looked around the open deck. "Do you bring blankets and pillows?"

Elizabeth chuckled. "Just sheets and our top mattresses. Fifteen to twenty women have been sleeping here the last several nights." She smirked and leaned close to Mother. "Even first class."

Mother's brow furrowed. "Isn't that rather dangerous?"

"It's quite safe, really." Natalie brushed her blonde hair from her cheek. "An older steward stands guard. There's also a stewardess."

I made a show of mopping my forehead with my napkin. An idea occurred to me that might help me find Mr. Clayton before he found me—or, even worse, before he found Mother.

I fanned my face. "It's so hot, even with the sun down."

"My goodness," Mother said, "you never used to comment so much about the heat."

Millie turned toward Mother. "Why not let Ruth and Marion sleep out here with us tonight?"

"Hurray!" Marion shouted. "Please, Mama?"

"We'll take good care of them, we promise," Elizabeth said.

I pleaded in silence, my spoon poised over my bowl. Mother dabbed Richard's neck and forehead with her handkerchief. "That's very nice, but I don't think—"

"They can put their mattress right beside ours, Mrs. Becker," Natalie said, "and we'll return them to you first thing in the morning."

I shut my eyes tight and fanned myself with new urgency.

"That will do, Ruth." Mother was clearly annoyed. "Very well, you may sleep out here if you stay with the ladies and do as you're told."

Marion waved her spoon in the air. "Yippee!"

As soon as we scraped the last drops of ice cream from our dishes, Marion and I hurried toward the cabin to put on our nightclothes. After admonishments from Mother about proper behavior, saying our prayers, and promising to come right back in the morning, it was time to drag our mattress up to the deck for our overnight stay under the stars.

Now I might have a better chance of seeing Mr. Clayton in the morning. Can I head him off before he speaks to Mother?

～〜～

From our mattress, Marion waved her doll at the sky. "Look at the stars, Sissy."

The vast sea of dark blue above our heads was studded with diamonds. I held her hand and pointed her finger at the Big Dipper, the way Papa had done with me, so she could follow its outline of seven stars.

"Look at the two brightest stars in the bowl of the dipper," I said. "Follow them up in a straight line."

"Why is the Big Dipper at home and here at the same time?"

"Because the earth turns, and we see different stars at different times. The stars are always in the same place. But the sky is so big that sometimes we can see the same stars from different places on Earth. The Big Dipper is part of a bigger picture in the sky, called the Great Bear. The dipper handle is the bear's tail. See it?"

She sighed. "Maybe. It's too big, Sissy. I can't tell."

Millie sat up on her mattress next to Marion. "Ruth, how do you know so much about astronomy?"

"My father taught me," I replied. I took Marion's finger again and pointed. "Follow those two stars straight up to that other bright star."

Marion laughed. "I see it!"

"That's the North Star. It's the end of the handle on the Little Dipper. It's kind of upside down."

She tilted her head to the side. "It's crooked."

"Yes, it doesn't look quite like the Big Dipper. But if you can find the North Star, you can find any of the constellations from there."

"Can we do this again tomorrow?"

"I don't know, maybe. Let's just enjoy it tonight."

Marion was quiet for a minute, then she asked, "When we gonna get to Sam Town?"

"Southampton? Not for a few weeks yet."

She rolled toward me and kissed me on the cheek. "Night-night, Sissy." She closed her eyes and folded her hands. "God bless Mama and Papa, and Sissy and Richard, and me and everybody in the whole wide world. Amen."

Amen.

Millie and her companions chatted softly on their mattresses. They'd tied up their hair with strips of cloth to keep cooler. Warm breezes passed over the *City of Benares*, much nicer than the dead air in our cabin. A whiff of someone's toilet water and the sound of soft breathing relaxed my tumbled thoughts.

We'd brought our pillows, and I took my journal and pen from beneath mine. Light from the stairwell and remnant of the quarter moon were just bright enough. I opened the journal to the front cover and re-read what Miss Knauss had written before she gave it to me.

Dear Ruth,

You're about to embark on an adventure of a lifetime. Use this journal to record your memories and feelings along the way. Someday, you'll reflect on them and smile, and perhaps even share them with your own children.

May God guide you on your journey and keep you in His care.

G. Knauss, March 6, 1912

Would I truly look back one day and smile? I couldn't imagine it—not while I still felt like I'd been thrown from a cliff and ordered to swim.

I stared deeper into the vastness of space. Papa had tried to guide me through life, just as the stars had guided the ancient mariners through unknown waters. Now, as I took this strange trek into the unknown without him, it was no wonder I felt lost.

SS City of Benares, Suez Canal
March 16, 1912

Sky Report: Tonight, a gigantic black canopy hangs high above me, covered in stars. The stars are like a full orchestra. Each instrument, no matter how insignificant it may appear, plays a role in the production of a great symphony. Each star over my head forms part of a constellation, telling a story against a black velvet canvas, the way Sajni's quilt squares tell stories amid countless tiny stars on black silk.

If the stars are an orchestra, making up symphonies of constellations with stories, perhaps there is a story for me, somewhere in those stars. If only the stars could be a path and show me the way.

CHAPTER ELEVEN

SS City of Benares, Suez Canal
March 17, 1912
Dawn

An awful scraping sound startled me awake. A crewman was dragging a stack of deck chairs behind our mattresses. I pulled the thin sheet over my head, but then I removed it five seconds later. The sun barely peeked over the horizon, but the sticky breeze promised another hot day ahead.

Marion lay sleeping perpendicular to me with her head on my leg. Millie stirred and pushed herself up on one elbow. I shut my eyes so she'd think I was asleep.

After the crewman vanished, Millie lay quiet, as did everyone else on the deck. *Now where is Mr. Clayton, and how can I find him?*

I extracted my leg from under Marion's head and reached for my dressing gown, wishing I'd thought to bring more appropriate clothing. I waved to the stewardess at her post against the wall. In slow motion, I crawled off the mattress.

Quick footsteps on the nearby stairs made me pause, and Jack appeared at the hatchway. "Miss Becker, are you here?" He spoke in a loud whisper. "Miss Ruth Becker?"

Uh-oh. I raised my hand.

"Miss Becker, your mother asks that you return to the cabin immediately."

No! Mr. Clayton must have paid her a visit. I would be chained to a dark wall somewhere in the hold with no breakfast. I'd read about rats on ships …

"I'm coming."

Millie sat up. "Ruth, do you want me to go with you?"

That was definitely not a good idea. "No, but would you please take care of Marion until I get back?" *If I come back.*

"Of course." She lay back on her mattress and turned to face my sleeping sister.

Wrapping myself in my dressing gown, I hurried to follow Jack. This was *not* my plan.

One deck down, a man sat in a chair, reading a book near the railing. I looked again at his face in the dim light.

Mr. Frank.

He glanced up as we approached. "Ruth! Are you all right?"

I couldn't let him suspect anything was wrong. I glanced at Jack, who clearly wanted me to hurry. "My mother wants me to come to the cabin, that's all."

Mr. Frank took one look at Jack and rose from his chair. "I'll come with you."

I started to follow Jack to the next stairway and called over my shoulder, "I'm sure everything's fine, Mr. Frank!"

"If he's your friend, Miss Becker, let him come," Jack said. "Your mother may need a hand with Master Richard."

Richard is the reason I'm being summoned? A mix of relief and anger filled me. My new sea legs grew wobbly.

Mr. Frank caught up to us. "What's wrong with Richard?"

"Better for Mrs. Becker to explain, sir," Jack whispered as we reached the passageway to our cabin. As soon as Jack tapped the door, Mother pulled it open.

"Thank you, Jack." She backed up so I could enter, appearing puzzled at the sight of Mr. Frank behind me. "Why are you here?"

"To be of some help, ma'am." He kept his voice low. "Is Richard all right?"

Jack stood to the side. "Will there be anything else, Mrs. Becker?"

Mother tightened the sash on her dressing gown. "No, I don't think so." Releasing a long breath, she held the door open wide for Mr. Frank. "You might as well come in. Everyone else has been here."

Richard slept in a rumpled ball in the middle of her bed. She wiped her nose with a handkerchief. "Is Marion all right? Where is she?"

"She's asleep," I said. "Millie was awake when I left and she's watching her."

Mother sank to the chair by the washstand. "I've been up all night. Richard's fever returned, and he had two seizures in two hours." She pushed her loose hair away. "I went to Jack's cabin and made him get the ship's doctor. He was here around four o'clock."

Mr. Frank moved closer to the bed and peered down at Richard. "How is he now?"

Mother's shoulders drooped. "I don't know. His fever's still high."

Richard rolled onto his back, eyes closed. I took in his pale cheeks and lips, trying to think of what to do next. "What did the doctor say?"

"He gave me something that helps prevent seizures in adults—he cut the dose in half—but I can't give it to him until he eats something." Mother clutched her handkerchief to her mouth.

The heat in the cabin was stifling. Richard let out a moan, and Mother jumped to her feet and checked his forehead. "He's so hot! I can't let him go through another seizure, but I can't get his fever down, and he isn't due to take the medicine for another two hours."

Mr. Frank felt Richard's forehead. "It is high, that's for sure." He looked around the room. "Let's try other ways, without medicine. Ruth, go ask Jack for a small tub or basin."

"I think there's one in the WC," I said.

"Good, bring it here. We'll fill it partway with tepid water, not cold."

Mother motioned to a wet cloth on her bedpost. "I've been sponging him off, but—"

"We'll give him some cool drinks if he'll take 'em," Mr. Frank said. "And we need to get the air circulatin' in here. Maybe we can fan him. Better ask Jack what he can bring, Ruth."

With Mr. Frank taking charge of the situation, I dashed out the door and headed toward Jack's cabin, five doors down. Finding Mr. Clayton would have to wait.

Jack and I returned with the basin from the WC and a pitcher of lukewarm water. Mr. Frank poured water from the pitcher over his wrist and into the basin. "Just right. This should be plenty."

Richard wailed and wriggled in Mother's arms. She held him firmly and knelt next to Mr. Frank beside the metal basin. "Are you sure it isn't too cold?" she asked him.

"It's room temp, I'd say. The way me wife would fix it for Michael."

Mother dipped Richard's feet into the water. Mr. Frank poured water from a cupped hand over Richard's legs. "Do you think he'll sit?" he asked her.

She lowered Richard a bit more until he sat in the basin, diaper and all, but he cried and reached for her.

"Hey, now, Richard." Mr. Frank's voice was calm and deep, just like Papa's. "This'll make y' feel better." He cupped his hand again to pour water over Richard's arms and back. "Ruth, prop the door open with that chair, and see if there's somethin' to fan the air."

Mother ran a wet cloth over Richard's arms. "But he mustn't catch a chill."

"O' course," Mr. Frank replied. "We only want to cool the room some."

With the chair holding the door open, I waved a towel up and down. Jack appeared at the doorway with a small tray of beverages and ice and set it on the washstand.

Richard cried louder, and Mr. Frank sang, "*Mary had a little lamb, little lamb, little lamb ...*"

My brother's cries lessened. He looked so small in Mr. Frank's hands. With wide eyes, he watched as Mr. Frank continued to sing and pour handfuls of water over his body.

My arms grew tired, and I stopped fanning the air. Mother sat back and rubbed her forehead. Her bottom lip quivered as her eyes met mine.

In an odd way, I felt as if I was seeing her clearly for the first time.

She's taking her son halfway around the world to give him a chance to get well, and all she wants is to get him through this long journey without a fuss.

Mr. Frank finished the song, and Richard gave him a weak smile.

Mother sighed. "Thank you. He seems better already."

"Let's take him out of this tub and give him somethin' to drink," Mr. Frank said.

I handed the towel to him. He wrapped it around Richard and gently lifted him from the basin. He rested his head against Mr. Frank's shoulder and closed his eyes.

CHAPTER TWELVE

SS City of Benares, Suez Canal
March 17, 1912
7:30 a.m.

Minutes later, Mr. Frank left. Richard lay asleep in his crib wearing a clean diaper.

Jack knocked softly on the open door. "Pardon me, Miss Becker. I had a feeling you might not make it to breakfast today, so I took the liberty of bringing your family something to eat."

On his shoulder, he carried a large tray loaded with three covered dishes, a steaming teapot, cups and saucers, and a carafe of water. He set the tray on Mother's bed with a quiet sureness.

Mother rose from her seat, obviously moved by the gesture. "How very kind of you, Jack."

I checked the passageway for any sign of Mr. Clayton. Instead, Marion's voice echoed from near the stairs.

"Someone's bringing Marion. I'll go help." I started down the passageway just as Marion, Natalie, and Millie came into view, lugging our mattress and pillows.

"Allow me," Jack said.

I thanked Natalie and Millie, and Jack hurried to put the room back together. When he left, Mother, Marion, and I ate our breakfast. I took Marion to the WC to wash and dress, and Richard woke when we returned. He laughed at us in surprise, as if to ask what we were doing there.

Marion reached into the crib and patted his back. "Richard, guess what? Me and Sissy slept outside all night."

Mother felt his forehead and cheeks. "He's cooler now, thank God." She offered him a drink of water and some hot cereal, and he perked up after a few mouthfuls. She gave him the anti-seizure medication, settled him back in his crib, then lay on her bed. "Ruth, I'd like you to stay in the cabin today. I've had no sleep, so perhaps I can get some with your help."

I didn't mind keeping out of sight. Michael would be staying in his cabin anyway. Maybe Mr. Clayton would be too busy and forget about me, and we'd avoid a confrontation. With everything Mother was going through with Richard, I could only hope he wouldn't show up.

Sajni's quilt made a good cushion. I opened it all the way for the first time since leaving Guntur and spread it over our bed.

"What should we do, Sissy?" Marion asked.

"How about you pull out all the books you brought, and I'll read 'em to you." *Did I just say* them *the way Michael does?*

Marion plugged her nose. "Richard …"

I lifted him out of his crib. His diaper was disgusting. *Great.*

"Go ahead and climb on the quilt while I change his nasty diaper."

"Thank you, Ruth," Mother said from her bed, her eyes closed.

Once Richard was fully clean, I let him crawl on top of the quilt next to Marion. I read to them quietly from Marion's books, and Richard rested on the pillow and played with her doll. I finished reading ten books. How else could I entertain them?

"Can I see your birds, Sissy?"

"*May* I? But you know the answer to that. Plus, they're wrapped in the trunk, and I'm not unpacking them."

Marion stuck out her bottom lip, then she moved her books. "Can you show me Sodgie's quilt pitchers?"

Richard sat up, patted his corner of the quilt, and said, "Kiki," his word for flower.

I guess I can do that. I pointed to the flower stitched onto the corner. "This is a lotus, India's national flower. Remember the pink-and-white ones behind our church? And this is a dancer."

Marion held her arms high with her palms together, like the dancer Sajni had so carefully stitched onto another square of the quilt. The dancer wore deep-teal pantaloons and slippers with a purple tunic. Tiny gold bracelets were embroidered on her arms, and Sajni had even added some *mehndi* to the dancer's dainty hands.

"And here's an elephant," I said. "They carry people and heavy things. They're also very smart and they live a long time."

Wait—what's this? Where Marion had been sitting, Sajni had finished the last three squares! How could I have not noticed them before?

The first was a red-and-black ocean liner against a sea of white, with four masts surrounding a single, red-and-black funnel. It wasn't quite the *City of Benares*, but I liked the look of it. Over the ship, my name was embroidered in silky red lettering, and next to my name, a violin.

The next square held a beautiful gold cross, outlined in white, and last, our bungalow, with Teddy asleep on the front step.

Sajni had thought of everything. She'd even added her initials and *1912* in the quilt's lower right corner. I traced the year with my finger and tried not to cry.

Marion bent to kiss the picture of Teddy, then brushed her hand over the saffron-yellow elephant and its curved white tusks. "I wanna go home, Sissy."

It occurred to me that she might have not understood all that was happening. I swallowed and whispered, "I know. But we're going to meet our grandparents, and Papa will come to be with us in America."

"Are you crying?" she asked.

I shook my head and sniffed. "I miss home, too." I rubbed her arms. "We'll be fine, though. I promise." *If only I could believe my own words.*

Marion wound a strand of her hair around her finger. "Can you help me write to Papa?"

Richard had fallen asleep. I settled him on the quilt with his baby blanket. Papa told me that day in his office to put the needs of others ahead of my own. Why were the "others" always my little sister and brother?

"Why don't you draw him a picture? I'll find some paper."

~

The rest of the morning matched our endless glide through the Suez. Mother woke from her nap, and I practiced several songs on my violin. I moved my fingers precisely along the neck, and with each draw of the bow across the strings, I became lost in my own world—the world of the Mission School and Mr. Liddle, my family bungalow, the stars and Papa, Sajni and my classmates and Teddy.

It was the world I knew and understood, predictable and peaceful. *How very far away that world is now.*

Richard napped off and on, thanks to the medicine. I helped Marion wash her hair while Mother wrote letters. I was hungry and ready to get out of the cabin to see our friends again. "It's almost dinnertime," I said. "Can we all go?"

"I don't want to take Richard to dinner," Mother said. "I'm going to do as Dr. Collins said and let him get as much rest as possible. You and your sister may go up, and I'll ask Jack to bring a tray."

I braided Marion's damp hair, almost as well as when Mother braided it. At least I would see Michael at dinner, and maybe I could talk to him alone. As Marion and I climbed the stairs to the deck, the ship rocked a bit. Had we hit something?

On deck, several passengers stood near the railing. I checked to see what held their interest. The sleepy Suez was gone, and a large body of slate blue water now surrounded our vessel, with no shore in sight.

Sometime during the day, when I was too busy in the cabin to notice, the ship had entered the Mediterranean Sea. The invigorating scent of fresh, open water raised my spirits.

"Sissy, we're movin' again!"

I lifted Marion and carried her to the railing. Choppy waves now slapped at the ship's hull. "I think we'll be rocked to sleep tonight."

I never thought I'd miss it, but after our eternal sojourn through the steamy Suez, I was ready for some rocking again. But the Mediterranean also meant I was farther from home.

A voice behind me made my stomach drop.

"Hello, ladies." Mr. Clayton stood in the middle of the deck. He beckoned me to step closer.

This is it. At least Mother will be spared hearing of my crime for now.

The Franks made their way toward us from across the deck. I set Marion down. "Go with Mr. Frank and Michael for a minute."

Mr. Clayton waved a hand toward the water. "Welcome to the Mediterranean Sea, Miss Becker. How are you and your family faring?"

I snuck a glance at Michael, whose face tensed when he saw us. I leaned toward Mr. Clayton so no one would hear. "Well, sir, my brother is sick with a bad fever. I don't want to worry my mother about anything else, so if you wouldn't mind, could you please not speak to her about … *you know.*"

He straightened and clasped his hands behind his back. "It is my understanding that Captain Drummond handled the situation. If there are no further infractions, I do not intend to speak to anyone about it again."

No lockdown in the brig? No plank to walk?

My sea legs swayed for a moment like underwater reeds. "Oh, there won't be any infractions, sir. I promise. Both of us promise."

I thanked him with a Mediterranean-wide smile.

CHAPTER THIRTEEN

SS City of Benares, Mediterranean Sea
March 17, 1912
6:30 p.m.

Marion dug her dessert spoon into the chocolate pudding with the same enthusiasm as a tiger pouncing on its prey.

"Your mum must be glad Richard's better," Mr. Frank said, "and jolly well pleased that we're through the canal." He nodded toward our view of the Mediterranean displayed through the dining room windows.

I swirled my pudding around before tasting it. "She's relieved, definitely. So am I."

Relief—the perfect word to describe the feeling in my chest, now that Mr. Clayton had wiped the slate clean for Michael and me. Maybe putting the Suez behind us was a sign of good things to come. *Better, anyway.*

Elizabeth's coppery tresses caught the glow in the room from the setting sun. How she managed to keep the Gibson Girl look every day amazed me. "We're certain to have some cooler breezes now," she said.

Millie dove her spoon into her own pudding. "Perhaps we won't need to sleep on deck anymore."

Marion bounced in her seat. "I wanna sleep outside again."

Millie laughed. "It was fun having you there, Marion."

"Girls are lucky," Michael said. "Wish they'd let fellows sleep outside. Our cabin stinks like wet shoes."

Not having Mother present made it easier for me to join in the conversation. "All the stars … that's been the best part of this whole voyage for me. But I'm ready to get off the ship."

"You'll have your wish the day after tomorrow," Natalie said, "when we reach Valletta. I read in *Ladies' Home Journal* that Malta has had quite a history."

"And we'll have most of the day," Mr. Frank said. "Her harbor's quite a sight."

"Valletta, Malta," I said. "Sounds like a fancy dessert."

Mr. Frank lowered his teacup to its saucer. "There's a nice ol' restaurant I've been to, not far from the docks. You like fish, Natalie? Would you like to go there for lunch?"

Even though I sat at the far end of the table, I couldn't miss the knowing look that flashed between Elizabeth and Millie.

Mr. Frank coughed and added, "All of us, of course."

Elizabeth barely hid her smile with her napkin. With a wide grin, Millie took a sudden interest in whatever was happening at the next table.

Michael interrupted, probably to save his father's embarrassment. "Last time, there was a whale of a storm and we couldn't even dock at Malta, so I haven't seen it meself yet."

His dad cocked his head. "Wait a minute. I think we're forgetting somethin'."

"But that'll be the third day, Dad." Michael flexed his wrist. "Please?"

"I'm done." Marion dropped her spoon in her dish with a loud clank.

"Use your napkin," I said. "Half your pudding is on your face." A round of laughter resulted. Marion stuck out her lip.

"Oh, look what I've done," Millie said, wearing a pudding mustache she had painted on her face. She winked at Marion.

Marion grinned and wagged her finger. "Use your napkin, Miss Millie!" We all roared with laughter as Rushab brought a fresh pot of Earl Grey tea to refill our cups.

Michael covered one side of his mouth as though he were trying to keep his dad from hearing. "Did you read my note?"

"I thought for sure Mr. Clayton was going to tell my mother," I whispered. "I asked him not to, and he said he wouldn't. But no more circus tricks."

He grinned. "Promise. I'll spend tomorrow with Dad and then pray I can get off the ship at Valletta."

After dinner, I was in no hurry to return to our cabin. Marion and I ambled along the outside decks, and she hopscotched across imaginary squares. I showed her a map of the Mediterranean Sea and Europe in one of the stairwells.

Our route was highlighted in red, and I pointed to Malta. "We're almost there."

She ran her finger along the rest of the red line, all the way to Southampton, England. "We got this much left? Is that a lot of days?"

"Yes. Many days." *An endless voyage.*

We wandered to the stern, and I took a chance and led her to the first-class deck area. Just as I suspected, no one seemed to care about two girls minus their parents. "We're in first class," I whispered. "Be Princess Marion."

She gave me a solemn nod.

Hand in hand, we strolled along the railing of the first-class deck. I moved us closer to a group of five women so I could admire their dresses—tiny sewn-on beads, silk and lace in pastel shades, with hems just above the floor, showing off coordinating beaded shoes. Each woman's hair was perfectly pinned.

"Edith," one said, "did you notice the hobble skirts in the last issue of *Vogue*? The designers must think women don't need to walk fast." They all laughed. Maybe Natalie could tell me what a hobble skirt looked like.

Nearby, a group of young men eyed the ladies. One man bravely approached. "Pardon me, ladies," he said, "but those gentlemen over there were wondering—"

"Let's go, Sissy." Marion pulled me away just as things were starting to get interesting.

An older couple crossed in front of us with two fox terriers, popular pets among the British in India due to the breed's ability to stand the heat. Except for my time through the Suez, that was a trait I shared with them.

Marion pulled me the other way to avoid the dogs, and I had to peel her off my leg. "Don't be afraid just because you were chased once. They're not all like that, you know."

"I still don't like dogs!"

We took three flights of stairs down to our deck. As we reached D-29, Mother placed a tray bearing a half-eaten plate of food in the passageway for Jack to retrieve. "Come see what we have, girls."

Inside our door, she pointed to a long electrical cord that snaked its way from a plug in the wall to … *a fan*! A swift breeze blew through the cabin, ruffling our sheets and the pages of Mother's book on her bed.

Richard bounced in his crib. "Boot! Mimi!"

Mother looked more awake than when we'd left for dinner. "Jack brought the fan. He said Mr. Clayton sent it. Isn't he one of the officers, Ruth?"

Marion planted her feet in front of the fan, allowing the breeze to blow her hair around.

I shrugged as if I had no idea. "I think so."

The man I'd assumed would sentence Michael and me to the brig had not only forgiven us, but he had also sent a fan to keep my family comfortable. I smiled at the gift, amazed at the turn of events.

"How was your dinner?" Mother asked.

Marion held her arms out to her sides. "We had pudding. And there's dogs on the ship, and Sissy and Michael did sumpin' bad."

My mouth fell open. "Marion!"

Mother folded her arms. "What is she talking about, Ruth?"

So much for thinking the whole rope-walking business was behind me. I had no choice but to act innocent. "Nothing. Marion, you're confused."

My sister swung her arms back and forth. "I heard you talkin' about circus tricks."

I forced a nonchalant chuckle. "We were talking about the circus and the tricks they perform."

Mother sighed. "Get ready for bed, girls."

After tucking in Marion and Richard, Mother turned to me as I brushed my hair. "You know, I misjudged Mr. Frank." She pulled pins from her hair and laid them on the dresser. "The way he helped with Richard this morning, when I couldn't think straight … Come to think of it, he's been nothing but kind and thoughtful to all of us from the minute we met."

I wanted to say I'd told her so, but I could only breathe a big sigh of relief. As Papa would often say, *Will wonders never cease?*

SS City of Benares, Mediterranean Sea
March 17, 1912

Sky Report: At last, I don't have to write Suez Canal ever again and I can practice spelling Mediterranean! Excellent night for stargazing. Orion the Hunter stands high in the east. Betelgeuse and Rigel compete for the brightest star award, as always. I found gigantic Perseus, too, holding onto the head of Medusa.

I showed Marion how to find Orion's belt. When Papa looks at the stars tonight, I'm glad he'll see Orion too. I hope he misses me, because I miss him.

And I hope he's sorry.

CHAPTER FOURTEEN

SS City of Benares, Valletta, Malta
March 19, 1912

The *City of Benares* floated into the crystal waters of Valletta's harbor. I stood at the railing as dozens of seagulls soared and exchanged greetings overhead.

Mother wore the only hat she owned—a beige one with a silk gardenia attached. She held Richard and pointed to a large white dome. "See the church?"

Richard was more interested in the seagulls. He waved at them until they dipped low, resulting in one of his belly laughs.

"I wanna see, Sissy."

I hoisted Marion high, and she placed her hands on the railing. "It's pretty here," she said. "Can we stay?"

Natalie, Elizabeth, and Millie joined us, each of them wearing stylish outfits and hats to match. I still preferred bows to hats, but my dress from the Guntur market now felt wrong. Its pale-pink bodice had faded from drying in the sun, and the wide collar started to itch.

Where was Michael? Would Mr. Frank keep him on the ship on this beautiful day? Rope walking was part of his profession, after all. If he hadn't taken all the blame for our little stunt, I could've been stuck in my cabin, too—or worse.

At least Mother hadn't made an issue of what Marion said she heard. I had to make sure nothing else went wrong.

We felt the bump and jerk of the ship's starboard side against the dock. As soon as the gangplank was set in place, the first-class passengers disembarked.

"Good afternoon, ladies!"

Mr. Frank made his way through the crowd, wearing a blue shirt and light gray trousers with suspenders. "I say, you all look lovely this fine day. Michael's on his way. We slept in and skipped breakfast. May we escort all of you?"

Yes. Michael was coming.

Natalie's blue eyes beamed. "That would be very nice, Robert."

I could tell Mother and Millie were trying to stifle their smiles. Was a connection really taking place between Mr. Frank and Natalie?

"We all have letters to post," Mother said. "That's our first priority."

Mr. Frank patted his coat pocket. "We do as well. Let's find the nearest post office. Then the restaurant I spoke of isn't far. They serve the best seafood around."

The passengers pushed forward to descend the stairs, and I craned my neck to see if Michael was on his way up. What was keeping him?

Marion jerked my hand. "I have to go, Sissy."

People on the stairs parted to let Michael squeeze through. "Pardon me. Sorry. Tryin' to reach me dad."

He finished stuffing the hem of his shirt inside his trousers. He wore his too-small cap, which I hadn't seen since the train to Cochin. It slipped off, revealing shiny, slicked-back hair, parted down the middle like the straightest of train tracks. He was more scrubbed than I'd ever seen him.

Mother led the way downstairs toward the gangplank. Once we were off the ship, it was an odd feeling to be on solid ground and not feel any vibrations through my shoes. We located the post office, mailed our letters, and I found a washroom for Marion. Mr. Frank put Richard on his shoulders. Mother wrung her hands until my brother wrapped his arms around Mr. Frank's neck and laughed.

Mr. Frank led us past formal gardens and beautiful homes. At one corner stood the most incredible building I'd ever seen. "The Royal Opera House," he said. "She's a beauty."

Millie shielded her eyes with her gloved hand. "It's like a palace!"

Set on a hill, tall columns topped with intricate carvings graced the entire front. A wide set of stairs behind the columns led to a grand entrance. A sign advertised an upcoming performance with a full symphony orchestra.

I could bet there was an enormous lobby that had an echo. What would it have been like to perform there?

I imagined rushing up those stairs with my violin case. The huge paneled door would open, and I'd walk way, way down the red-carpeted aisle to the stage, to the first chair to the left of the conductor. A hush would fill the hall as he tapped his baton on the music stand …

I'm in Malta, of all places, where no one knows me, and no one cares that I play violin. A wave of sorrow threatened to pull me under once again. I hummed the scales and pretended to play them as fast as I could, my fingers mimicking the movements.

Michael groaned. "This is great, Dad, but I'm starving."

Natalie took Mr. Frank's arm. "Lead on, Robert."

He wore an ear-to-ear grin. Michael's jaw dropped, and I hummed the rest of the way to my first Maltese lunch.

~

It was late evening when we returned to the *City of Benares* for the next leg of our journey. My stomach felt odd, and my dress grew itchier by the minute. I couldn't wait to get to our cabin and take it off.

On deck, Mr. Frank slipped Richard into Mother's arms. "Thank you very much," she whispered. "We'll see you tomorrow."

Marion could barely stand, probably tired from her big restaurant meal, plus a stop for gelato and a romp in the park. I lifted her, and she relaxed her head on my shoulder. She must have gained ten pounds overnight.

By the time we reached our cabin, it hurt to take a deep breath. "I think I ate too much," I said. I let Marion fall back on our bed, and I rubbed my stomach.

Mother laid Richard next to Marion and removed her hat. "Please don't stand there. Help me get them undressed."

A stab of pain gripped my middle. *Uh-oh.*

I barely made it down the passageway to the WC before losing my entire lunch. I sat with my back against the cold wall of the tiny room, knees drawn to my chest. I prayed no one would knock on the door, wanting to come in.

My stomach rolled like a crippled ship on a stormy sea. Sweat poured down my forehead and wet hair stuck to my neck. I ran my hands across my angry midsection, and each breath made it hurt more. Another wave of nausea took control, and I was helpless until it finished its course.

The steam engines began their low drone, signaling our departure. The walls and floor vibrated, everything inside me churning in unison. I'd miss seeing the Valletta harbor as we pulled away, but I didn't care.

I hated Malta and the ship and all the reasons I was there. I hated Mother and Papa for ripping my life to shreds, Marion for constantly bothering me, and Richard for not getting well.

Someone help me. I can't do this anymore.

CHAPTER FIFTEEN

SS City of Benares, Algiers, Algeria
March 25, 1912

Dear Sajni,

Our ship dropped anchor in Algiers today, but it's raining too hard to disembark. To think I'm on the shores of North Africa, and I can only admire it from the harbor—not that there's much to admire. The sky and water are a matching dark gray. Rain is streaking down the windows that enclose the second-class dining room, where I currently sit with Marion while she draws pictures.

Six days ago, we docked in Malta, and I became ill from food poisoning. I'm not even sure what I ate, but most of it tasted like fish. After that, I didn't feel so well. I skipped dessert, even though it was gelato and lemon cake, and spent most of the night in the WC.

Richard's fever spiked, and he's had more seizures. Mother called for Dr. Collins, and she is keeping him quiet today. Sometimes I think she misses Papa more than I do, especially with Richard so sick.

While he naps, she's washing clothes in the bathtub we share with other passengers and hanging the clothes around the cabin to dry. I now have knickers hanging on my bedpost.

Mr. Frank says that, in England, women who are sent to India to find husbands are called the "fishing fleet." I don't think the women we've met went for that reason, not that they wouldn't like to marry someday. They've told me so much about their university that I'm starting to wonder if college may be in my future. But I do want to continue with the violin, no matter what.

I love the new squares on the quilt! The trip across the Atlantic will be colder, especially at night, which is hard to imagine after the stifling heat of the Suez Canal. It topped India's heat any day, if you can imagine.

Please give these pictures of our ship and our friends to Papa from Marion. I helped her write your name on the picture she drew for you.

Your loving "sister,"
Ruth

~

Two days later, the *City of Benares* reached the port of Gibraltar. After three solid days of gray skies and rain, the sun finally made an appearance, and I couldn't wait to go ashore at our last Mediterranean port.

In the cabin, Mother finished tying a bow on Marion's braid. "Whatever happens, stay with Ruth," she instructed. "Hold her hand, and don't let go. Ruth, please don't take your eyes off her."

"I won't." I pulled my other black stocking on and checked under the bed for my shoes. I hummed "Onward, Christian Soldiers" instead of saying something I'd regret.

"I hate to stay on board," Mother said, "but Richard simply isn't well enough today."

Shoes in hand, I wiggled out from beneath the bed and buckled the shoes onto my feet. Mother brushed off my dress with her free hand. "Do be careful, Ruth. Please stay with the adults."

Marion and I grabbed our sweaters and pecked Mother's cheek as we left. My sister skipped down the passageway, pulling me along. "This'll be a fun day, Sissy."

Natalie, Millie, Elizabeth, Mr. Frank, and Michael greeted us at the gangplank. The women wore light coats over slim skirts, and I was glad I had my thick sweater. Sunlight danced on the harbor waters, and a cool breeze ruffled my hair and tickled my cheeks.

We followed other passengers down the long dock toward the town. A lively *oom-pa-pa* from an accordion and tuba thumped from up ahead where a crowd had gathered on the far side of the town square.

"Michael, look." Mr. Frank pointed beyond the crowd as we approached. "It's a circus."

I stood on my tiptoes in time to see a man do a somersault in the air. Onlookers cheered. I stared in awe. How did he do that? Except for juggling by The Great Frank and Son, Marion and I had never seen a circus before.

"Let's go!" Michael slipped through the crowd with ease and led us to the opposite side of the square for a better view. On the grass, a band played trumpets, tuba, accordion, and drums. We zigzagged between people until Marion could stand with two little girls and the rest of us could see fairly well.

Two men now spun around on separate trapeze bars, positioned about ten feet off the ground. They hung by their knees, then their ankles, and then their hands, and they flew through the air trading bars.

The crowd roared and applauded, and I yelled right along, "More, more!"

Natalie turned to Mr. Frank. "Can you do that?"

He squeezed Michael's shoulder. "We both can."

"Fancy that!" Elizabeth said. "If you ever perform in London, we all shall come."

I checked on Marion. She and Millie clapped and hopped up and down with the other little girls. Papa would've called Millie a child at heart.

The acrobats now faced each other and juggled long wooden pins, tossing and catching them, throwing one in the air every few seconds and spinning around without dropping even one pin.

"They're almost as good as us, Dad," Michael said.

Mr. Frank laughed. "I don't know, I think we could learn a thing or two ... but I'd like to see 'em try juggling eggs."

The acrobats bowed to the audience, and one of the performers held up his hands. "Thank you, ladies and gentlemen. We hope you enjoyed the show! The next act begins in ten minutes." With that, they hurried behind the makeshift curtain near the band.

"They was good!" Marion said.

I turned to our friends. "I didn't know they would speak English."

"Most Gibraltar folks do, but many people here are Spanish," Mr. Frank said. "Spain borders Gibraltar at the North."

Millie tucked loose sections of her wild hair underneath her hat. "Does anyone remember what time the ship departs today?"

Elizabeth imitated the stern voice of Captain Drummond. "All passengers must be aboard by four o'clock."

Mr. Frank touched Natalie's arm. "Would you like to see more of the circus?"

She smiled at him and her girlfriends. "To be honest, we were thinking of doing some shopping." She waved her gloved hand toward a long row of shops and cafés across the grassy area where we stood. "You're welcome to join us while we get something to eat and look around."

"I wanna stay and see the next act," Michael said. "But you can go, Dad."

I wanted to stay too. "Could we wait here with Marion? We've never seen anything like this."

"No harm in that, I s'pose." Mr. Frank reached for his wallet. "If you get hungry, here's money for lunch. We'll meet you 'round the square, say, three o'clock?"

Michael pocketed the bills. "Aye aye, sir." He saluted. "Fifteen hundred hours."

Natalie took Mr. Frank's arm, and the four of them crossed the grass together. The band struck up a quick tune to introduce the next circus act. The crowd parted, and four men dressed in identical red outfits rode in on something like bicycle seats that had only one wheel attached.

"Blimey!" Michael shouted. "Unicycles!"

Marion returned to her spot up front near the performers, and Michael and I did our best to inch closer. The little girls had left, and three taller boys took their place next to Marion.

The unicyclists rode around in circles several times, then they each rode forward and backward, up and down wooden slopes. They had me mesmerized. How did they keep their balance, avoid running into each other, all the while smiling and waving at the same time?

If that wasn't enough, an assistant lit the ends of four long sticks and tossed them to the men on the unicycles. Soon, all four juggled the flaming sticks with each other. The heat warmed my face every time one whizzed by.

Marion reached around one boy's leg and pulled at my dress. "Sissy, I'm hungry."

"In a minute. Watch the show."

The crowd cheered. A dark-haired woman on a unicycle rode to the center, dressed in a sequined red shirtwaist and matching knee-length trousers. She circled the four men who continued to juggle the burning sticks. The band launched into a slower, more dramatic melody that was punctuated by drumrolls.

Next, the four fire-juggling men spread out to form a circle around the woman and her unicycle. She stopped pedaling and placed her hands on her seat. Balancing on the wobbly unicycle, she bent over and slowly raised her legs until her feet pointed to the sky.

The crowd broke into deafening cheers and applause.

"That's amazing!" I clapped hard and looked over one boy's shoulder. "Marion, what do you think?"

She wasn't there.

I turned to Michael. "Where did she go?"

He pointed to the spot where she'd been. "She was there a minute ago."

I tugged one boy by the arm. "Did you see that little girl?"

He yanked his arm back and shook his head. Michael questioned the other two boys. They shrugged and turned back to watch the performance.

"Marion!" I called, searching in front and behind the people near us.

Michael moved to the left, calling her name. I went to the right, shouting questions at spectators. "Did you see a little girl in a blue sweater and pinafore? She's my sister, she's this tall."

Some didn't appreciate the interruption. Most responded with shrugs or blank stares.

Michael caught up with me. "I can't find her."

Impossible. Marion was right *there.*

He clenched his fists. "I don't know how we could've lost her."

"She knows she isn't supposed to wander off!" I noted the dozens of gawkers who watched the unicyclists finish their act. "You don't think someone took her, do you?"

"Those fellows looked a bit dodgy, but we would've heard or seen somethin'."

I moaned. "We have to find her *now.*" I gripped his shoulder. "She said she was hungry. Maybe she went looking for your dad."

Michael and I sprinted across the grass toward the shops. Shoppers crowded every store we passed. Cafés bustled with loud conversations and waiters carried full trays. Where to start? Every minute could be crucial.

I dashed into a toy store and scanned the children who milled around the displays—but no Marion.

"Excuse me, have you seen a little girl about this high?" Michael faced the elderly store clerk and held his hand at waist height.

The man looked at him over his spectacles. "Young man, there are little girls in my shop all day."

"She's lost, sir." I tried to keep my voice steady. "She's only four."

He scratched his short gray beard. "*Lo siento.* I hope you find her."

Michael placed his hands on the counter. "Sir, if you see her, her name is Marion Becker. Please keep her here and send word to the *City o' Benares*. She sails at four o'clock."

We returned to the walkway outside. I willed myself not to panic—not yet.

Michael pulled my sleeve. "Let's try the next one."

Inside the teashop, the spicy scents transported me back to India. Natalie would've liked this store—maybe they'd been there. I marched up to the counter and interrupted the clerk. "I'm looking for my sister. She's about this tall, she's wearing blue, and she has a long braid." I searched her face for a sign of recognition.

"No little girls today," the clerk said in a matter-of-fact way, as though it was a daily routine for people to look for lost children.

"Maybe you saw me dad," Michael said. "He's with three ladies."

"Yes, I saw them," the clerk said. "They were here about a half hour ago. The ladies each bought tea."

I pulled Michael by the arm and called over my shoulder. "Thank you!"

The next three shops were less crowded. We peeked in the windows, looking for anyone we knew, but no luck.

"Maybe they're in this café," Michael said. We checked the outside tables and walked toward the rear of the busy café.

A slender young waiter carrying an empty tray stopped us. "May I help you?"

"Yes, I'm looking for my little sister. She's ... and I'm looking for our friends."

Michael jumped in. "Me dad and three ladies. They might've had a little girl with 'em."

The restaurant aromas made me ache from hunger, and my hands shook. Where was my sister?

The waiter checked with an aproned man who counted money at a large wooden buffet, then returned to where we stood. "He thinks he saw a man with three pretty women, but no little girl."

Back on the sidewalk, Michael flexed his wrist. "They were here—we know that much."

"That doesn't help at all." My throat closed with emotion. *I won't cry, I won't cry.*

Michael shrugged. "Maybe they found each other and she's with 'em right now. What time is it?"

My worry intensified by the second. "There's a big clock in the square. If it's close to three o'clock, maybe your dad's looking for us."

The circus performers and band in the square were now replaced by a mime. He was dressed head-to-toe in black with a painted white face, entertaining a small crowd. But there were no little girls wearing blue.

The clock chimed half past two, and my stomach churned with hunger and fear all at once. *Where are you, Marion?*

Michael ran a hand through his hair. "They said they'd come and look for us. Maybe we should wait here."

I sagged against the clock tower. "But it doesn't seem right to just stand around and wait."

Michael raised his hands. "Don't leave this spot! I'll be back by three, no matter what." He ran back the way we'd come until he was swallowed by the crowd.

Why didn't I hold Marion's hand like I had promised Mother? The clock chimed three-quarters past two. I looped counterclockwise around the clock base, wishing I could unwind it and go back to when we arrived. What if they were all together, having fun somewhere, while Michael and I wasted the whole day playing a horrific game of hide-and-seek?

A gust of wind hit my face. I hung my head and kicked at the clock's cornerstone. *What a rotten sister and daughter I am. If anything happens to Marion*—I covered my face with my hands and squeezed my eyes until hot tears overflowed. *Please, God …*

A police officer! I checked the square for someone in uniform. It was nearly three o'clock, and Michael would be back. *Should I wait for him?*

At the opposite edge of the square, people crisscrossed near a group of flagpoles, oblivious to the fact that a four-year-old girl was lost. Then my heart skipped two beats. Walking in my direction below the flags were Mr. Frank, Natalie, Millie, and Elizabeth.

Marion wasn't with them.

CHAPTER SIXTEEN

Gibraltar
March 27, 1912
3:00 p.m.

I ran through the busy square, waving to get the group's attention. Natalie waved back before a puzzled look crossed her face. Then the women hiked up their skirts and rushed toward me with Mr. Frank.

"What's wrong?" he asked. "Where are Michael and Marion?"

Millie put her arm around me until I caught my breath. "We … can't find Marion. I was hoping she was with you."

Elizabeth's eyes widened. "Oh, no! We have to find her!"

Three loud bells bonged in the clock tower. No sign of Michael yet.

I tried to calm myself with a deep breath. "She disappeared during the circus performance. We looked everywhere, and some people thought they saw you, but no one saw Marion."

"Where did Michael go?" Mr. Frank asked.

"To look some more. He was supposed to meet me at three o'clock."

"There he is." Mr. Frank lifted his arm in a wave.

Michael sprinted across the grass toward us. "Dad!"

Mr. Frank embraced him and held him at arm's length. "Where's Marion?"

Michael's face was ashen. "I don't know. I've searched everywhere."

I scanned the crowded square again. "I was about to look for a policeman, but—"

Natalie waved to a man hobbling behind a souvenir cart and hurried over to him. Her straw hat blew off. "Sir, do you know where we can find a policeman?"

The man waved his hands. *"No hablo ingles."*

Mr. Frank scooped Natalie's hat from the ground and stepped closer. "Police?"

The vendor studied our frantic faces. *"La policia?"*

Mr. Frank nodded. *"Si, Senor! Policia."*

The man gestured toward the shops and said something else in Spanish. Then he rummaged in his pocket, pulled out a cracked fountain pen and unfolded a wrinkled piece of paper from his cart.

"What's he doing?" Elizabeth asked. "We don't have time for this!"

Mr. Frank looked over the man's shoulder. "He's drawing us a map."

He drew a building with a circle around it one street behind the toy shop. We thanked him and headed across the square, located a side street, and raced to the station. All of us panted for breath when we burst through the doors. Behind the front desk, a surprised uniformed officer knocked over his cup of tea.

He blotted the spill with a rag. *"Cuál es el problema?"*

Mr. Frank spoke in sputtered gasps. "We lost a little girl in the square today."

The officer folded his hands and rested them on the desk. "Description, *por favor.*"

I stepped forward. "She's my sister. Her name is Marion Becker. She's four and has brown hair in a braid." My throat caught. "Sir, we don't have much time."

He scratched his bald head and shoved away from the desk. A ring of keys jangled from his back pocket as he shuffled through a doorway at the rear of the small office. Where was he going?

The clock over the doorway read half past three. "Sir," Millie called. "Please. Our ship departs in less than thirty minutes!"

Finally, the sounds of jangling and shuffling returned. The

policeman reappeared—holding Marion's hand.

She let out a squeal and ran toward me. "Sissy, where was you?" She hopped into my arms and wrapped hers around my neck.

My knees nearly buckled as relief washed over me. Michael and the others broke into cries of joy and embraced each other.

"Why did you run off?" I asked.

"Sorry, Sissy." She hopped to the floor.

Mr. Frank signed a paper to verify we had claimed Marion, and with eighteen minutes left until four o'clock, we rushed back toward Gibraltar's harbor.

I pictured Mother pacing the decks and wringing her hands. What would she do with me when she heard the whole story?

Millie and I grabbed Marion's hands as we hurried through the square. "You gave us all quite a scare, little lady," Millie said.

"I was hungry, and Sissy said to wait but I couldn't wait, so I went to find you."

I jerked her hand. "But Mother told you never to—"

Millie interrupted. "Let her tell us what happened, Ruth."

"I didn't see you anywhere, but a nice lady took me to the peaceman." Marion bobbed her head. "They gave me ice cream, and I got to work on a puzzle, but it was too hard."

Mr. Frank caught up to Michael and me. "Did you and Ruth ever eat?"

"No, Dad," Michael said. "How could we?"

"If only we'd known! We shopped and had lunch," Natalie said. "Then we stopped in the maritime museum."

My stomach had unknotted, and as we neared the *City of Benares*, all I wanted was something to eat and to unwind in our cabin. But I had to face the music with Mother. She would learn the whole truth. *And she should.* I'd heard enough about child kidnappings to know anything could've happened.

Mr. Frank turned to me. "Would y' like me to go with you and talk to your mother?"

"I'll come as well," Natalie said, "if it will help."

"Yes, thank you." It would help. But how could I tell Mother I let my sister get lost in a foreign country?

We crossed the gangplank just as the ship's horn blasted, announcing its departure. Our next stop: Southampton, England.

Marion and I led Mr. Frank and Natalie down to our cabin. My palms perspired like I'd held them underneath a faucet.

Mother opened the door. "It's about—"

"Mama!" Marion rushed in and wrapped herself around Mother's legs.

Mother placed her hands on Marion's head and glared at the three of us. "Did something happen?"

"Mrs. Becker, I'm sorry to surprise y' like this," Mr. Frank said. "Everything's fine now."

Mother looked baffled. Marion ran to Richard, who was playing in his crib.

Natalie moistened her lips. "Mrs. Becker, we—that is, Mr. Frank and Elizabeth and Millie and I—left Ruth and Michael with Marion at the square and went to the shops."

"I never should've left 'em, ma'am," Mr. Frank said. "They lost sight of Marion and, well, she was missin' for a bit."

The ship's engines vibrated in perfect time to my stomach growling. I dug my fingernails into the doorframe. Things were always ten times worse on an empty stomach.

Mother's face reddened. "She was *missing*?"

I stood straight but looked at the floor. "We were watching some circus performers, and she was fine, and a moment later she was gone. But we found her, and she's okay now."

Mr. Frank held his palms out. "I'm to blame for this, Mrs. Becker. Ruth did everything she could to find Marion. Michael did too. Ruth was the one who thought of going to the police."

Mother held up both hands. "That's quite enough. Thank you, both of you. Ruth and Marion and I need to sit down so I can hear the entire story. We'll see you in the dining room."

When they left, I managed to fill Mother in, and Marion supplied her version of what happened. Mother interrupted with only a few questions.

Finally, she folded her arms, and her voice was as slow and steady as the trip through the Suez Canal. "You both disobeyed me, and I am very disappointed. We will talk more after dinner."

None of us spoke on the way to the dining room. Even Richard seemed to sense the need to be quiet. On deck, the winds had strengthened. According to the route map in the stairwell, the *City of Benares* now eased toward the Straits of Gibraltar, where only eight miles separated the continents of Africa and Europe.

A couple walked ahead of us, the man holding his hat and gesturing toward port side. "That must be Morocco," he said. "As soon as we pass through the straits, we'll enter the Atlantic and head north."

Even though I was starving, I wanted to take in the view—plus I needed a few minutes to calm down after this horrendous day. "Let's look for a minute, Mother."

She let out a soft groan but crossed the deck with Richard and Marion in tow. "It *is* beautiful."

With the wind pushing at our backs, we gazed at the shoreline and towering mountains of Morocco, the ancient African nation. The setting sun cast a glow across the land, and all of the geography books in the world could not compare to witnessing it with my own eyes.

But I'd still trade it for India.

~∽~

Marion and I spent the next day in captivity. Because of what had happened in Gibraltar, Mother's decision was to keep us prisoners in the cabin for the rest of the voyage.

Except for meals, my last five days on the *City of Benares* would be spent scrubbing diapers, babysitting, and practicing violin. And I couldn't talk to Michael. Marion got a lecture, too, and she burst into tears and promised she'd never go off alone again.

That afternoon, Marion beat her fists on the wall next to Richard. "When's dinner?"

Mother entered the cabin. "Stop that, Marion! I didn't mean to take so long. Elizabeth's dress needed more mending than she could handle." She put away her sewing supplies and glanced my way. "May we hear some music? How about 'Spring Song?'"

"No, I'll play something else." Since leaving Malta, I'd practiced daily, but "Spring Song" was out of the question. *She still doesn't understand.*

Mother settled on her bed, and I played what I remembered from a much sadder piece—a Chopin "Nocturne," to match my mood. Marion danced with Richard in her arms until he pushed himself down.

As we prepared for dinner, the *City of Benares* rolled slowly to port, rose in the air, rolled to starboard, and dropped. My hungry stomach mimicked the ship's groaning and moaning once again. *So, these are ocean waves! Will we rock like this all the way to Britain? I might not sleep at all.*

SS City of Benares, Atlantic Ocean
March 28, 1912

Sky Report: We have more daylight now, and due to the circumstances, I was prevented from waiting on deck after dinner for the stars to appear. We're going to London for a week before we sail on the Titanic, and I should be able to see some stars in London. But I'll certainly see them over the Atlantic if the skies remain clear. All I know tonight is that I'm ready to reach Southampton and for this voyage to end.

Sometime during the night, Mother sat up and rearranged her pillows.

I whispered to her, "Are you awake?"

"Yes, why?"

I turned on my side so I could lie facing her. "I've been thinking about all the people we've met—the Franks, the ladies, Mr. Clayton, Jack, and things they did for us that they didn't have to do. And other people too. The vendor in Gibraltar was one. And the lady that took Marion to the police."

I waited, hoping she wouldn't bring up my lack of responsibility again.

Instead, she took a deep breath and exhaled. "God often puts people in our path to help us, Ruth. And sometimes He uses them to teach us things."

Had I learned anything from those I met?

"I know this hasn't been easy for you," Mother said. "And I'm sorry."

After all this time, she'd apologized.

CHAPTER SEVENTEEN

SS City of Benares, Southampton, England
April 3, 1912

Our ship navigated the River Test as it approached the busy Southampton harbor. My heart thumped faster with every passing minute as the cold wind assaulted my face and hands. What a difference from India and the Mediterranean! I stuffed my hands inside my coat pockets, tucking my fingers around Papa's handkerchief.

Millie stood at the railing beside me, shielding her eyes from the bright sun with a gloved hand. "What do you think of your first look at England, Ruth?"

"To begin with, I didn't know there would be this twisted passage up to Southampton."

"At least it's not as bad as the Suez Canal," Millie said with a short laugh. As usual, several of her wayward curls had escaped her hat.

"And I didn't expect all the factories and big ships either." They added a gritty scent to the chilly, salty air.

"I heard a great many ships are stuck here because of the coal strike," Millie said. "But it should settle before you depart for America. I must say, I've so enjoyed getting to know you and your family, Ruth. I do hope things go well for you in the States. You're a brave girl."

Her words almost made me tear up. She was the brave one, fighting for women's rights and planning to be a doctor. Papa had told me to be brave, but I still didn't see myself armed with courage.

Mother crossed the deck from the stairway, carrying Richard and holding Marion's hand.

"Don't forsake your dreams," Millie whispered before Mother was upon us.

"I feel like we're almost home," Mother said. "You must be thrilled, Millie."

Millie caressed Marion's cheek. "Yes, it's been a long trip. It will be splendid to sleep in my own bed again without feeling anything move."

Wearing warm coats, Natalie and Elizabeth joined us at the railing, soon followed by The Great Frank and Son. As a prisoner these last days, I'd missed the fun Michael and I had together. And he felt like a true friend, even though we had only met a month ago. What could I say to this crazy acrobat who had helped me survive this part of my journey?

He came to my side, his too-small cap snug on top of his head. "I hope it's all right with your mum if we talk now."

I smiled, fiddling with Papa's handkerchief in my pocket.

"Captain Drummond told us the *Titanic* is on its way here from Belfast," Mr. Frank said. Dr. Collins had removed the stitches from under his eye, and the wound looked less scary. "It appears we'll miss 'er, though."

"Look over there," Natalie said. "It's the *New York*."

"And there!" Elizabeth said. "The *Philadelphia* and the *Adriatic*."

"They've enlarged the harbor since we left for India," Elizabeth said. "We heard it was to accommodate the *Titanic*."

Even in their simpler traveling clothes and warm coats, the women still looked fashionable. If I ever saw another copy of *Vogue,* I would think of them, and I would always remember their sweet dispositions and silly jokes.

Mr. Frank placed a gentle hand on Richard's head. "Michael and I'll keep Richard in our prayers, Mrs. Becker." Richard squeezed Mr. Frank's finger. "He seems cheery today."

"Yes, thank God," Mother said. "Thank you for all your kindness, Mr. Frank. And good-bye, Michael. You have brought much excitement to this journey."

I was so glad she left it at that.

Across the gangway on the loading platform, people rushed about, porters waited to transfer luggage, and taxis lined up to whisk passengers away to their destinations.

Mr. Frank leaned down, facing us. "Ruth, Marion, it's been a jolly good pleasure."

"Bye, Mr. Frank," Marion said, hugging his legs.

"Stay close to your sister," he told her. Next, he turned to me. "Thank you for being a good friend to Michael." He shook my hand in farewell. "Enjoy the *Titanic*, and best o' luck."

What would this voyage have been like without Mr. Frank? "Thank you for everything," I said, "and good luck with the circus."

He followed Natalie and her friends toward the stairs. Michael and I watched his father kiss Natalie's hand, and she lifted her handkerchief to dab her eyes.

I nodded in their direction. "I hope that goes well."

Michael grinned. "He sure does fancy her."

"I'm glad we met on the train," I said. *Oh, that sounded brilliant.*

"You're a bricky girl, Ruth. We had some adventures."

I hoped *bricky* meant something nice in Biggleswade. "Be careful on those tightropes," I said, and we both laughed.

"I'll be expectin' a letter. I want to hear all about the *Titanic* and America." He stuffed his hand into his back pocket. "And I have something for you." He held out the black pawn from his chess set. "I wanna give you this—to remember me by."

I lifted the wooden piece from his palm. "But how can you play without it?"

"It's me lucky spare," he said. "And I have a confession. You know how we ended up together at Table 18? I kind of arranged that."

"I had a feeling. But I'm glad you did."

The *City of Benares* maneuvered into her Southampton slot and thudded against the docks. Now that we wore our coats and had our belongings to carry, we moved slower than usual down the stairs.

At last, my feet left the ship and touched English soil. Captain Drummond and several of the officers stood at the foot of the gangplank, bidding passengers farewell.

When it was our turn, Mr. Clayton shook Michael's hand. "Good to meet you, Michael. No hard feelings, I hope?"

"No, sir." Michael smiled. "Good-bye, sir."

Thankfully, Mother had turned to Captain Drummond and didn't hear their exchange.

Mr. Clayton offered his hand to me. "Godspeed, Miss Becker."

"Godspeed to you, Mr. Clayton, and thank you for the lifesaver."

"I beg your pardon?"

"The fan." I smiled. "My mother said it was a lifesaver."

He tipped his hat. "Glad to be of service."

A few crew members hurried down the gangway. Rushab came forward. "Good-bye, Table 18. Safe journeys."

We gathered in the noisy waiting area until all the trunks were unloaded and tagged for their next destinations. Our black trunk was retagged "RMS *Titanic*" and sent to a holding area.

Mr. Frank stopped a porter for help with their trunks. They would take the next train to Biggleswade. When a taxi pulled up next to the gangplank, Mr. Frank beckoned Michael.

I rolled the pawn between my fingers. "You better go," I said.

Michael leaned over and gave me a quick kiss on the cheek. Before I had a chance to react, he took off with his usual speed, dodging passengers and luggage carts, and climbed into the backseat of the taxi where his father waited.

London, England
April 3, 1912
Dear Sajni,
  Today we boarded the Southampton-to-London train, which was everything the Guntur-to-Cochin train was not—clean, modern, cool, and fast. It even smelled good! Millie, Elizabeth,

and Natalie rode with us to London's Waterloo Station. There were signs everywhere that advertised the Titanic, the ship that will take me to America on April 10, one week from today.

Finally, we stood below the station's grand entrance and it was time to part ways. We embraced, Mother shed a few tears, and we all promised to write each other and send postcards.

The longest voyage is behind me, but my future looks no clearer than it did the day I left Guntur. If anything, I'm even more confused and conflicted. I wish you were here with me. But the quilt is a special link to you and to all that we share.

Michael kissed me good-bye on the cheek today! Never would I have imagined it when you and I first watched him juggle at the Guntur station.

Your loving "sister,"
Ruth

CHAPTER EIGHTEEN

Southampton, England
Wednesday, April 10, 1912

I never thought I'd say this, but during the entire week in London, I missed being rocked to sleep by the waves. And now, at long last, we were back in Southampton for the final leg of our journey to America.

Our week in London was a whirlwind, as Mother wanted us to see all the sites that she and Papa had visited on their way to India—Kensington Palace, Buckingham Palace, Madame Tussaud's Wax Museum, the London Zoo, and Parliament.

We borrowed a pram from the hotel for Richard, thank goodness! Despite visiting all the tourist attractions, the highlight for Marion was probably watching an organ grinder with his pet monkey. Mine was eating authentic bangers and mash in a real English pub, and Mother's, by far, was attending the Easter service at the breathtaking St. Paul's Cathedral.

Our "boat train" from London's Waterloo Station slowed to a crawl as it neared the station in Southampton, carrying passengers bound for nearly every corner of the world. Outside our window, a cacophony of noise met us, like an orchestra warming up—trains chugging, peddlers shouting, and cars honking—as they inched between throngs of people on foot or bicycle.

Reporters and photographers peered through the train windows. The train attendant surveyed the crowd. "They're lookin' for celebrities who might be boardin' the *Titanic*. Thank God that horrible coal strike is ended. Today's a big day for this country, I daresay."

I turned to Mother. "Will we see any celebrities?"

She scrutinized the mob outside. "We may, but I'm not sure I'd know a celebrity if I saw one."

As soon as we exited the train, we were immediately engulfed in the chaos. Porters pushed dozens of loaded luggage carts, adding to the noise. *Our trunks better make it on board.*

Everyone looked to be determining where they should go amid the confusion. Highly fashionable ladies and gentlemen stood out in the crowd, accompanied by attentive servants. Reporters descended on them while passersby gawked. Were these the celebrities, in their beautiful coats and high hats?

Colorful posters that advertised the *Titanic's* maiden voyage hung on every available wall and column:

FIRST SAILING OF THE LATEST ADDITION TO THE
WHITE STAR FLEET
THE QUEEN OF THE OCEAN
TITANIC
WORLD'S LARGEST OCEAN LINER
MAIDEN VOYAGE
SOUTHAMPTON TO NEW YORK
DEPARTS APRIL 10, 1912

A station worker shouted into a megaphone and waved his arm to our right. "*Titanic* passengers that way. All others follow me."

Mother had to shout for me to hear. "Carry Richard, please. I'll take Marion. Stay close!"

We were swallowed up in a sea of people. We bumped one another with our belongings as we shuffled forward to the end of the platform. I missed the London hotel's pram already.

Another station worker directed those of us who had *Titanic* tickets down a wide pavement, toward docks marked *White Star Line.* The tops of several ships rose against an azure sky. Some had tall funnels, others only masts and rigging. Their striped flags whipped in the wind, reminding me of our dishcloths in India when Mother hung them outside to dry on washdays.

Here I go ... another ship, another voyage.

America—not the land of my dreams by any stretch, as it was for so many leaving their homelands. To me, America was a place with a huge question mark hanging over it, a place where I still had no plan, and nobody knew me. Even my grandparents only knew *of* me.

But I'd endured the long journey on the SS *City of Benares*, strange as it was. Not only did I survive, I grew sea legs, saw incredible places, tried new things, and made new friends. Maybe I'd learned something from Michael, besides the basics of how to walk a tightrope. He taught me that some things weren't always as bad as they seemed.

I supposed I would make friends in America—eventually. But they wouldn't be Sajni, and everything would be different. I ground my teeth, thinking of Papa and why I was about to board another ship.

"Is it over there, Darling?" A young woman walking ahead of us wore a yellow silk coat and a wide, matching hat. She took the arm of the man beside her and pointed to an enormous ship that had three funnels. The White Star Line's flag—white background with a red star—flew from a short mast at her bow.

"No, that's the *Majestic*," the man replied. "One of *Titanic*'s sister ships. And there's the *New York*."

The *New York* had been in the harbor the week before, when we sailed into Southampton. It was smaller than the *Majestic*, but still bigger than the *City of Benares*. An American flag flew from the *New York*'s stern. I hadn't seen the Stars and Stripes since my social studies lessons at the Mission School.

I pledge allegiance to the flag of the United States of America ... I miss India ... This is so hard to believe.

We descended a small set of stairs, walked between two low buildings, and followed a bend toward Berth 44.

A man lifted his bowler hat high in the air. "There she is! That's the *Titanic*."

I strained to catch my first glimpse of the already-famous ship. People who were on all sides of us gasped at the sight of her. Even Richard twisted in my arms to see what all the commotion was about.

Four massive, black-and-gold funnels gleamed in the sunlight and towered above us. The ship was taller and wider than any I'd seen before. I never imagined anything so overwhelming! *If only Michael could see this.*

Marion tried to see over the crowds. "We're almost there," I said. "It's as big as a palace. Bigger than ten—no, fifteen—*City of Benares.*"

Mother tried for a better view. "Oh, my. I don't understand how something of that size can even float."

We were then ushered into a large building. The mayhem back at the train station was nothing compared to what met us—camera bulbs flashed and popped, white-gloved policemen blew their whistles, baggage handlers and White Star Line employees shouted orders to one another. Passengers by the hundreds waited in several lines, talking and laughing together.

The day seemed bigger than Christmas, maybe even more celebrated than a royal coronation—at least in Southampton. Today was the day the largest and most elaborate ship that had ever been built would take her maiden voyage. Despite all my trepidation about America, now that I had seen the *Titanic*, I had to admit that the enthusiasm of boarding her was contagious.

A man who wore a White Star emblem on his lapel helped sort us out. "Second class," he called. "This way!"

We waited behind a family who had three small boys. My arms ached, but I boosted Richard higher. After a fifteen-minute wait in line, our tickets were stamped.

"Gangway upstairs and to your right," the employee told us.

Elbowing our way through the crush of humanity, we ascended our stairs, and entered the gangway. It extended over the docks far below and was supported by a huge scaffold next to the ship. Hundreds of portholes ran right and left as far as I could see, above and below us. Two more gangways led to the ship at lower levels. It felt more like we were entering a tall building through a sixth-floor window rather than boarding a ship.

Piano music drifted from somewhere on an upper deck. I'd never dreamed musicians would be aboard! Even before we reached the shiny new hatchway, whiffs of fresh flowers and new paint filled the chilly air.

A crewman greeted us at the threshold. "Welcome aboard the *Titanic*."

I suppose I can handle a week here ...

We entered a large room with a tile floor and polished oak paneling. Its elaborate carvings, framed paintings of ships, and brass-trimmed electric lights gave it the feel of an elegant hotel. I took in all its grandeur as Richard squirmed in my numb arms.

Marion's eyes widened as she spoke in a hushed tone. "Oh, Sissy."

Mother gave it a quick appraisal, then interrupted a young crewman who was directing passengers to their cabins. "I'm Mrs. Allen Becker, and these are my children."

He leafed through pages of papers. "Becker, Becker ... Yes, Cabin F-4." He located the key in a tiny compartment of a huge shelf along the wall, handed the key to Mother, and motioned toward the passageway behind him. "This is Deck C. Take the stairs down three flights to Deck F."

Three flights?

"First, can you direct me to the purser's office?" Mother asked.

The crewman gestured forward. "This way toward the bow, starboard side. One of the younkers will show you." He lifted an index finger, calling for a younger seaman.

But my weeks of living on a ship paid off. "It's all right—we'll find it."

At the purser's window, I read the name that was pinned on the jacket of the dark-haired man who assisted passengers—*McElroy, H., Chief Purser.*

"I want to leave some money here," Mother said to him. "I doubt I'll need it before we arrive in New York."

He handed a slip of paper and a pen to her. "Simply fill out this receipt. Will you be renting any deck chairs for the voyage?"

"I don't think so," Mother replied. "I don't plan to leave the cabin often."

A large diagram of the ship was attached to the side of the purser's window. The *Titanic* had ten decks, from the top Boat Deck down to the Lower Orlop, where all the ship machinery was housed. Deck F, where we would sleep, was also called the Middle Deck. I'd never even been in a building that size.

Scattered throughout the top decks was the grand dining saloon, gymnasium, swimming pool, and library, just for starters. The *City of Benares* didn't have any of those! There was also a Promenade, a Veranda Café, and a Grand Staircase. What could that be like?

The complicated design showed some rooms that were more than one deck high. Certain passageways ran almost from bow to stern, others stopped and started again, and many areas were designated for first, second, or third-class passengers only. I would have to steer around that if I were to see the whole ship.

Behind the purser's window, a yellow canary chirped in a white cage.

"Is that your bird?" I asked.

Mr. McElroy smiled. "No, miss. He belongs to a passenger. He's only going as far as our first stop at Cherbourg, France. His name is Petey."

Marion tugged the fold of Mother's skirt. "Can I see the bird?"

"Will there be other pets onboard?" I asked.

"Yes, I expect there will be several, miss."

Mother handed an envelope that contained money to him, as well as the top portion of the receipt. "I'm not a bit happy about going on this ship."

"Why is that?"

She frowned at Petey. "Because this is the first voyage it's ever made."

Mr. McElroy regarded Mother with his gentle brown eyes. "The *Titanic* has watertight compartments, and if anything happens, they will keep the ship afloat until we can get help. There is absolutely nothing to worry about."

Mother's faint smile told me she didn't feel any better. She reached for my brother. At long last, I could trade him for Marion. My tingling arms thanked me.

We made our way through the crowded passageway and retraced our steps toward the stern. Signs directed us down to the far stairs. At Deck E, a white iron gate blocked anyone on that level from using the stairwell. Surely it would be opened at some point.

The next level down on Deck F, ornate brass sconces lit the soft white walls every six feet—a far cry from the bare lightbulbs on the *City of Benares*. People hurried along the passageway, some speaking in languages I didn't understand, but all of them were wide-eyed and seemed eager to locate their cabins.

A steward helped us find F-4 just as a man unlocked the cabin door directly across the passageway. Clinging to his coat were two curly-haired little boys, the bigger one speaking what sounded like French. The man laughed and led them inside.

Our cabin was as large as our hotel room in London, and every single feature was polished and perfect—from the shiny brass light fixture overhead to the thick, dark-red carpet. Just like the *Titanic* itself, everything was brand new, right down to the crisp cotton sheets and sparkling clean washbasin. The room had a fresh scent, like school on the first day.

Marion released her grip on my hand and dashed to the floral-printed sofa. "It's so big!"

"And there's a porthole! Are you sure this isn't first class?" I circled the room, brushing my fingers across the furniture, bedding, and upholstery. "This doesn't feel like a ship at all. It's more like a little house."

"It *is* lovely," Mother said with a relieved sigh. She set Richard on the floor next to the carved walnut desk. "Look, girls—bunk beds. Although, on a ship I believe they're called *berths*."

"I'll take the top," I said. "With the porthole next to it, I won't have to guess if the sun is shining or if it's dark out."

Marion plopped down on the bottom berth and folded her arms. "*I* want the top."

"You will sleep on the bottom," Mother said. "And please get your shoes off the bed."

Finally there was an advantage to being the oldest sibling.

Marion fell back and tried to reach the underside of the top berth by raising her legs in the air and pointing her toes.

Mother laid her jacket along the full-size bed across from ours. Another small bed with a low railing sat at an angle. Richard would love the freedom of not having a crib.

She set him on her bed. "We have one more diaper—I hope it's enough until our trunk arrives. Go explore if you'd like, but not too long, and please don't get lost."

I glanced at the china clock on Mother's bedside table. "It's almost noon, and the ship is scheduled to launch. Let's go watch all the fun, Marion!"

CHAPTER NINETEEN

RMS Titanic, Southampton, England
Wednesday, April 10, 1912
11:40 a.m.

I led Marion back up to Deck C. We took a passageway toward the bow, climbed another set of stairs, and exited the stairway on Deck B, also known as the Bridge Deck. A sign that read *Café Parisien* pointed starboard.

A crewman stopped us. "Children, after we launch, this section will be for first class only."

"We'll remember." I tugged Marion's hand and hurried past him. Mother hadn't mentioned sticking to the second-class areas, and why should we see only part of the *Titanic*? I was determined to see everything, even if it took the whole voyage.

Passengers stood three or four deep along the railings, waving handkerchiefs and calling to the well-wishers who lined the docks. Papa's handkerchief nestled safely in my coat pocket, but I wouldn't risk letting it go.

I pushed Marion ahead, squeezing us between an older couple and a family that had a girl about my age. The girl wore a long coat that matched the sky, with an ink-black fur collar and cuffs.

She sized me up. "Are you in first class?"

What was it about first class? Things weren't this regimented on the *City of Benares*.

I looked around with authority, like I was supposed to be there. "This is Deck B, isn't it?"

Her glance swept the ceiling. "Of course it is."

"Then yes, I am." I pointed to the joyous crowd. "Look, Marion. They're all waving to us."

We waved and hollered to the hundreds remaining on land. Calls of "good-bye" in various languages rang out. Camera bulbs flashed, and I marveled that I was on the *Titanic*, waving to reporters. *I could end up in a newspaper photo!*

Bells clanged, and a few visitors rushed back to shore via the gangways. Hatchways were shut. Then three whistle blasts sounded, loud and long, making Marion and me jump and cover our ears. The deep vibration of the engines worked its way up through the deck, and tugboats towed our great ship away from the pier. Marion stomped her feet and laughed as the *Titanic* began to move.

The crowd on the dock grew quiet. I looked across the harbor to see what had them so concerned.

The ropes holding the stern of the *New York* had snapped, allowing the ship to swing out toward the *Titanic*. Passengers near me gasped, and I leaned over the railing to see the two ships miss each other by no more than a few feet.

"That was close," the older man next to us said to his wife. "We almost had a collision."

She clutched the handkerchief she'd been waving to her chest. "That is *not* good, Isidor."

It took some time for the tugs to get us underway again, and people grumbled that we were already off schedule. But soon we were coasting along through Southampton harbor, passing the same buildings and factories we had seen the week before. They appeared smaller now from my higher vantage point.

Two decks below, a girl stretched her arms along the railing. Her long blonde hair was tied back in a kerchief, and her dark dress hung unevenly below her tattered coat. She turned around and dropped her head back, squinting at all the faces along the railings above her. Was she a steerage passenger? Where was she from, and why was she going to America?

I smiled and lifted my hand in a slight wave. She nodded, but then she moved away and disappeared from my view.

"Can we go now, Sissy?"

We went back the way we came, but a gate now divided first-class decks from those below. I fumbled with the latch, and the gate swung open. I closed it and led Marion away. A sign on the second-class side of the gate read *No Admittance*.

Hmm. I would need to figure out the system when I went exploring.

~

When we returned to Deck F, our cabin door stood open. I heard Mother's voice. "Set it anywhere, just so it's out of the way, please."

A young man dressed in a white jacket backed out the door, pulling an empty cart. "Ah, you must be Miss Ruth and Miss Marion. I'm John Hardy, chief steward in second class."

"Pleased to meet you," I said. Marion swung my arm with her hand and gave him a shy sideways glance.

"Girls, our trunk is here," Mother said. "Come help me unpack."

Mr. Hardy called back into the room before he left. "Let me know if you need anything, Mrs. Becker. And if you require a stroller for Master Richard, please ask. My cabin is across the way and one door to the right. Good afternoon."

"Did you hear that?" I removed my coat, then Marion's. "I think a stroller's the same as a pram."

Mother tipped her head toward Richard. "Someone likes his little bed but not enough to nap."

My brother sat in his bed, drooling onto the new white sheet. He shook his head with a look of determination. "No, no, no, no ..."

I lifted my violin case and Sajni's quilt from our brown trunk. I hugged the quilt to my chest and set the violin case beside the wardrobe. "I think Mr. McElroy has postcards of the ship at the purser's window. Can we buy a few and send them tonight from Cherbourg?"

"That's probably a good idea," Mother said. "We'll get them before dinner."

I unfolded the quilt and tossed it on top of my berth. "I might need this tonight."

"Yes, the sunshine is deceiving," Mother said. "There's a chill in the air, but those vents in the wall will pump warm air into the room."

Marion shoved a pile of clothes into an open drawer of the wardrobe. "When do we eat?"

I laughed. "I don't know, but I can't wait to see the dining room."

My sister gave her joyful approval. "I wanna see the food."

Richard dozed off while we unpacked. I had a whole drawer to myself! I left an old pair of shoes in the trunk with my green dress, which was still tucked around my wooden birds.

Faint music drifted in from somewhere down the passageway. "There's the bugle Mr. Hardy told me about," Mother whispered. "That means it's time to dress for dinner."

I glanced toward the door and grinned. "They're going to blow a bugle every day?"

"For lunch *and* dinner."

The bugle woke Richard from his brief nap. *Well, it was nice while it lasted.*

"Ruth, change his diaper and give him a drink of water from the washbasin. I'd like to use the WC now before someone else needs it."

"Oh, I discovered something," I said. "There's a water closet and a separate room marked *Toilet.*"

With a few trips back and forth, it took us an hour to get ready. Marion and I wore new dresses Mother had bought us in London. Marion's mint-green dress had a white collar with matching cuffs. According to her, it was exactly like "Miss Elizabeth's."

Mine was simple, but in the new straighter style that had a higher waist and in a color I'd never worn before—a soft peach. *Would Natalie think it makes me look more grown up?*

Wanting to save money, Mother didn't buy anything for herself in London. But she looked lovely in her "Sunday only" outfit—a light brown skirt, lacy white shirtwaist made in India, and a flared jacket to match the skirt with white rose-shaped buttons. I'd always liked it, even though she'd worn it for years. As if reading my thoughts, she caught my gaze and smiled.

We purchased several postcards and took them to a writing table near the purser's window. Mother wrote one to Papa. I'd brought along Michael's and Natalie's addresses and I wrote to them and Sajni. I hadn't written Papa since we left Guntur. I still wasn't ready to write.

"We'll be in Cherbourg in a few minutes, Mrs. Becker," Mr. McElroy said. "Hand those to me when you're finished so I can put them with the outgoing mail."

"Is Petey ready to go?" I asked him. The canary bobbed his head at his reflection in the little mirror inside his birdcage.

"I believe so, Miss Becker. He's been very quiet since we left Southampton."

~

On Deck D, our dining room was big enough to hold all of the nearly 300 second-class passengers at one sitting. I couldn't help but wonder—was this a ship or a floating castle?

We followed a young steward across the patterned tiles. "We call this the 'dining saloon,' Mrs. Becker. My name is Calvin, from Southampton. I'll be your dining steward for the voyage."

Calvin wore his hair parted down the middle, like Michael did. As he led us to our assigned seats at a long table, I admired the huge oil paintings adorning the oak paneled walls.

"Here you are," he said. "These three seats will be yours, and I'll bring a high chair straightaway."

Mother shifted Richard to her opposite hip. "Girls, take your seats."

Our red leather chairs were bolted to the floor and swiveled so we could get in and out. Marion pushed herself forward and back until I made her stop.

Snow-white linens covered the tables. Each place setting consisted of sparkling white china, painted with royal-blue flowers surrounding the flag with the red star emblem. The words *White Star Line* were painted below the flag.

I ran my finger along the plate's edge. *I will be the first person in the world to eat off this plate.*

Three forks, two knives, and three spoons per person would not be a problem, thanks to plenty of practice on the *City of Benares.* Marion grinned, lifting her correct fork for the first course.

"Good memory, Marion." *Even if you sometimes remember things you shouldn't.*

Across our table sat another family—a round man with his even rounder wife, and their son and daughter, who were on the way to a similar girth as the parents.

"How do you do?" the man greeted Mother. "I'm Jacob Simmons. This is my wife Edith and our twins Peter and Priscilla."

"We turn seven on Sunday!" Peter shouted, holding up seven fingers. I immediately found him to be annoying.

As Mother made introductions, Marion whispered in my ear, "Do I have to talk to them?"

"Only if you want to."

"No whispering, girls," Mother said.

Mrs. Simmons announced, "We're on our way home to Boston from a visit with my mother in Yorkshire." She pronounced it *Yuckshuh*—another British dialect to get used to—different from Michael's, and different than any I'd heard in London.

Mother kept her response brief. "We're moving home to Michigan from India, where my husband runs an orphanage. He's joining us in the States as soon as he can."

When the steward returned with the high chair, Mr. Simmons asked him, "Have you worked aboard other ships, Calvin?"

Calvin brightened. "I served aboard the *Olympic* for two years, sir, and the *Adriatic* before that, both under Captain Smith. There's no finer captain, if I may say so."

"Pity he's retiring after this voyage," Mr. Simmons said.

Calvin left and returned with a tray of ice waters, lemon wedges, and a platter of tiny round toasts topped with various spreads and perfectly diced vegetables.

"Ah, the hors d'oeuvres." Mrs. Simmons patted the table. "Set that plate right here, young man."

Calvin wisely brought a second hors d'oeuvre platter, followed by a parade of courses. First, a consommé, then turbot, mutton cutlets, potatoes, peas, and Crème Reine Margot. I had no idea what it was, but I liked it.

We weren't finished. Next came a choice between beef sirloin, roast duckling, or filet of veal.

Marion turned to me. "What are you gettin'?"

"Let's ask for the beef. I could never eat a duck, and I don't know what veal is."

A man in a black tuxedo played the grand piano near the dining room entrance, and somehow the music made all the food taste even better.

Marion pushed the table to make her chair turn. "I'm full."

"But your favorite part is next," I said.

"Dessert!" She laughed, letting her chair swing back.

I read from the menu card. "Pudding *and* ice cream. And tarts and things."

Marion lifted her dessert spoon in preparation and sighed with contentment.

After sampling three desserts, I was ready to crawl back to the cabin. But after so much feasting, I wasn't sure I could stand.

"It's a good thing they have so many passageways and decks on the ship," Mother said with a smile. "We'll need the exercise to work off these enormous meals."

Mrs. Simmons gave her a cold appraisal. Mother blushed. "I only meant if we wish to do so."

⌒

I talked Mother into getting our coats and going up to Deck C to see the lights of Cherbourg, France. The *Titanic* was too large to dock there, so two small tenders transported passengers and supplies to and from the ship. As one tender unloaded, passengers stood ready to board for Cherbourg. I imagined they were disappointed in being unable to spend even one full night onboard.

A man held Petey's cage. Two crewmen loaded sacks of outgoing mail aboard the tender. "There go our postcards," I said.

The lights from the *Titanic*, the departing tender, and a glow from the buildings along Cherbourg's coast camouflaged all but the brightest stars. We roamed the deck, but Marion and Mother were soon yawning. Richard rubbed his eyes. I longed to keep exploring, but I couldn't hide my own yawn.

Down in F-4, I tucked Marion under the clean sheet and added a blanket from the top of the wardrobe. Behind the blankets were four white adult-size life belts.

"These take up too much room," I said. "Shall I move them?"

"No, leave them alone," Mother said. She settled Richard in his bed and unpinned her hair.

I turned out the overhead light and climbed up to my berth. Light from the passageway shone from under the door. Once I'd covered up with the sheet, a blanket, and Sajni's quilt, I turned to the porthole centered next to my bed. The water line came to just below the window. Maybe in the morning, I would see fish.

The engines came to life as the *Titanic* headed for Queenstown, Ireland, her last stop before steaming across the Atlantic. I felt the vibrations in the bedpost. We began a smooth ride, without the rocking motion I'd grown to like on the *City of Benares*.

So far, everything about the ship proved beyond what I'd imagined. *If only I didn't have the Great Unknown waiting at the other end of this voyage.*

RMS Titanic, Cherbourg, France
April 10, 1912

Sky Report: Clear skies, many stars. Last quarter moon. Cassiopeia the Queen visible low in the North.

Papa would love this ship, also known as a queen—the Queen of the Ocean. I can't wait to see what unfolds over the next six days.

CHAPTER TWENTY

RMS Titanic, Atlantic Ocean
Thursday, April 11, 1912

A hard *whap* of water against the porthole woke me early. The *Titanic* moved at a good clip across the water. Between the splashes, nothing but sunshine.

On the way to the dining saloon for breakfast, we followed the man from across the passageway and his two young sons. They kept turning around to smile at us until finally the man stopped and spoke to them in French. To Mother, he said, "Pardon, madam. Little ones."

"That's quite all right," she said. "I have little ones as well."

He paused at the stairs and lifted the smaller of the two boys in his arms. "Forgive me. I am Michel Hoffman."

Mother reached out to shake his hand. "Mrs. Becker."

As we entered the dining saloon, I said to her, "Hoffman? That doesn't sound French."

"Well, if he wants it to be Hoffman on this voyage, then Hoffman it is."

We joined the Simmons family again and feasted on eggs, grilled ham, sausages, baked apples, jacket potatoes, and honey-slathered scones. To Mother's surprise, we all ate more than we usually did for breakfast, even Richard.

Mrs. Simmons plucked another scone from a tiered platter, and two more for Peter and Priscilla. "Everything is so delicious, I hate to waste it."

I had to agree with her on that.

I was still in awe of *Titanic*'s marvels and wanted to see it all.

"Could Marion and I do some exploring before lunch?"

"This is a very big ship," Mother said. "You may go, but don't lose your sister."

Marion and I set out immediately after breakfast. I soon learned that Deck B, where we had stood for the launch from Southampton, was the highest deck allowed for second-class passengers, but then only in certain areas. At times when it seemed we could walk bow to stern, we ran into gates and signs that read *First Class Only.*

Mr. Hoffman came around a corner, pushing his youngest son in a stroller. The older boy tried to stop the stroller and climb in with his brother. I didn't need to understand French to figure out their father was telling him to behave, or else. But I did know the universal signs of a temper tantrum forming.

"May we push them around in the stroller?" I asked. "We'll let them take turns."

Mr. Hoffman smiled in gratitude. "Oh, *oui.* Zat would be nice." He spoke in French to his oldest son who looked at us and nodded.

Their father watched while Marion and I took a few turns pushing the boys, one at a time, up and down the deck as fast as we dared. The boys soon wore ear-to-ear grins. So did Mr. Hoffman. *Crisis averted.*

Marion and I descended one flight of stairs to Deck C so I could review the diagram at Mr. McElroy's office. We poked our heads in the second-class library, which I would save for another day. Then I found another diagram posted nearby that had a red circle indicating our current location.

What I really longed to see was on Deck D. "Let's find the grand dining saloon, Marion. Breakfast should be finished, so maybe we can have a look."

Heading down one level and toward the middle of the ship, the inside passageway widened. Were we close? We came to a dead end and tried another passageway, only to hit another dead end.

The dining saloon had to be on the other side. Turning toward the port side, we followed another passage around that ended at a stairway.

Maybe this was a shortcut. "Up or down?" I asked Marion.

"Up!"

We walked around on Deck C again and passed the purser's office, a door marked *Private,* and some cabins. A steward in a white jacket emerged from around the corner.

I had to think fast. "Sir, we're lost. We're trying to get to the grand dining saloon. Our mother thinks she left her handbag under her chair."

"It's closed until luncheon, miss. Your mother may check with the head steward at the main entrance. He's responsible for any lost items."

"Thank you." I pulled Marion around a corner.

Marion placed her hands on her hips. "That wasn't true, Sissy."

There's nothing like an accusing four-year-old to set one straight. "You're right. We'll have to look for it later." I no longer felt any movement or the engine vibrations. "I think we've dropped anchor. Maybe we can see Ireland now."

Along the starboard promenade designated for second class, Marion stood on the first rung of the railing and pointed to the approaching tender. "Here come more people. Are they all going to America?"

"Yes, and most of them will probably stay there."

"Like us!" Marion said.

My stomach tightened in empathy. "Yes, like us."

I tried to see the faces of those aboard. Most stood and stared at the *Titanic,* but several others turned around for a last look at their homeland. I could almost read their thoughts.

Beyond the tender, gray cliffs gave way to the ocean. Above the cliffs were lush green hillsides dotted with tidy homes, spring flowers, and a tall church steeple. If Ireland had been my home, I wouldn't have wanted to leave either.

One deck down on D, several passengers gathered, including the girl in the tired clothes I saw the day before. A small boy held her hand and pointed to the shore. She laughed, caught his other hand,

and swung him around in a circle. Two younger girls joined them. They all had the same blonde, wavy hair. Siblings, for sure.

The oldest girl glanced up to where we stood, and I smiled. She did, too, but then her sister tripped and she bent to help her.

I desperately wanted to meet her. "Marion, let's go downstairs."

By the time we descended the stairs to the outer third-class deck and found our way to the right place, the girl and everyone with her had gone.

Marion held her palms out. "Maybe it's time t' eat."

"Already? I didn't hear a bugle or anything."

The second tender pulled up close to the *Titanic*'s hull. I stepped to the railing and watched more passengers come aboard.

I checked a wall clock. We *had* missed the bugle. We found a place to wash our hands along the passageway and made a dash for our dining room. The older of Mr. Hoffman's sons waved to me from their table near the center of the room.

Mother and Richard were already seated when we reached our table. "I'm sorry we're late." I paused, trying to catch my breath. "The ship is much bigger than I expected."

Mr. Simmons laughed as he tucked a napkin into his shirt collar. "It's good for the appetite, isn't it?"

Mother tied Richard's bib. "You should have paid attention to the time, Ruth."

"What have you seen so far?" Mr. Simmons asked me.

Peter spoke before I had a chance. "We just went to the libary." He made a face, causing Priscilla to giggle.

I wanted to correct him about his pronunciation, but instead I unfolded my napkin and answered his father. "Passageways and stairways mostly. And a few outside decks."

Calvin set a loaded tray on a stand near the end of our table. Mrs. Simmons grabbed a roll and passed it to Priscilla. "Have we left Queenstown yet, Calvin? I don't feel any movement."

He checked his wristwatch. "We're to be underway soon, I believe, ma'am."

None of us could eat everything he brought us, not even the Simmons family. I wrapped a few sweets in a napkin for later.

Once we were outside the dining saloon, Mother shook her head at my gooey treasure. "I'm not sure that's allowed, Ruth."

"I saw Mrs. Simmons do it."

She murmured so Marion wouldn't hear. "That woman is a glutton."

Marion dragged her feet. "I'm 'zausted."

"A little rest will do you good." Mother turned to me. "But I don't imagine you need a rest."

"No, definitely not."

I now had a couple of hours to myself for whatever I pleased. I brushed my teeth and clipped part of my hair back in a tight barrette. I grabbed my coat, journal, and a pen. "Have a good nap, everyone."

In the passageway, the gentle hum of the engines reached my feet. That meant we were about to leave Queenstown and would soon head out into the open ocean. Next stop—New York City.

I raced ahead of other passengers to the stairs and up to Deck C. Then I took a chance and pushed the elevator button.

Three ladies emerged from a nearby cabin, all sporting huge frilly hats and discussing whom they hoped to see at dinner. I hid behind them.

The elevator door opened and a tall lift boy spoke from inside. "Going up?"

His long arms stuck out a little too far from his white jacket sleeves. He looked straight ahead, like the guards at London's Buckingham Palace.

I followed the ladies in amid a haze of perfume. One said, "Promenade deck, please."

The ship's diagram had indicated the Promenade was on Deck A. I kept my head down and stifled a sneeze.

First class, here I come.

~

As the lift boy opened the elevator door to the Promenade, a brisk wind tried to push me back. I followed the ladies out into the bright sunshine, where the most elegant of fashion shows was in progress.

Ladies meandered about in silky frocks intricately adorned with beads, lace, pearls, and jewels. Some wore furs and carried parasols and small trimmed pouches that matched their dresses.

And the hats! I'd never seen so many in one place, in a variety of colors and trimmed with veils, flowers, fringes, and even colored feathers. Some were over two feet wide. I would have to describe them in my next letter to Natalie.

I hope they're pinned down well, or they'll take flight over the ocean any minute.

Several young maids tended to their employers or waited together near the railing. Dressed mostly in simple black dresses and shawls, some were wide-eyed and talkative. Others pulled at their skirts or yawned, as if they'd rather be back at their ladyships' English estates or French chateaus than on the biggest cruise ship in the world.

Gentlemen chatted with the ladies or walked together, carrying iced drinks or teacups atop saucers. Like many men I'd seen in London, they wore long overcoats or fancy, pinstripe suits with vests, and shirts with pointed collars instead of rounded ones. Most wore dark caps or bowlers.

The *Titanic* was the size of a small city! The Promenade alone looked larger than Guntur's entire business district, maybe even larger than the town square in Gibraltar. I slipped between some occupied deck chairs to the wide-open area on the starboard side.

The hills of Queenstown faded in the distance. Ahead, the ocean reflected the sun across the entire horizon. The unstoppable, unsinkable *Titanic* charged westward, in complete command of the sea. With one hand on the railing, I turned my face to the sun, shut my eyes, and inhaled the chilly air. I felt like a wise and powerful seagull, flying at full speed over the blue world below.

Nearby, two men's voices prompted me to open my eyes. A man held a leash that belonged to a small, longhaired dog the color of cinnamon. Its tail resembled a big feather, like the feathers on some of the ladies' hats.

A ship's officer bent to pat the dog's head. "He's a fine little Pekinese, sir." The officer wore a black coat that had two rows of brilliant gold buttons.

"Why, thank you." The man with the dog extended a hand to the officer. "Henry Sleeper Harper. Harper Publishing, New York."

The officer stood to shake his hand. "First Officer William Murdoch."

"A pleasure. And a splendid ship you have, Mr. Murdoch."

"Thank you very much. Enjoy your day, Mr. Harper." Mr. Murdoch bowed slightly before heading away.

Mr. Harper lifted the dog and held him against his dark overcoat. The dog turned his little black face toward me and wagged his plumed tail.

I had to laugh. "May I pet him?"

"Yes, of course," the man said. "You are American?" His dog wagged its tail harder and reached out a paw.

Michael had reminded me I was American. "Yes, I am." I moved closer and let the dog sniff my fingers, then I scratched its chin. "What's his name?"

"Sun Yat Sen, named after a Chinese politician I once met. Isn't he handsome? He won a top prize at a dog show in France last week. I'm Henry Harper."

I scratched behind the dog's silky ears. "I'm Ruth Becker."

"If I may ask, where are your parents, Miss Becker?"

While I petted his prize dog, I told him about India, my family, and why we were on our way to America.

"Tell me something." He leaned a little closer. "You're not in first class, are you?"

Squinting, I peered up and down the Promenade. "At the moment, yes." I smiled and smoothed hair away from my face. "May I walk him for you? I'll be careful."

"Henry, what are you doing out here?" A sophisticated-looking woman who had streaks of gray at her temples hurried toward us. She wore a pink wool suit with a wide, fur-trimmed hat.

"Pardon me, Miss Becker. I'm being hailed." Mr. Harper turned toward the woman. "Simply showing off our little prize winner, my dear."

Mrs. Harper gave me an icy glare. I pulled my hands away from Sun Yat Sen.

"There's someone in the lounge I would like you to meet, Henry," she said. "Hammad can take Sun now."

"Of course." He warmly nodded to me. "Good day, Miss Becker."

As they left, Sun Yat Sen waved his tail like a miniature flag. *There goes my chance to walk a famous dog.* He poked his head around Mr. Harper's arm. I was positive he smiled at me.

CHAPTER TWENTY-ONE

RMS Titanic, Atlantic Ocean
Thursday, April 11, 1912

Strong winds kept most passengers on the Promenade from walking too far toward the stern. I passed a glassed-in area. Inside, behind tall windows, men and women sat at carved tables. Some read books or wrote letters, while others visited over tea.

More passengers claimed the wooden deck chairs outside as the sun rose in the sky. Above me, white steam escaped from three of the ship's funnels. On the Boat Deck, I counted eight lifeboats.

Following an inside passageway, I passed the Veranda Café. It resembled pictures of Paris I'd seen in school. A doorman greeted a well-dressed couple and led them inside to a white wicker table behind potted palms. I lingered outside the windows, imagining having ice cream there with Sajni.

The doorman returned. His pleasant expression disintegrated the moment he saw me. He pushed the door open and stood in the entry. "Children do not belong here without supervision!"

I quickened my pace and headed farther toward the stern. I had probably pushed my luck far enough on the Promenade for the moment. What were folks doing down in the third-class areas? Maybe I could find the girl.

I went all the way back to the purser's office on Deck C to check the ship's diagram, the closest one I could find. From there I took the stairs down one flight to Deck D, home of our own second-class dining saloon and the first-class *grand* dining saloon, which was still at the top of my Must-See list.

From what I remembered of the diagram, third-class passengers could use the portion of Deck D closest to the stern, where I'd first seen the girl.

Three small boys ran in front of me at the landing. A group of teenagers chatted at the railing and watched the spray from the ship's tail. Several younger boys sat in a circle, playing a noisy game of jacks on the varnished wood floor. Their coats were tattered, and one wore only a sweater and trousers that had holes in the knees.

Neither the girl nor her siblings were around. *Should I try another deck?* She could've been anywhere, maybe even in her cabin. I was probably wasting my time.

I ran my hand along the polished railing, unsure what to do next. My feet hurt from walking for so long. Even so, I loved having time to myself. Maybe I could find a deck chair and write in my journal—only I couldn't, because Mother hadn't paid for a deck chair. Maybe I could find a vacant one and use it for a short time.

I hadn't been to Deck E yet, so I descended the stairs. At first glance, it looked like a copy of Deck D above, except with no deck chairs. I trudged back up two flights to Deck C. *Now to find an empty chair and rest my feet.*

Near the railing, two vacant chairs sat in the sun. As I headed toward them, I caught a glimpse over the railing of another small deck below on D. The girl stood facing the wind, tying a kerchief beneath her hair.

Before I could think if it was all right or not, I called down to her. "Hello?"

She raised her head and squinted. "Hello."

What now? We couldn't talk with a twenty-foot space between us. I smiled, not knowing what else to do.

She cupped her hands around her mouth. "Can you come down?"

I held up a finger. "Give me a minute."

I hurried back to the stairs.

"You're quick," she said, when I hopped off the last step. "I'm Ann O'Hara." Definitely Irish. I envied her dimpled cheeks.

"I'm Ruth Becker." I'd wanted to meet her, and now I wasn't sure what else to say.

"I saw you up there yesterday, Ruth Becker." She pointed up two decks and narrowed her eyes. "You aren't stayin' in first class, are y' now?"

I loved the way she added a little twist to her vowels and lingered over her *r*'s. I instantly relaxed. "No, second. My sister and I were exploring. She's napping right now, and I'm thoroughly enjoying it."

Ann laughed as we walked to the railing. "I know all about that. I have four younger sisters and a little brother. My big brother Tim is sixteen, two years older than me." She raised her chin. "He got a job on board, right before we sailed. He's washin' a million dishes in the kitch … *galley*. We haven't seen him much. He sleeps with the crew."

We both rested our arms on the railing, facing the wide blue ocean. "Why are you going to New York?" I asked.

She lowered her voice. "Here's the short of it: My father died last year in a train accident, and my mother's had a horrible time. Her cousin in New York wrote and asked if she'd be willin' to bring us all to her big house over there. So, we scraped together what we could, sold our house to a couple of teachers, and here we are."

I watched the foamy waves that rolled away from the ship. "You make it sound so easy."

She gazed across the water. "Mercy, no. It's hard leavin' our home and the country we love."

I've happened to meet someone who knows exactly how I feel.

"You seem sullen. What's wrong? America's home, right?"

After I explained everything, Ann tucked a long strand of her hair underneath her kerchief. "Don't you miss your father, even though you're still upset with him?"

"Yes, I miss him, but I haven't written to him yet." I turned from the railing to admire the immaculate deck. "He was so excited about us traveling on the *Titanic*, and I didn't care what ship it was. But now I'm glad he picked this one for us."

I stuck my hand in my coat pocket to touch Papa's handkerchief. *How dare I fuss about him making me leave India, when Ann no longer has a father at all?*

~

Dinner that evening was another feast. I was ready to try all the delicacies, from the first course to the last.

Mother surveyed our vast dining room and the dozens of stewards who rushed about with loaded platters. "How do they make so much food for over two thousand people?"

Mr. Simmons raised his water glass. "More than that, if you include the crew."

Calvin held a platter of beef tenderloin for Mrs. Simmons. She stabbed a thick slice with the meat fork and dropped it on her plate. "At least we're getting our money's worth."

"I'm almost full." Marion patted her stomach. "But caramel pudding's coming."

Mother gave my fussy brother some of her meat and buttered beans. "Tell me more about the girl you met today. Did she and her family board at Queenstown?"

I swallowed some milk. "No, they went to Southampton to say good-bye to an aunt, so they boarded there instead. We're meeting again tomorrow."

"Pardon me, ladies," Mr. Simmons said. "Captain Smith himself is heading our way."

Moments later, the *Titanic's* captain stood beside my chair. I gawked at the shiny brass buttons and medals on his uniform and his tidy white beard. His smile seemed honest and unhurried.

"Good evening, everyone. I'm Captain Edward Smith. I hope you're enjoying yourselves. Do you have any questions about the ship?"

I had so many questions. But what did I most want to know? "Yes, how many crew members are there?"

"I believe the number is 885, give or take a few."

I never would have guessed there were that many. Where were they hiding?

He greeted Marion and Mother. "Are you ladies finding everything to your satisfaction?"

"Oh, yes," Mother said, "Get us to New York in one piece, and I'll be happy."

The captain gave her an easy nod. "I think I can guarantee it, madam." He moved to the other side of our table, shaking hands with the Simmons family and those next to them.

A quartet of tuxedoed musicians entered the dining room. Three carried violins, and the last man toted a cello. They took their positions near the center of the room and began a gentle melody that I knew from my lessons with Mr. Liddle.

The fingers of my left hand pressed imaginary strings. *How Papa would love to be here with us, enjoying the music on such a glorious ship.*

Instead, he'd soon attend the Spring Festival, along with other missionary families in Guntur. During the violin competition, someone would say, "Such a shame your daughter Ruth couldn't be here."

"Yes," he'd reply. "Yes, it is."

RMS Titanic, Atlantic Ocean
April 11, 1912

Sky Report: Sliver of last quarter moon. The stars over the dark ocean tonight seem even brighter and larger than over the Arabian Sea. Too many to count. I even found Hercules and Aquila tonight. It's comforting to see them and so many familiar constellations, though I'm so far from home.

It's very cold and getting colder. I found warmth today, though, in a friend. Ann O'Hara is from a tiny village in Ireland. She described it as having a long name and about a hundred folks, "including the ones in the cemetery."

She never had music lessons, but she loves to sing. "Music's powerful," she said. Tomorrow, we'll explore Titanic together.

CHAPTER TWENTY-TWO

RMS Titanic, Atlantic Ocean
Friday, April 12, 1912

Ann skipped the last step on the stairs and leaped to the third class area of Deck D. "Sorry I'm late. I was giving baths, and we had a long wait. There's only two bathtubs for all seven hundred in third class. And it's gettin' a wee bit noticeable, if you know what I mean." She waved the air in front of her nose.

I leaned against the stair rail. "Maybe you could use ours, but we have a line sometimes too."

Ann buttoned up her dark-brown coat. "We'll survive. By the way, I happened to hear they don't use the word 'steerage' aboard the *Titanic* the way they do on other ships. They just call us third class, but it's the same thing. We're still known as the poor immigrants that had to be checked for diseases before we could board."

I wrinkled my nose. "Was anyone turned away?"

"Good question. That'd be sad now, wouldn't it? So, where should we explore first?"

"The grand dining saloon, for starters. It's on this level, but I haven't found it yet."

Ann glanced toward the passageway that led to the bow. "But isn't that first class?"

I drew my fists to my chest. "Yes, but I just want to *see* it, maybe peek in a window."

She gave a waggish grin. "Let's not be dawdlin', then."

The passageway was deserted as we passed beneath the *First Class Only* sign. I showed Ann everywhere I'd searched before. "It makes no sense that I can't find it."

"I'm not sure why we're running into dead ends," she said. "It must be enormous, and I'm thinkin' these are its outside walls." She tapped her finger on her chin. "But I have an idea. Ever hear of Scotland Road? Tim showed me last night when he got off dishwashin' duty."

She beckoned me to follow her. "It's a passageway for the crew to get wherever they're goin' quickly. It runs nearly the length of the ship. It's on Deck E, so we have to take the middle stairs, not the back ones 'cause there's a locked gate."

"Yes, I noticed that."

"Someone said the gates keep us in our place." She dismissed it with a wave.

I followed Ann to the lower deck, then through a swinging door with a small round window. She waved her hand with a flourish. "Welcome to Scotland Road."

One wide passageway stretched nearly all the way from bow to stern, with doorways along both sides. Crew members hurried about, pushing carts or carrying trays, luggage, or linens. One dull-eyed crewman carried a small dog crate that contained a yipping Chihuahua. Stewards, stewardesses, errand boys, and cooks called to one another.

"This is amazing," I said. "I wondered where all the staffers were hiding. Now I see how they deliver things so fast and where they go when they disappear. But how do we get to the dining room from here?"

Ann pointed through the foot traffic to the opposite wall. "Tim's this way, where they wash all the dishes. I'm thinking he'll know."

We entered a steamy room that was lined with large steel tubs. Ann pointed to a set of shiny double doors. "The actual cookin' takes place through there and up on Deck D."

Two teenage boys in food-spattered aprons hurried by. "Hey, you lasses shouldn't be here," one said.

The other turned around with a grin. "Tim's sister, right? He's back in the dish room, but hurry before the boss sees you."

We passed carts and tables that were piled with dishes until we reached a blond boy on a stepstool. "Ann, what are you doin'?" He set a stack of dinner plates on a shelf and climbed down. "I only brought you here yesterday so you could see where I work. Even that was risky."

"We'll be quick. This is my friend, Ruth. How do we get to the grand dining saloon? Is it through the galley?"

Tim stiffened. "What? You can't be goin' up there."

Ann stared him down. "Never mind that. Show me."

He moved the stepstool out of the way. "If you get caught, I didn't see you."

He led us back out to Scotland Road, then to a wide unmarked door. "It's a shortcut." He checked behind him and waved us in. "Have fun."

Through the door, we took a stairway up, two steps at a time. The fear I had of being discovered—plus the lure of adventure—made my heart pound in my ears. We entered a small service area at the top of the stairway and rushed past serving carts that were stacked with neatly folded tablecloths and napkins.

"I feel like a spy," I said.

"You *are* a spy," Ann answered.

A white door stood at the other end of the service area. I pushed it open a few inches and held my breath.

The entire playground at the Mission School for Girls would've easily fit inside the grand dining saloon. It spanned the total width of the ship, from port to starboard. Wide windows on both sides provided ample natural light and amazing views of the Atlantic Ocean.

Dark-green padded chairs surrounded dozens of tables. Each was set for a lavish dinner, including crystal goblets and enough sparkling silverware for at least seven courses.

"This rug ... it's beautiful," Ann said.

"It reminds me of a Persian carpet." I looked from the patterned rug to the intricately carved white ceiling. "Like frosting on a cake."

Ann let out a short breath. "No cake these eyes ever saw."

A door at the far end opened, and two stewards entered with a metal cart. Their voices echoed off the high ceiling.

Ann and I hid behind a table. I spotted a door across the room to our left. "This way," I whispered.

We scurried on tiptoe for at least a mile, between the tables and over the plush carpet.

"Now I know how a mouse must feel," Ann muttered.

The double oak doors held glass panels with elaborate swirls of iron scrollwork. I gently pushed one door, and it opened with a whispery *swish*.

Ann dropped her hand on my shoulder as we exited the grand dining saloon. "Whew!"

Her eyes widened. Another room spread out before us, with a gorgeous white ceiling and rust-colored carpet. Chatting passengers relaxed at a few of the many tables. How would we get out of there?

Ann nudged my arm. "How about that way?"

To our right was a double oak staircase at the base of which a carved cherub held an electric lamp. High over the staircase was a huge glass dome that had scrollwork to match the dining saloon doors. It looked as if it extended all the way to the top of the ship.

"It must be the Grand Staircase I saw on the ship's diagram," I whispered. "We've come this far. We might as well try it out."

"Oh, good Lord and St. Patrick, please make us invisible."

We snuck along the edge of the room and ducked behind a large potted palm. Two men walked by, engrossed in conversation.

"We're almost there," Ann said. "Keep going."

We sidestepped about ten more feet to the bottom of the immense stairway. I stopped to take in its splendor.

But rather than act like intruders and risk breaking into fits of laughter, why not walk up the stairs as dignified as possible? Maybe we'd be less noticeable. At the very least, we'd enjoy ourselves before we got caught.

I smoothed my dress, placed my sweaty right hand on the massive banister, drew myself up to my full height, and tipped my nose in the air. Ann did the same, and together we waltzed up *Titanic's* Grand Staircase, step by magnificent step.

We stopped at the landing to admire the carved golden clock set in the wall. I could tell Ann was trying not to break into laughter.

I cleared my throat and did my best impersonation of Mr. Clayton from the *City of Benares*. "I say, do you have the time, Miss O'Hara?"

Ann nearly burst but covered her mouth with both hands.

A man coughed from somewhere in the room below us. I checked the clock and did a double take. "Uh-oh. It's time for me to get back."

~⌒~

Marion swung the door open to the cabin. "Sissy, I been waitin' for you."

Mother cradled Richard and rubbed his back. He pulled on one ear and whined. "He's getting a fever," she said. "You could have returned sooner and taken Marion out. She's been climbing the walls."

Her disapproving tone negated all the fun of the previous hour. Well, almost.

I removed my shoes and climbed up on top of Sajni's quilt. "Ann and I lost track of time. I'll take her in a minute, as soon as I change my shoes."

Through the porthole, I had a good view of the clear sky and a few wispy clouds. The bed vibrated gently as always, and the ocean splashed against the glass as the ship plowed through the Atlantic. I stretched my arms and legs and rubbed my sore feet.

"See to it you're back when the bugle sounds," Mother said. "I won't be taking Richard to dinner. I'll give him a bath and see if that helps, but he keeps tugging on his ears, so they must be hurting him."

I slid to the floor and rummaged through the trunk for my other shoes. *How can I make her less upset with me?* "Should I ask Mr. Hardy to bring you something to eat?"

"Yes, if you can. That would be helpful."

I yanked my old shoes out from under the green dress and stuffed it back down to keep my bird collection safe.

Marion and I found Mr. Hardy's younger assistant exiting the cabin next door. I didn't know his name.

"Excuse me, could you help us?" I asked. "Our mother can't come to the dining room tonight because our brother is sick. Is there anything you can bring for them to eat?"

"Room service isn't available in second class, but because your brother is ill, I'll see what I can do. Maybe I can bring sandwiches and soup, if that's all right, and some fruit?"

"Oh, yes." I smiled. "And tea?"

"Of course." He turned to go, then added, "And I'll see about a slice of cake."

Marion and I set off for the stairs. "Want to meet my friend Ann? She has younger siblings."

"Okay," she said. "Hurry up!"

One deck below us, I knocked on G-15, Ann's cabin number. A pretty woman answered the door, her hair graying blonde and her eyes matching the ocean.

"You must be Ruth," she said. "Ann's been tellin' us about you. And who's this?"

"My sister, Marion. We're pleased to meet you, Mrs. O'Hara."

Ann came to the door. "Come in, you two, and meet everyone."

Their cabin was almost the same size as ours, but it was packed with beds and children. Ann led us to a lower berth. "This is Alannah, Ava, and Catherine." The girls peeked up from their books and grinned.

Ann pointed to the berth above. "That's Thomas, and Cadie's over there. She'll be two on Monday." Cadie sat sucking her thumb on a child-size bed that was similar to Richard's. They all had blond hair and dimples like their big sister.

Mrs. O'Hara had an easygoing disposition and a bubbly laugh. "We're a close family, and as you can see, that's a handy thing. But our Tim is thrilled to have a job upstairs, and not only for the money. He has a bit more room with three other lads than he would here."

A small washbasin with a single shelf above it stood against the wall between a pair of bunk beds. One battered trunk rested against another bed. There was no room for a wardrobe or anything else. With Deck G below the water line, they didn't need a porthole.

"You have a little brother, also, I'm told," Mrs. O'Hara said.

"Yes, he has a fever and an earache today."

She clapped her hands once and rested them on my arms. "I have something that always helps my children—if your mother's willing to try an old Irish remedy."

"She might be willing to try almost anything at this point."

Mrs. O'Hara wove her way to the old trunk and lifted its lid. She rummaged through clothing. "Here 'tis."

She handed me a small package wrapped in brown paper. "My own mother used this when I was a wee one, and I swear by it. It's black sheep wool, and it works like a charm. Tell your mother to place some of it in whatever ear is hurtin' him." She closed my fingers over the package.

"Are you sure? I don't want to take it if it's your last."

"Your brother needs it, Ruth dear. Take it, and for heaven's sake, get out of here and go have some fun."

Ann dropped her hands to her sides. "I hope you won't mind—I have to bring company this time."

"That's fine," I said. "Who wants to come?"

Thomas hopped down from his berth, and Catherine set down her book. "It's our turn," she said.

We stopped by Cabin F-4 so Mother could meet Ann, Thomas, and Catherine. Richard, asleep in his bed, was flushed with fever. I gave Mother the package from Mrs. O'Hara and told her what to do.

Mother unwrapped it and gave it a sniff. "Well, people in India use stranger remedies than this."

~

On the aft area of Deck C, the late afternoon sun eased the chill from the wind. Marion, Thomas, and Catherine joined another group of children in a game of tag.

Mr. Hoffman passed by and said hello. His sons gave me shy grins and pulled him to the railing.

Ann and I walked toward the railing on the third class "promenade." She stepped onto the lowest rung and stretched her hands high.

"You're just tall enough for that not to look safe," I said.

She laughed and stepped down. "You're probably right." She glanced over her shoulder. "A shove from one of 'em and I'm fish bait."

A tall boy sauntered by and smiled at Ann. Orange-red hair poked out from under his wool cap. She lowered her eyes, and a faint blush crossed her cheeks.

"Who's he?" I asked.

Ann covered her cheeks with her hands. "I don't know his name. He's in the cabin down from ours." She regarded the boy as he joined a group across the deck for a game of ring toss. "If he wants to introduce himself, he's more than welcome."

We faced the ocean again, and I closed my eyes against the wind, feeling our enormous vessel plow through the water.

"Ruth!" Ann jostled my arm. I opened my eyes as she pointed out to sea.

I saw nothing unusual. "What is it?"

"I think it's a whale. It went under now—wait."

I concentrated on the spot where she pointed until something like a shiny, black hill emerged above the water's surface.

"I see it!" A second one appeared beside it. "Look, there's another!"

"How beautiful," Ann said. "They're swimmin' with us."

The whales didn't stay long. "They probably can't keep up," I said. "Did you ever dream the *Titanic* would be like this?"

Ann turned around to watch her siblings and Marion chase each other. "I had no thought about what to expect, but that's how it is for most of the folks in third. We're all takin' a risk on America, but we're hoping for a better life."

"It'll be a whole new world for both you and me."

Ann rested her back against the railing. "You sound worried."

My hair blew across my face, and I swept it back. "I told you I didn't want to leave India. I had a good life there."

Catherine and Marion held hands and chuckled. I marveled at how they could understand each other's accents.

The wind lifted Ann's kerchief, and she held it down with one hand. "Ruth, y' have to believe you'll have a good life in your new home too. God won't stop takin' care of you."

How could she believe that, with her father gone and her family having so little? I shielded my eyes from the sun to get a better look at her face.

Her genuine smile and calm manner told me she meant every word. She spread her arms apart. "No matter what happens, I'm in God's hands."

RMS Titanic, Atlantic Ocean
April 12, 1912

Sky Report: The "Northern Crown," Corona Borealis, lying between Bootes and Hercules, is usually hard to find, but tonight its stars are especially bright. I found Gemini too! When Gemini (the Twins) appears, it's a sign to sailors of a safe voyage ahead. If I see Captain Smith again, I'm going to tell him about Gemini. And I'll suggest that Titanic provide a telescope for stargazing on all future voyages.

CHAPTER TWENTY-THREE

RMS Titanic, Atlantic Ocean
Saturday, April 13, 1912
Morning

Who needed an alarm clock or bugle when my sister was on board?

Marion's curls bobbed as she shouted and ran ahead of us to the stairs. "Time for breakfast!"

"Hold the handrail, Marion." Mother carried Richard, who waved to the two ladies following us.

"What a happy boy you are!" one of the ladies said.

"He wasn't so happy yesterday," Mother said to them. "He had a terrible earache and fever."

The woman smiled. "It's remarkable how they bounce back so quickly, isn't it?"

Mother leaned toward me. "Thanks to that Irish sheep."

We all breakfasted like royalty on eggs Benedict and Belgian waffles with warm strawberry sauce. Mother returned to the cabin, and I took Marion and Richard down to the "O'Hara Hideaway," as Ann called it.

She opened the door. "Ah, it's about time I get to meet the littlest Becker. Hello, Richard." Richard covered his eyes to hide from her. Marion scooted past Ann to hug Catherine.

"Is your mother here?" I asked.

"She's down the passage with Cadie's diapers. I'm doin' arithmetic with the others."

I handed Ann the package of sheep's wool. "Here's what was left over. Tell her Richard is doing better. My mother said to thank her for the help."

"She'll be glad to hear it," Ann said. "Let's try to meet later, maybe after lunch."

Back upstairs on our deck, Marion and I found Mr. Hardy and asked him for a stroller. He showed us to the service elevator so we wouldn't have to carry it on the stairs.

I twisted side to side in the elevator. "Let's find the gymnasium today."

Marion copied my twists. "What's that?"

"It's where people exercise. There's a swimming pool too. It's on the Boat Deck, way up on top. I hope they let us see it."

We left the service elevator on Deck C and went to the passenger elevator. The lift boy waited alone at the open door.

"Boat Deck, please," I said, pushing the stroller inside.

The boy coughed. "That's, uh, first class."

That hadn't kept me down so far. "That's correct." I concentrated on the glass-covered dial above the door.

He did a quick scan of the passageway, pulled the door shut, and up we went. "My shift ends in five minutes," he said, "so you're on your own coming down."

We exited onto the Boat Deck. Marion laughed when she saw how high we were. "Sissy, look at the ocean!"

I understood her amazement. Far below us, the dark blue waters of the Atlantic stretched on forever, giving a sense of how small the ship was in comparison.

A bracing wind pulled and tugged our clothing. Richard rocked in the stroller seat and squinted at the cloudless sky. I found his knitted hat inside his jacket pocket and tugged it over his ears.

The deck was crowded with passengers taking in the sunshine and the glorious ocean views. Couples bundled in long coats strolled together arm-in-arm. Others relaxed in deck chairs, covered with blankets called steamer rugs.

We crossed from port to starboard. Maids supervised romping

children, and a group of four older women held their brimmed hats against the wind. One suggested hot tea, and the women all moved inside. A roar from a rowdy game of shuffleboard drew a few onlookers.

Four dogs walked on leashes beside their masters. Marion moved away, peeking around my coat as they passed. One lady in smoky-gray fur carried a tiny white dog. Wearing its own little red cape with a fur collar, the dog released a string of shrill barks. The lady held his mouth with her gloved hand and cooed in his ear.

After I pushed the stroller around to the port side again, I counted the lifeboats. *One, two, three, four, five, six, seven ...* There were eight, exactly like on the starboard side, plus a smaller one.

"What are they for?" Marion asked.

"We had them on the *City of Benares*, too, in case something happens and—"

A hatch opened, and a black-coated officer stepped onto the deck and glowered at us. "Children are not allowed in this area without adult supervision. Also, it is only for first-class passengers."

Here we go again. Was I wearing a "second class" sign?

"Actually, sir, we were—"

"Miss Becker, is Mr. Lightoller bothering you?"

I turned to see Mr. Harper draw near. He led Sun Yat Sen on a leash, and a man in a long overcoat walked with him. The dog wagged its fluffy tail and pulled on the leash. Marion clung to my leg.

The officer greeted the men. "Mr. Harper, Colonel Gracie. You know this young lady?"

"As a matter of fact, we are well acquainted," Mr. Harper said. "I've asked Miss Becker to take Sun Yat Sen for a walk so that Colonel Gracie and I may discuss some business matters."

Was I hearing correctly?

Mr. Lightoller didn't hesitate. "Very good, then. A pleasant day to you, gentlemen."

I exhaled and bent down to pet the dog. "Thank you, Mr. Harper."

Marion loosened her hold on my leg. She reached out a tentative finger. Sun Yat Sen licked it then sniffed Richard's foot.

Richard reached down to touch him. "Dobbie."

Mr. Harper chuckled. "It is *I* who must thank *you*, Miss Becker—that is, after you and the little ones deliver Sun Yat Sen to my suite. Shall we say, in thirty minutes? Cabin D-33."

"Oh, yes. I'm … we would love to!"

He offered me the leash, and I wrapped it around my wrist and turned to leave. Sun Yat Sen beat his tail against Richard's leg. This would be much more fun than seeing the gymnasium.

We walked the dog all over *Titanic*'s Boat Deck, greeting everyone we passed. Marion made me stop every few minutes so she could play with him.

"I thought you were afraid of dogs."

"I'm not afraid of Sun Sun."

According to a clock on the bulkhead near the wheelhouse, thirty minutes had passed. I pushed Richard into the elevator, and Marion held Sun Yat Sen.

"Deck D, please," I said.

The new lift boy reminded me of Michael, with his freckles and dark hair. He was more interested in petting the dog than questioning my class status.

I let Marion knock on the door to D-33. A dark-skinned man answered. He could've been Rushab's twin from the *City of Benares*, minus any hint of joy in his face. He reached out for Sun Yat Sen. "Mr. Harper wishes to give you his kindest regards."

Mr. Harper called from somewhere inside. "Hammad, for heaven's sake, show them in."

The man grimaced, then he held the door open for us. I pushed the stroller into a large sitting room that had a crystal chandelier and fireplace. Marion held onto the back of my coat.

Mr. Harper entered through an archway that was framed in thick velvet drapes. "Come in, come in. Did Sun behave for you?"

"He was perfect," I said.

"He was good," Marion the Reporter said, "but he had to go."

"I hope it wasn't a problem?"

"Somebody came and swept it all up." Marion mimicked the crewman with the pan and broom.

Mr. Harper bent down to Richard's eye level. "This must be the young master who's been struck ill."

Hammad unleashed Sun Yat Sen and set him on the carpet. The dog trotted over to a little bed near a window that was much larger than our porthole. Was that a silk doggie pillow?

Mrs. Harper arrived and planted her feet outside the doorway. "Hammad! What are these *children* doing in our suite?"

"We really must be going." I quickly turned the stroller toward the door, and Marion followed at my heels. Mrs. Harper stood to the side, her mouth widened in surprise.

"Good-bye now, Mr. Harper!" I said. "Have a lovely day, Mrs. Harper."

CHAPTER TWENTY-FOUR

RMS Titanic, Atlantic Ocean
Saturday, April 13, 1912
Afternoon

As we left the dining saloon after lunch, Mother appeared to gain a spark of energy. "I'm taking Marion and Richard to the library. Mrs. Simmons told me there's a children's play area inside. Do you want to come?"

I stopped in the stairway landing before heading down. "Ann wants me to meet her and her sisters, but I'll be back before the bugle."

The little O'Haras would've enjoyed the library, if third-class passengers were allowed. But what Ann had in mind sounded like much more fun.

At the O'Hara Hideaway, I met Ann, Ava, and Alannah. They took me to the third-class general room, on the stern end of Deck C. Men and women sat at long benches and round tables throughout the room, talking and drinking tea and beer.

"Everyone relaxes here between meals and in the evening," Ann said. "There's always someone playing music and folks dancin'."

We stood against the far wall, where several young people milled about, some holding glasses of beer.

Two men jumped to a raised platform with their violins. One shouted, "Find a partner, lads and lasses. Here we go!"

They struck up a happy, quick-tempo tune. As if mesmerized, half the men in the room set down their glasses, grabbed girls' hands, and began to dance around the platform.

Ann, her sisters, and I clapped along with other bystanders. A man with blondish whiskers pulled a chair over to some barrels in the middle of the room. Someone handed him a pair of drumsticks, and a young man in a ragged sweater joined him, beating on the barrels with the palms of his hands.

I studied the nimble fingers of the fiddlers. How did they play so fast and dance in place at the same time? I had a feeling most of what they played was improvised. I'd never heard anything quite like it, and I'd never seen people jump up and dance at the first suggestion of a song.

Ann cupped a hand over my ear. "You should've brought your violin."

"I don't know how to play like this." I clapped and stomped my foot to the rhythm. "I love it, though!"

The red-haired boy stood across the room with his pals, looking our way. "There's your friend," I said to Ann.

Ann folded her arms. "He's too shy to come over."

The dancers swirled around me, laughing, eyes shining. The revelers were from many different countries, but the music was a language everyone understood. If any of them feared for their future in America, their faces didn't show it.

Ann reached for my hand and Ava's, and I took Alannah's. We danced in a circle, spinning one way and then the other. We copied the other dancers, bringing our hands together high, backing away, and coming together again, until finally the song ended and we all let go, holding our stomachs and laughing.

Everyone clapped and cheered. Someone gave a loud whistle. Others called for more music, so the musicians started another tune that was as lively as the first.

"This is amazing," I said between songs. "First and second class don't know what they're missing." We got cups of water and stayed until the fiddlers were replaced by a man who played bagpipes.

I walked the girls back to their cabin. "Tomorrow's Sunday," I said. "There's a church service in the morning for *all* passengers. You'll never guess where."

"Not on deck, I hope," Ann said. "It's gettin' chillier every day."

I couldn't wait to see her face when I told her. "They announced it at lunch. It's in the grand dining saloon."

"What?" Ann's green eyes shone. "You mean I went to all that trouble of findin' Tim and sneaking you in there when we could've waited and seen it legally?"

"I'm afraid so." I laughed. "But you should come. Bring your family."

"I'll see what my mother says. I think they're havin' a Mass down here as well."

~~~

Back in F-4, Marion stamped her foot as I tightened the bow on the back of her dress. "I'm tired of getting dressed up just to go eat dinner. I wanna see Sun Sun."

I'd told Mother about our little adventure up to the Boat Deck that morning so it wouldn't come as a surprise. "Sun Yat Sen. You should learn his proper name. He's probably having a fine doggie dinner tonight."

Mother tied Richard's shoes. "You had no business in first class. You're lucky that dog's owner didn't have you both removed."

I turned Marion around and straightened her collar. "Mr. Harper wouldn't do that."

Marion pulled away. "Mrs. Harper isn't very nice."

"What do you mean?" Mother asked, lifting Richard from her bed.

"She didn't realize Mr. Harper let us walk the dog," I said, "but he explained it to her."

Marion shook her curls. "She doesn't like me."

"She's probably not used to being around talkative little girls," Mother said.

At least Mother wasn't *too* angry. Maybe she was accepting my waywardness—at least until we reached New York.

At the dinner table, Peter and Priscilla Simmons fought over whose turn it was to pass the salt. Mr. Simmons finally put a stop to it. "Not one more word, or you will be taken to the cabin without any dinner."

The twins and Mrs. Simmons looked at him as if he'd gone mad. Mother covered a smile with her napkin, and I pretended to fix my shoelaces.

Richard smacked the high chair and teased Marion. "Mimi, Mimi, Mimi ..."

"Richard," Marion said, "you're givin' me a headache."

As I ate the main course of beef Wellington, creamed spinach with bacon and walnuts, and Parmesan new potatoes, my foot tapped to the beat of a song from the party that afternoon down in third class.

I might be able to play some of the music if I practice. Maybe I could ask one of those fiddlers for help in a day or so.

Marion tugged my sleeve. "Look who's here, Sissy."

Four members of the *Titanic* orchestra arrived, set up their chairs and instruments in the center of the dining room, and played a waltz. They followed it with two Irving Berlin songs—"After the Honeymoon" and "Angels"—a big contrast from the type of music playing in the general room down below, but it was still the kind I knew and loved the most.

Calvin brought a dessert platter of chocolate and vanilla éclairs.

"One of each, please," I said when he reached my side.

Mother looked at me above her spectacles. "Choose one, Ruth."

I did my best not to roll my eyes. "Vanilla, then."

Calvin placed a vanilla éclair onto my plate with his tongs. When Mother turned to clean Richard's hands, he slipped me a chocolate one too.

The quartet, led by the wavy-haired violinist, began a new song, and my throat caught at the first few notes. Of all the songs in the world, why that one? It was "Spring Song"—my own, never-to-be "Spring Song" that I would've played in the Spring Festival at home.

I had to bite my lip to stop the tears. *What kind of mean joke from God is this?* I'd felt a little better for a few days and hadn't thought much about home and Papa and the festival. Now, my heart ached with every quarter note. I wanted to run from the dining room. But running wouldn't change the fact that I was moving to America and I'd never, ever play that song for an audience. I stayed and choked down my tears.

Mother's eyes held a look of concern. Maybe she realized my agony.

Following the applause, I breathed easier and took a bite of each éclair. The musicians played one more waltz, sweet and perfect.

Richard twisted in his high chair. Mother untied his bib. "Time to go," she said.

"Would it be all right if I come in a few minutes? I'll bring Marion." I glanced over to the orchestra members as they chatted with passengers. "I'd like to meet the lead violinist."

"All right. But come back to the cabin right away."

Marion and I left the table. I took her hand and approached the musicians. The one I wanted to meet had his back to me.

"Pardon me," I said. My palms started to sweat on cue. I let go of Marion's hand and wiped them on my dress.

The wavy-haired man turned, straightening his tuxedo jacket.

"I only came to say ... how much I enjoyed the music."

"That's very kind of you." He extended a hand. "I'm Wallace Hartley."

"I'm Ruth Becker." I shook his hand and blurted out a question that had been on my mind. "What's the title of the song they play on the bugle?"

Mr. Hartley laughed. "That's 'Roast Beef of Old England.'"

"Sissy plays violin!" Marion announced.

Leave it to you, Marion.

Mr. Hartley raised his eyebrows at me. "You play?"

I stammered, feeling heat rise in my cheeks. "Um ... yes."

"Sissy can play 'Spring Song.' She was gonna play it at the festibal, but we had to leave. She's gonna play in a orchasa someday!"

I stared in disbelief at this child who had just somehow managed to share all my pain with a complete stranger—*Titanic's* orchestra leader, of all people.

"Marion, stop. Don't bother Mr. Hartley with this." My face burned. *This was a big mistake.*

Mr. Hartley set his violin case at his feet. "Do you have your violin with you?"

I nearly choked. "It's in my cabin."

"Bring it with you tomorrow to the second class lounge, after the church service in the grand dining saloon."

RMS Titanic, Atlantic Ocean
April 13, 1912

Sky Report: Short view of the sky tonight due to cold air temperature. Still clear, and earlier winds have calmed. Cassiopeia and the Dippers are brilliant, no moon visible.

How am I supposed to sleep tonight? Mr. Hartley told me to bring my violin with me tomorrow, and that must mean he'll ask me to play. I'm so honored! On the one hand, I could've strangled Marion for blabbing to him that I can play. But I wouldn't have this opportunity otherwise. I just pray I won't forget everything I know, and he won't be sorry he asked me.

CHAPTER TWENTY-FIVE

*RMS Titanic, Atlantic Ocean
Sunday, April 14, 1912
Morning*

I hurried down to the O'Hara Hideaway before breakfast to tell Ann about Mr. Hartley and his invitation. Laughter and chatter filtered through the closed door. When I knocked, Ann came out to the passageway and shut the door behind her so we could hear each other.

"Ruth, that's so exciting!" She gave me a hug. "I wish I could come see you play, but we're not allowed up to the lounge."

"Why not come to the church service? Then you might be able to come to the lounge from there without anyone noticing."

Ann twirled a piece of her hair. "Even if we were invited, my mother doesn't want to take all the wee ones to first class. We're goin' to Mass down here—Tim, too." Her eyes took on their usual glint of mischief. "But I'll pray about it. Maybe something will come up."

I gave her directions to the lounge, just in case. Even if Ann managed to get past all the gates and signs and reach the lounge, would she be allowed in? Classes never officially mixed, but I'd had some luck in that department.

Ann's Irish. That should help.

～

During our colossal breakfast in the dining saloon, an announcement was made that the lifeboat drill, previously planned for 11:00 a.m., had been canceled.

"I wonder why?" Mother asked.

Mr. Simmons poured thick maple syrup over a stack of pancakes. "Not necessary and too many activities on the schedule, I reckon. Much too cold also."

A lifeboat drill was the last thing on my mind. I picked at my food, but I still had to attend the church service before I would see Mr. Hartley.

After breakfast, we followed several passengers to the grand dining saloon. My violin case beat against my leg, keeping time with my heart, where anxiety and excitement battled it out.

"Right this way, ladies and gentlemen." Two stewards directed us through a doorway and a short passageway. How had Ann and I missed this? It wasn't half as interesting, though, as taking the scenic route through Scotland Road.

As we filed in, Mother carried Richard and admired the room's carved ceiling. "Isn't this beautiful?"

I couldn't keep it to myself. "Yes, I've already been here once."

"Me and Sissy couldn't find it," Marion said.

Mother's jaw went rigid. "Yet you found it with Ann, I suppose."

I shrugged. "Her older brother helped us."

"I can't blame you, but rules are rules."

"I won't do it anymore." There were plenty of other first-class areas I had yet to visit, including the gymnasium, the Turkish baths, and the Palm Court, for starters.

The dining tables had been moved out of the way, and the green-cushioned chairs placed in rows for the service. We found three chairs near the back, and I carefully set my violin case beneath mine.

Maybe I should've told Mr. Hartley I couldn't come. What if he wanted me to play something I didn't know?

"Performance jitters," Mr. Liddle would say. *"Normal and to be expected."*

I tried to ignore my sweaty hands as I practiced a slow-breathing technique he'd taught me.

"Are the O'Haras coming?" Mother asked as Richard examined

her cross pendant. "I'd like to properly thank Ann's mother for her help with Richard."

"No, they're going to Mass in the general room."

Some of the first-class passengers began to arrive, all of them dressed in fine apparel. Mother recognized a few from the newspapers and pointed to a graceful woman wrapped in a dark fur coat.

"That must be Dorothy Gibson, the film actress. Mrs. Simmons told me she was aboard. And the gentleman there with the mustache and the young wife—I'm certain that's John Jacob Astor, one of the richest men in the world."

Richard squirmed, and Mother let him stand in front of her chair. I'd dressed him that morning in his red-and-blue Sunday outfit with an extra undershirt for warmth. Marion and I wore our dresses from London, but I wished I'd added my sweater. I shivered and rubbed my arms.

Captain Smith strode to the front of the room. "Good morning, ladies and gentlemen. Let us begin."

Everyone stopped chatting and stood. The captain started us off with a song from a pamphlet we had been given at the entrance. We took our seats again as a minister opened in prayer and gave a short message.

Captain Smith then led us in the Lord's Prayer. When we finished, we sang, "Eternal Father, Strong to Save." Mother's hand visibly trembled as she held onto the pamphlet.

When the service ended, I turned to her. "What's wrong?"

"It's that song," she said. "That line about saving those in peril on the sea—I don't care for it."

~∽~

After the service, we made our way to the second-class lounge, which doubled as the library, where Mother had taken Marion and Richard the day before. Glass shelves with books by the hundreds lined the walls. Dark woods, stuffed furniture, and tapestries made the long room feel cozy. The sun made a striped pattern along the carpet through the pale gold curtains. Passengers read or wrote letters at small tables and scanned the shelves.

There was no sign of Ann. The orchestra members sauntered about, browsing the books. Two of the musicians were not the ones who'd performed in our dining room. My palms were wet rags, my heart a bass drum.

Mother took Marion and Richard to find seats. I clutched my violin case and went over to Mr. Hartley toward the front of the room.

He tightened the bolt on his portable music stand. "Miss Becker! Are you ready to play with us?"

I swallowed. "Yes, if you'd like me to, sir."

The other musicians approached. "Fellows," he said, "allow me to present Miss Becker. She's going to join us on a song or two."

They introduced themselves, but their names went in and out of my head.

"Let's start with something simple, shall we?" Mr. Hartley asked me. "Is there anything particular you'd like to play?"

I struggled to open my case. "I'm … I'm sorry." I took out my violin and bow and set the case to the side. They waited for my response, but my mind went blank. What could I play?

The room filled with more people. Some gave me amused looks, no doubt wondering what the girl with her mouth hanging open was doing with the orchestra.

I took a deep breath and remembered a song they had played the first time I heard them in the dining saloon. I'd practiced it a few times in our cabin. "How about 'Ah, Sweet Mystery of Life?'"

"Very good," Mr. Hartley said. The musicians readied their instruments. I stepped to the end of their semi-circle and lifted the violin to my shoulder.

Mr. Hartley counted quietly. "One … two … three … four."

As soon as we began, the notes came to mind, and my fingers cooperated. Halfway through, I relaxed. I'd forgotten how much I missed playing music in a group. When we finished, Mr. Hartley and the others smiled at me. I'd played well and had their approval. But this was just a warm-up.

I barely heard the polite applause from our audience while Mr.

Hartley directed us to play two more songs. As I drew my bow across the strings for the final notes, I glanced up to search for Ann.

More passengers, including several children, had entered the room. I hoped they were drawn in by the music. Mr. Hoffman, standing near the bookshelves with his two sons, smiled and waved.

Still no Ann.

Mr. Hartley bent close to my ear. "You're an excellent violinist. Would you play 'Spring Song' for us?"

I froze.

What? I'd barely been able to listen to the orchestra play it the night before. "Spring Song" belonged in Guntur, not here. It was *my* song. Playing it on the *Titanic* would be like saying good-bye to my old life. And I wasn't ready for that.

The door from the passageway opened, and a small group entered amid loud whispers. Ann led them, followed by five little O'Hara children. Would they be allowed to stay? A young crewman stalked over to Ann, rebuke on his face.

Mr. Hartley laid a hand on my shoulder. "Miss Becker?"

Ann sternly whispered something to the crewman, who folded his arms and backed away. *She must've given him a little Irish talking-to.*

Since she was there now, *maybe* I could play my song. I cleared my throat and pushed up my sleeves.

"Yes," I said. "I'm ready."

The musicians waited for me to begin. I inhaled and took my time exhaling, hoping to slow my heartbeat. I stole a glance at Ann, who greeted me with a triumphant smile. I drank in her encouragement and let it wash through me inside.

I raised my violin to my shoulder and lifted my bow. With eyes closed, I began to play "Spring Song," sweet and clear. The song transported me back to Guntur, with Papa on the veranda. *Oh, Papa, if you could see me now ...*

A tear escaped, and I missed a few notes. My bow wouldn't move. The only sound came from my thumping heart.

The orchestra stepped forward and joined in, as if supporting me to keep me afloat. I recovered, drawing from their strength, and played "Spring Song" with more passion and finesse than ever before. Together, the *Titanic* orchestra and I played the song through to the pure final note.

The room nearly split from the thunderous applause. People across the lounge rose to their feet and gave a standing ovation. In the back of the room, Mother lifted Richard high so he could see. As he clapped, Marion bounced up and down on her toes, cheering and waving her arms.

The orchestra members smiled and thanked me as though I'd done a good deed for them. Mr. Hartley said, "A splendid job, Miss Becker! A true pleasure."

I had to steady myself on his music stand. "Thank you, Mr. Hartley. Thank you for letting me play."

Ann and her siblings approached me with hugs and congratulations—I instantly had at least one child on each leg. "You were fantastic," Ann said. "When you said you could play, I had no idea!"

"I don't think I could've played that song if you hadn't come when you did. How did you manage it?"

"I confessed to my mother that you and I had sneaked into first class." She grinned. "She was stunned, of course. I told her you were playing your violin here today. So, after Mass, she winked at me and said, 'Ann, don't you and the children have someplace to be?' But I'm sorry we're late. We had to take a few detours. And it's quite a long walk, especially with this brood."

I laughed, appreciating all her efforts. "What did you tell that fellow at the door?"

Ann cocked her head toward the doorway, where the young crewman stood. "I told him you're our sister, and he better let us stay or our big, strong brother would be delighted to throw him overboard."

Mother waved to me. I wanted to introduce her to Mr. Hartley. To Ann, I said, "Let's do something after lunch, all right?"

Two scowling stewards headed in our direction from the entrance.

Ann quickly agreed and rounded up her crew. "I think we've overstayed our welcome. Come down and get me. And bring Marion and Richard this time."

~

Never was there anyone so famished in the history of the world as I was after my *Titanic* musical debut. Of course, I was in the right place, because we were presented with a magnificent buffet lunch.

The Simmons twins and their parents followed me to the buffet line. "We heard you in the library today, Ruth," Mrs. Simmons said. "You never told us you play violin. You were wonderful!"

"Yes, very impressive," Mr. Simmons said. "What an honor to play with the orchestra."

I couldn't stop smiling. "Thank you. I almost—"

Peter pushed his sister into the buffet table, the collision causing a serving utensil in the dish of filet mignon to bounce and hit the floor. I jumped out of the way before the sauce could splash onto my dress.

"Hey, look what you did!" Priscilla said.

Peter laughed. "You did it!"

Mrs. Simmons caught both of them by their wrists. "That's quite enough, you two. Keep your hands to yourselves, for heaven's sake!"

Marion opened her mouth to say something, but I interrupted before she could. "I think I see pudding!" I bent down and whispered, "I'm glad you have good manners." After lunch, I asked her, "Want to go visit the O'Haras?"

"I just wanna see Catherine," she said.

"She'll be there." I turned to Mother. "I'll take Richard too."

"All right, but stay inside. It's much colder today, now that we're in the middle of the North Atlantic."

It *was* colder. An icy wind skimmed the passageway. Ann let us squeeze into her cabin, then she turned to Alannah, Ava, Catherine, Thomas, Marion, and Richard in the stroller. "How 'bout some dancing?"

We took their squealing and bouncing as a *yes*, ushered them up to Deck C, and followed the music from there to the general room.

An accordion player had taken the stage. Everyone danced or clapped along to the infectious energy of the music.

Ann's siblings and Marion soon joined hands and jumped into the center of the action. They finally wandered back to us with pink faces, all complaining of thirst, so we shepherded them and got cups of cold water for everyone.

The red-haired boy stood propped against a post across the room. His friends elbowed him and sent plenty of glances in our direction. At last, he headed our way, urged on by their friendly taunts.

"Don't look now," I said to Ann, "but you're about to meet your favorite redhead."

She wrinkled her nose. "What?"

He tapped her shoulder, and she turned around.

"May … I have the next dance?" He blushed and bit his lip.

Ann glanced at the stage and back to him. "I don't even know your name."

"Oh, sorry." He shuffled his feet. "Jerry. Jerry Hawkins."

"I'm Ann O'Hara. And, yes, y' may have the next dance, Jerry Hawkins."

She took his hand as the music began. After a rough start, they soon swirled around the floor with everyone else. The rest of us clapped along.

Alannah turned to me. "I don't think my sister's ever danced with a boy before."

When the song ended, Jerry walked Ann back to our group and returned to his friends. They made a big show of teasing him.

Ann's cheeks had turned a warm shade of pink, and she tucked a strand of hair behind her ear. "That was interesting."

"I hope he asks you again. I'd love to stay, but I promised to get back before the bugle."

Ann pretended to look down her nose. "You may return to second class, if you must. Let's meet tomorrow. It's Cadie's birthday, so we'll have a party."

"Maybe it'll be warmer too." I embraced her in a hug. "Thank you for coming to see me play today."

She gave me an extra squeeze. "It was important to me. I'm glad I did."

The ship vibrated more than usual on our way back to the cabin. I hummed along with the bugle as I parked the stroller next to F-4, thinking that "Roast Beef of Old England" would not be too popular in India.

Inside our cabin, the heat that came through the vents felt wonderful. Mother perched on the end of the sofa and bit the thread off a button she was sewing back onto my coat. "What did you and the O'Haras do?" she asked.

"I danced and danced." Marion twirled across the room and bumped into the sofa.

Mother checked the other buttons. "And how was Richard?"

I placed him on the floor beside her. "Good. He loves the music."

"I'm so thankful. I pray he'll be all right until we get to Michigan."

Marion flopped back on the sofa. "How many more days?"

I untied my shoes. "Today is Sunday. We're due to arrive in New York on Wednesday. That's three more days on the ship. Then we take another train."

Was it possible that this never-ending journey would come to an end after all?

Mother put away her sewing. "Let's get ready for dinner, girls. I've heard they're serving an extra-special meal tonight. Marion, your blue jumper is all that's decent. I'll do some washing tomorrow."

All of my clothes were dingy and wrinkled. I opened our trunk. Down near the bottom, I found my dark-green dress wrapped around my birds. I pulled it out and unfolded it on Mother's bed. It was a bit fancy, but not for the *Titanic*. It was also the warmest dress I owned.

Marion came to the bed, wearing her chemise. "Can I hold one of your birds, Sissy? Please?" She rubbed my back with her chubby hand. "I'll be careful—I promise."

"No." My response was automatic. I'd hoped to place the birds back in the trunk without her noticing.

But the disappointment in her eyes made me reconsider. She'd been a good sport, more or less, throughout this mad journey. And she was a little more patient than the whiny girl who had boarded the train in Guntur.

Or maybe it was *me* who was different.

I ran my fingers through her curls. "Help me carry them to the desk. You can look at them while we get ready."

Her eyes gleamed as she gently carried a bird in each hand to the desk. After lining up all ten for a bird parade, she stood back and clasped her hands. "I like them so, so much, Sissy."

I volunteered to carry Richard upstairs to dinner, joining the Simmons family on the stairwell. Two pimple-faced stewards hurried past us, taking the steps two at a time. "How's everyone doing this evening?" one asked.

"You all look splendid," the other called over his shoulder. "Enjoy your dinners!"

"They must be late for work," Mr. Simmons said, "but they're certainly in good spirits."

"I've noticed that today," Mrs. Simmons replied. "They're all in better moods than usual."

Mr. Simmons knocked hard on the paneled wall. "She's an excellent ship, doing what she was designed to do. That'll make a happy crew. We've traveled over five hundred nautical miles since yesterday, and rumor has it that Captain Smith might try to get us into New York a day early."

Mother's voice was shaky. "Wouldn't that be something?"

Mrs. Simmons checked the ornate watch pinned to her dress. "We're certainly moving fast, but I'm thankful the ocean is calm."

Her husband patted her shoulder. "Nothing stands in *Titanic*'s way, my dear."

For my main course that evening, I chose the curried chicken and rice, hoping the curry would add a taste of India. We had the usual overwhelming number of side dishes, then plum pudding, ice cream, nuts, fresh fruit, and several types of cheese.

To add to the festivities, Calvin brought a small chocolate birthday cake to the table for Peter and Priscilla. Three other passengers had birthdays as well. After the stewards sang "Happy Birthday" to them, Mrs. Simmons cut small slices of cake for the twins, Marion, Richard, and me. The stewards then cleared the tables and led the entire dining room in a hymn sing-along.

As we followed the Simmons family back to the stairs, loud laughter and singing came from outside on the third-class deck. "Listen to the whooper-ups!" Mrs. Simmons remarked. "They don't seem to mind the cold."

It was later than usual when we reached our cabin. Mother got Richard and Marion ready for baths and bed. I had an urge to take a walk, despite the cold. "I'm going up on deck for a bit. I'll be back soon, I promise."

"Button up your coat all the way," Mother said.

I was sure Ann wouldn't be out among the "whooper-ups" in third, so I took the stairs up to the second-class section of Deck B. A few other passengers braved the temperatures and wandered the outside deck. My breath came out in little puffs—another new experience I would describe to Sajni.

The cheerful notes of "Everybody Two Step" came from inside the glass-enclosed area. I poked my head in and peeked around a group near the doorway. Mr. Hartley played violin with the three musicians who accompanied him the first night in the dining room—a violinist, a bass player, and a pianist at the grand piano.

Everyone swayed to the merry music. As the applause and cheers drowned out the last few notes, I yawned. It had been a long yet victorious day.

A moment from when Sajni and I said good-bye in Guntur came back to me. *"Ruth, I believe you will still play in an orchestra one day, just like Mr. Liddle told you."*

I grinned. Sajni had been right.

Millions of stars filled the black April sky as I made my way along the deck, headed toward the stairs. And then, for the first time since I left home, the constellation Virgo appeared. Papa had taught me the story of Virgo—that it represented the reunion of a mother and daughter—and its appearance was a sign of spring. Perhaps it was a sign that Mother and I were growing closer too.

I had to admit it—I'd been stubborn long enough. It was time to write to Papa.

I composed a long letter to him in my mind, telling him all about the *Titanic*, my orchestra debut, and all the stars I had seen so far—more stars than he and I had ever observed together in Guntur.

In the morning, I would write the letter and mail it to him from New York City. But now, Sajni's quilt beckoned me to bed.

RMS Titanic, Atlantic Ocean
April 14, 1912

Sky Report: Quite sure I see Saturn tonight, and finally Virgo, playing her Spring Song for me in the great star orchestra. No moon. Much too cold. How can there be so many stars? Every constellation must hold thousands more than I ever imagined. There's truly so much beauty to be seen, even during the darkest of nights.

CHAPTER TWENTY-SIX

RMS Titanic, Atlantic Ocean
Sunday, April 14, 1912
11:45 p.m.

I woke to an eerie silence. Reaching for the bedpost, I felt for the vibrations that always lulled me to sleep, but my berth was still. Nothing splashed at the porthole. I lay in the dark under my quilt, straining to hear the hum of the engines. But there was none.

Mother stirred in her bed. I turned to see her silhouette against the wall in the faint light from under the door.

"What's wrong?" I whispered.

"I'm not sure. I thought I felt the bed move." She wrapped a dressing gown around herself and went to the door. Someone scurried past as she opened it.

"Mr. Hardy, has something happened?" Her voice lowered in concern. "Why are we stopped?"

"All is well, Mrs. Becker," he said. "There's been a slight accident. They're going to fix it, and we'll be going on in a few minutes."

"An accident?" Her voice rattled.

"It's nothing, I assure you." He hurried away.

Mother returned to her bed and sat on its edge. "This is very odd." Even as she whispered, I sensed her tension.

I closed my eyes and hunkered down under my quilt. Two minutes passed. The only sound came from Mother tapping her fingers on the mattress. Why wouldn't they start the engines?

Footsteps thumped overhead, and Mother got up again. She

opened the cabin door.

Mr. Hardy's urgent voice echoed from down the passageway. "Everybody on deck with life belts at once!"

Mother stepped partway out the door and nearly screamed, "What?"

I pushed myself up on my elbows to see Mr. Hardy pause at our door. "Get your life belts on, and get up to the Boat Deck now, ma'am."

"But you said—"

He'd already moved down the passageway, pounding on doors and shouting the same orders over and over. Mother slammed our door and flicked on a light. Marion moaned from her bed.

I threw back my covers. "What time is it? Why can't we wait for them to fix it?"

Mother stammered. "It's … it's almost midnight. We … better do what he says." She went to the wardrobe. "Don't bother getting dressed. Just grab the coats!"

I slid to the end of the berth to climb down. "But—"

"Do as I say, Ruth."

Richard cried, so I took his coat and hat from Mother and lifted him to her bed. "It's all right, Richard. Time to get up."

Marion moaned again and draped her blanket over her head.

"Guess what, Marion?" I said. "We're going to the Boat Deck."

"Shoes, too," Mother said. "At least we all still have our stockings on." She tossed Richard's shoes to me and sat on Marion's berth. "Come, Marion. Here's your coat and shoes."

With Marion and Richard ready, Mother and I donned our own coats and shoes. My old nightgown hung way below my coat. If only I could hide it.

Mother grabbed our key and carried Richard out the door. "Hurry, please!"

I ushered Marion into the passageway, which was filled with people scurrying toward the stairs. Our door clicked shut. "We forgot the life belts," I said.

"Never mind now," Mother said. "Let's hurry."

Marion squinted under the passageway light and reached for my hand. "Sissy, what are we doin'?"

I was fully awake now, excited more than anything. "Remember where we walked Sun Yat Sen? Wait 'til you see all the stars tonight."

Richard quieted as he looked wide-eyed at the crowd. Most of the passengers had their coats, but some only wore their dressing gowns and stockings. They'd tossed their life belts on without bothering to tie them and carried their drowsy babies and small children.

An older man grumbled to his wife. "What's all this fuss about anyway?"

The small boy from three doors down rubbed his eyes. "Daddy, I'm tired."

Where were the Hoffmans? Maybe they had already started for the upper decks.

A girl around Natalie's age pinned up her hair as she walked beside her sister. I'd met them in the WC line a few days earlier. "I heard something, but I thought I was dreaming."

"We'll see what they want us to do," her sister replied. "Perhaps we can return to our beds soon."

Mother kept her head down, her mouth in a tight line. I took all of it in, like a distant observer, curious to find out what would happen next.

"Is the elevator working?" a young mother asked.

Someone informed us they'd been turned off. People filled the middle stairwell, and more joined us on each level as we trudged up to the Boat Deck. Some chatted or joked, and others asked questions no one could answer. One woman turned around and headed back down.

Biting cold air blew through the open door, leading from the stairwell out to the Boat Deck at the top of the ship. I shuddered and tightened my hand around Marion's.

First-class passengers mingled in groups, annoyance and fatigue plaguing their eyes. Many of the ladies wore their beautiful hats and long, fur-trimmed coats over nightgowns or dressing gowns. Some men were fully dressed, as if ready for an all-day outing, while others had tossed their coats over their nightclothes. Nearly everyone wore their life belts.

I hunched my shoulders forward in an attempt to keep warm. I should've added more layers beneath my coat. Mother led us to a wall that had an overhang to shelter us from the cold, while passengers continued to pour onto the deck from the stairwells.

Two of the ship's officers strode through the crowd. One was Mr. Murdoch, the man who had talked with Mr. Harper the day I first met him and Sun Yat Sen.

Mother clutched my arm. "There's Mr. Astor. Maybe he knows something."

A fuzzy gray-and-white dog pulled at the leash in his hand. Mr. Astor approached Mr. Murdoch. "Why bring us up here in our life belts? My wife and I are freezing."

Mr. Murdoch backed away. "We're seeing to the problem, sir." With that, he and the other officer hustled up the stairs that led to the wheelhouse above the Boat Deck.

The familiar opening bars of "Everybody Two Step" wafted from the center of the deck. Soon, the puzzled and angry faces around me relaxed. Mr. Hartley and his orchestra had arrived to ease everyone's minds. Their music lifted the mood, even though we still didn't have any solid information.

Where were Ann and her family? As far as I could tell, not many third-class passengers were on the stairways yet. It was not an easy task for anyone to navigate the passageways to the correct stairs. The people in third class had never seen the Boat Deck, and so many of them didn't even speak English. Would the crew help them if we were in danger?

Marion pressed against me and wrapped her hands in the folds of my coat. "I'm cold and sleepy, Sissy."

Two men paused in front of us, and I strained to hear their words. "An iceberg off the bow," one said. "They're trying to contact any ships in the vicinity over the wireless."

"That explains it then," the other man said.

Mother covered her mouth, fear shading her eyes.

Did he mean an iceberg was nearby, and we stopped so we wouldn't run into it? The men walked on toward the glassed-in sitting room. Maybe they'd allow second-class passengers to wait in there. "Mother, what if we—"

Another officer approached from the bow and snaked through the clusters of passengers. "Ladies and gentlemen, may I have your kind attention? As a precaution, Captain Smith has ordered that we begin loading the lifeboats. Again, this is only a precaution. Women and children first!"

Mother grabbed my arm and shook her head in panic. "No!"

A woman fiddled with her hat. "The lifeboats?"

A man with her said, "Whatever for?"

"I simply refuse to get in one of those boats!" An elderly lady limped away with her cane.

A woman who held a crying baby turned to her husband. "Dear, please find out what is going on."

A mother scolded a young woman who appeared to be her children's nanny. "Cassie, you must stop complaining! We are all cold, for heaven's sake."

"It's only a precaution," a man said to his tearful wife. "You heard the man."

The orchestra played another lively tune. Near the bow, three crewmen and an officer uncovered a lifeboat. Passengers backed away, shaking their heads. Two more sailors raced to the next boat. Never had I imagined they'd be needed.

"Ruth, please." Mother was nearly crying as she handed me the long brass key to F-4. "Go back to the cabin and bring some blankets. I hope we won't have to get into the boats, but we will need to stay warm while we wait."

The stairwell was jammed with passengers and crewmen as they rushed up and down. My foot missed the first step, and I reached for the railing to steady myself. The ship was tilted at an odd angle, tipping toward the bow but listing to port.

If we were sending wireless messages, other ships would certainly come to help. If only I could find Ann. It would be fun to wait together and see how the night turned out.

If the *Titanic* was truly unsinkable, Captain Smith was only being extra-cautious by ordering passengers into lifeboats until the damage could be fixed. None of the crew was wearing life belts. Maybe they knew they weren't really necessary.

I worked my way down to Deck C, where a crowd surrounded the purser's office. Mr. McElroy held his hands up on his side of the window.

"I'm terribly sorry, but we cannot allow any more withdrawals tonight. Your valuables will be safe here until the emergency has passed." He shut the window. People shouted and banged on it, demanding their money and jewelry. Mother's small amount of money was still there as well, but I was not going to remind her.

I waited on Deck C's half-landing for a break in the traffic flowing upstairs toward me. "Miss, you should be going up, not down," a passing steward said. "It isn't safe. And where is your life belt?"

"It's so cold on the Boat Deck." I tried to step past him. "I'm going back for some blankets."

"Miss, it's—"

A man grabbed him by the arm. "Will you help me? I can't find my son."

The steward turned to help him, so I continued down and around the stairwells. One more set of stairs and I would reach Deck E.

A group of young men tore up the stairs in my direction. "It's flooding forward," one said. "Don't even try it."

I caught a glimpse below of the door on Deck E that led to Scotland Road. Water trickled in from underneath.

Where was it coming from? Did we actually hit that iceberg? And what about Tim O'Hara and all the crew that lived and worked together? I prayed they'd already escaped up the back stairs that Ann and I had taken to the grand dining saloon. I wanted to look for her, but I first needed to find another way down to our cabin on Deck F.

I backtracked up to Deck D. The entire level was steeped in commotion, passengers and crew scurrying about, shouting, and asking questions. Still, even amid the chaos, some people joked, and others sat in the alcoves, playing cards or reading books. Maybe they knew something the others didn't.

I ran slightly uphill toward the stern, to the far aft stairway that led down to Deck F. As I descended the stairs and passed the locked gate at Deck E, I breathed easier when I saw no one on the other side. I reached Deck F easily, and except for the slant toward the bow, it looked the same as it did on any other night.

Two passengers raced by without even a glance toward me. Behind them came the two fiddlers from the third-class general room. They dashed past me, followed by two other men. One waved his arms and spoke in Spanish. Maybe their cabins were on Deck F as well, but that seemed to be a good sign for third class. *They're getting through.*

At F-4, I let myself in with our key. I yanked the plaid wool steamer blanket off Mother's bed and checked the clock on the nightstand— almost one o'clock in the morning. I'd never been allowed to stay up that late.

I grabbed another blanket from Marion's bed so that she and Richard could share it. From my berth, I pulled Sajni's cozy quilt for myself. Should I bring the life belts? How would I carry them with the blankets?

My violin case rested against the bedpost. *Maybe I should take it, just to keep it safe.* But what if this was all unnecessary and we would come back later?

I could barely manage the blankets, but I grabbed the case anyway. My birds had tipped over on the desk where Marion left them. My favorite little hummingbird lay on the carpet. I reached down to stuff it inside my left coat pocket.

What else? Should I add something to wear under my coat?

A low groan came from deep inside the ship. Through the porthole above my berth, I had no trouble seeing the water line near the top of the glass.

That was enough for me to know I had to leave. I turned out the light and shut the door.

CHAPTER TWENTY-SEVEN

RMS Titanic, Atlantic Ocean
Monday, April 15, 1912
1:05 a.m.

A family of five ran by in the passageway. Mr. Hardy appeared from around the corner as I reached the aft stairs. "Miss Ruth, I thought you went to the boats!"

"We did, Mr. Hardy. But I came back for blankets."

"Where's your life belt?"

"I couldn't—"

A woman rushed past us with her baby as the ship emitted another groan.

"Never mind," he said, and pushed me toward the stairs. "Promise me you and your family will get to a boat. God be with you!"

On my way back up, a crowd had gathered behind the locked gate at Deck E. Three men pushed against it. Where had they been when I'd passed the gate minutes ago? Were they only just now getting word of the emergency?

One man spoke in a heavy foreign accent. "Miss, you help?"

I rattled the gate. Locked, as always. Maybe there was a latch.

I dropped my blankets and violin. I couldn't find a latch, so I pulled and pushed, but the gate wouldn't budge.

I gestured forward. "Go back! Find the other stairs and get up to the Boat Deck. To the lifeboats."

The men argued, clearly not understanding. Then a flash of blonde hair rounded the corner behind them.

"Ann!" I jerked the gate back and forth.

She gripped Thomas' hand. "Ruth! What is happening?"

"They're loading the lifeboats. You need to get to the Boat Deck. Now!"

Ann glanced behind her. "We're trying, but nobody knows where to go. They're running everywhere or blocking the way." She lifted Thomas. "Water's seeping in … My mother insists on finding Tim. I can't leave her. I better go back to where I left her and the others."

"Hurry! Tell her Tim might've gone up already. Scotland Road is flooding."

With widened eyes, she turned and ran back down the passageway carrying Thomas in her arms.

"Follow her!" I told the crowd at the gate.

If anyone could get through the maze of the lower levels and up to the Boat Deck, Ann O'Hara could. But I knew she'd never leave her family. She'd need to convince her mother to bring everyone, even without Tim, if necessary.

The men at the gate turned away, shouting, shaking their fists. A few of them followed Ann, but the rest took off in other directions.

If only there was some way I could help—but how? I retrieved my belongings from the floor and continued back up to the Boat Deck.

The *Titanic* growled louder and longer, like a wounded lion lashing out in fury. I ran through the Deck D passageway near the grand dining saloon. The faces of those I passed now bore harsh expressions of urgency. There was no more time to waste.

The stairwells were packed, and some tried to elbow their way through. What if I reached Mother and there were no more boats? No, I refused to think such a thing. We *would* get on a boat, and the O'Haras would be up any minute. Other ships would come, and we would all be rescued.

But a growing fear darkened my thoughts. I clung to the blankets and inched my way up the stairs behind the slow-moving crowd until finally I reached the Boat Deck, swarming with people. The huge white plank floor tilted at a greater angle toward the bow.

A man who carried a suitcase bumped into me and stumbled away. With my teeth chattering, I hurried to the spot on the starboard side where I'd left my family. My breath caught in shocked surprise.

They were gone. Gone, too, were the four lifeboats closest to the bow. Only a smaller collapsible boat remained.

Where were they?

A shrill whistle came from somewhere near the wheelhouse. Then a white streak of light sped toward the sky, followed by a bright explosion over my head and a loud *pop*. All across the Boat Deck, people's anguished faces reflected the bright light.

"They're firing distress rockets," a man said. "We must be in some sort of trouble after all."

I had to find my family. I peeked into the sitting room, but they weren't there. Then I found the gymnasium, after wanting to see it all week. A man looked up in surprise from the rowing machine, as if I'd interrupted his exercise regimen. Another man rode a mechanical chair and chatted with the attendant.

What was wrong with them? Didn't they know we were in danger?

I turned in circles on the deck, searching for some sign of Mother or my siblings. Not far away on the open deck, the full eight-piece orchestra continued to play, led by steady Mr. Hartley. I recognized the tune as "Alexander's Ragtime Band," but no one seemed to be listening.

Why didn't they stop playing and get to the boats?

I rushed past them toward the stern, dodging passengers and crew members. A good deal of shouting came from the port side as I neared the huge domed window that comprised the ceiling over the Grand Staircase. The sound of three quick gunshots made me jump. Women screamed. What was happening?

Mother wouldn't have gone over to the port side without me, not unless she was ordered. I stayed on the starboard side and ran to the next set of lifeboats closest to the stern. Crewmen assisted in loading the first boat on my left. Dozens of men stood back, watching as women and children were helped into the boat.

I pushed my way through and scanned the frightened faces of

those in the lifeboat. In the center seat, Mrs. Simmons huddled with a tearful Priscilla and Peter. At the railing, Mr. Simmons waved and blew them kisses. Why wouldn't they let him go too?

He and the crewmen helped two more ladies climb into the boat, and they began to unwind the ropes that held it in place. I couldn't stay. I had to find Mother.

I ran to the crowd that was gathered near the second boat as it was being lowered. Mr. Murdoch and another crewman released the ropes from the davits.

There, in the packed lifeboat, four feet away from the *Titanic*, Mother crouched near the edge, her face twisted in terror. Another woman held Marion and Richard on her lap.

I shoved myself against the railing. "Mother!"

She saw me and screamed. "Ruth! Get in another boat!"

A crewman in their lifeboat made eye contact with me. I raised a blanket over my head and managed to throw it to him. He caught it midair and passed it to Mother.

The lifeboat jerked and dropped about a foot. Everyone in the boat groaned, almost in echo to the guttural groaning that still came from deep inside the ship.

I pushed away from the railing. Where was I supposed to go? Why couldn't I find a boat that wasn't already full? Why weren't there more boats?

Maybe I should try the port side. But we're tilting ... so many people ... I can't do this! My mind whirled at panic pace.

Someone pulled me by the arm. I looked up to see Mr. Murdoch. He pushed me toward the next lifeboat ten feet away. "Quick, get in that one."

Women, children, and several men already filled the boat, which was marked with the number *13* on its side. How could I possibly get in? Mr. Murdoch was wrong—I didn't see any room at all.

An officer who was directing crewmen at the davits reached for me. With one smooth motion, he wrapped his arms around my waist and hoisted me toward the boat.

I could only hold on for dear life to my quilt and blanket. Someone in the lifeboat grabbed my leg, but I had no place to put my feet. I lost balance and fell across someone's lap.

The officer shouted from aboard the *Titanic*. "Two more, then let 'er down!"

CHAPTER TWENTY-EIGHT

*Lifeboat 13, Atlantic Ocean
Monday, April 15, 1912
1:35 a.m.*

A girl wrapped in a heavy shawl and with a baby in her arms took my hand. She couldn't have been much older than I was. Without a word, she helped me squeeze onto the bench next to her. A woman was helped aboard, followed closely by a man who held a baby.

Our loaded boat dangled in space far above the ocean, like a seat on a Ferris wheel, swinging in the air. I gripped my bench with one hand, the blanket and quilt with the other. I held perfectly still, hoping that would somehow keep the ropes from breaking, and I avoided looking down at the ice-cold Atlantic that was waiting to swallow me up.

With several jerks on the ropes, our boat creaked toward the ocean's surface. Then the men who lowered the boat let out too much rope on the stern end behind me. We tipped backward. I clung tighter to the seat, choked with fear.

Several women let out shrill screams. "What's the matter with you?" a man yelled up to the crewmen. "You wanna tip us all out?"

The boat leveled. Then they let the bow end down too soon. My legs and arms shook with terror as people near me screamed and shouted.

The ropes caught, and we stopped.

"Sorry, sorry," someone from above yelled. "We have it now!"

The crewmen and the officer who were still on the ship adjusted the pulleys and ropes. We jerked up and down until our boat was finally horizontal with the *Titanic*. Then we were lowered to Deck A, where two more passengers climbed on. Those who were already in the boat shouted in protest. I was sure the boat would break in half.

A crewman jumped in, and the girl beside me cried out as the lifeboat creaked with the added weight. Someone on deck called to him. "You're in charge of this one, Fred."

Fred made his way to a seat at the tiller. "Down we go."

I barely breathed. The enormous and beautiful *Titanic*, still fully lit, slipped by to my right. Portholes revealed empty cabins. Thinking of my family and Ann, I lost track of which decks we passed.

As we continued our descent, we passed cabins that had their lights still on but were nearly filled with water. In one cabin, a chair, a stuffed animal, and forgotten papers floated by. Was it Deck F where I'd slept with my family? That meant Ann's Deck G was flooded.

Without warning, a huge gush of ice-cold water burst from a large pipe on the hull of the *Titanic* and shot straight at us. I ducked, but the water sprayed my head and across my back. In front of me, two women screamed.

"It's the condenser," Fred shouted. "Use the oars to push away from it!"

Hugging my quilt and blanket, I tried to lower my body as much as possible while passengers pushed, yelled, and screamed. Finally, someone managed to get ahold of the oars and shove us away from the oncoming water. Moments later, the bottom of the lifeboat smacked the ocean's surface.

With my wet head and back, the cold sunk its teeth in. I pushed soaked hair away from my face. The torrent from the pipe had shoved our boat toward the *Titanic*'s stern. Passengers moaned and wept, calling for help. I trembled from my lips to my toes.

Now, a huge shadow descended over our boat, and Fred jerked his head up. "Hey, watch out! Stop!"

Another lifeboat creaked straight for our heads from above. I screamed along with the others, "Stop! Stop!" A deep voice shouted, "Dear God, no!"

How would they hear us way up on the Boat Deck? The lifeboat came close enough for me to reach my hand up and touch the bottom. I pushed on it with every ounce of my strength.

We were about to be crushed.

Angry, frightened voices called out for help, and it was impossible to tell if they came from the lifeboats or from high on the ship. Then a man yelled, "It stopped! But we have to get away!"

Our boat, now on the water, was still connected to the davits up on the Boat Deck. A young man in the bow of our boat tried to help Fred loosen the ropes. "They're jammed! We need a knife."

"Hang on!" Another crewman inched forward and pulled a knife from his back pocket. He and Fred together sawed frantically at the ropes until they released. The men used oars to push us out from under the other lifeboat and away from the ship.

"Is everyone all right?" Fred asked.

A few people muttered replies, but most, like me, were silent and shaking. It took me a minute to catch my breath. Maybe I could bear the cold, if only there weren't any more deathly scares.

Another rocket lit up the sky and burst overhead. In the few seconds of extra light, I looked around for other lifeboats near us, but they were too far away for me to see any faces. Where was my family?

Besides the crewmen and rowers, about eight or ten other men sat in my lifeboat. The rest were women of various ages and several children. None were Ann or her family members.

"We better row fast, gents," Fred said. "When she goes under, if we're too close, she'll pull us right down with her."

When she goes under?

A blond-haired man took one oar. The other oar was already in the hands of a man who wore a life belt. They rowed us away from the ship with steady strokes through the eerily calm sea.

All lifeboats from the starboard side of the *Titanic* now floated in the water, and Mother, Marion, and Richard were in one of them. But where? It wasn't possible to see the port side or to even tell if those boats had all launched, but the top decks of the ship were still loaded with passengers and crew.

My shoulders trembled. There must have been more boats. *Ann, where are you?*

The *Titanic* was still fully illuminated. If not for the obvious dip at the bow and lifeboats that spread in every direction, she looked like she'd merely stopped to celebrate the starlit evening.

Where was the iceberg that had caused all of this? The ship must have skimmed past it before the engines were stopped. Now, nothing but the *Titanic* floated in the dark ocean—as still as a pond, Papa would have said. And our lifeboats were the sitting ducks.

Mr. Hartley and his orchestra continued to play from somewhere on the top of the ship, while the girl beside me rocked her fussy baby. A tear rolled down her cheek as she tried to soothe him with a song in a foreign language.

The music filled the night, adding to the beauty of the starry heavens and the brilliant ocean liner. How was it possible that, while those men played their instruments, so many others were fighting for their lives?

Would the music help to calm the passengers who swarmed the decks and stood at the railings? Part of me wished to be there with Mr. Hartley—playing my violin, serenading the passengers once again with the gentle notes of "Spring Song."

I let out a gasp. *My violin.* I glanced around by my feet, but the sinking feeling in my chest already told me it was useless.

I had set the instrument down when I'd tried to open the gate where I saw Ann, and when I turned to leave, I only gathered the blankets and quilt.

I'd left my violin on the *Titanic*—the one thing that might have given me a future with an orchestra. My most treasured possession was probably floating down the Deck E passageway.

Tears burned my eyes as I hugged my knocking knees. How could I have left it? But more important than the violin was my family. All that mattered now was their safety. *I need you, Mother. When will I see you?*

Fred spoke loud enough for us all to hear. "Let's see how many we have here. I'll start, and we'll count off 'til everybody says a number.

Ladies, please count for your children. One ..."

We counted out loud, and those who sat near the non-English speaking passengers counted for them. I counted myself along with the girl next to me and her baby.

The last person in the stern said, "Sixty-four."

"Is that everyone?" Fred asked. "All right, sixty-four."

He poked through a storage area near the bow, searching for a lantern or any supplies, but he found nothing. "There's supposed to be biscuits and such in here." He dropped the storage cover back into place and told the men to stop rowing. "I think we're safely away now, fellows."

The man who held the oar on the port side wore a long dressing gown and overcoat. He reached a hand out to the other rower. "I'm Lawrence Beesley," he said. Then he shook hands with one of the crewmen in short pants. "Were you working below in the boiler room?"

"Yeah, I'm a stoker. Name's George." His teeth chattered as he cocked his head toward another man closer to Fred. "So is James here."

George rubbed his arms. One finger was covered in blood, and the blood smeared over his short sleeve. "We had to get out when they shut the watertight doors, and I cut me finger somehow. But the other blokes ..." He lowered his head.

How could these two men stand the cold in their short-sleeve shirts and short pants? I was mostly covered in my blankets, and the people pressing in on every side should've kept me warm, but my whole body still shook with chills.

The blond man with the starboard oar introduced himself as Dr. Washington Dodge. "My wife and son are on another lifeboat. Officer Lightoller was in charge on the port side, and he wasn't letting any men on the boats. The women made a fuss—some wouldn't go without their husbands. I made my wife go. Most of the men stood back and refused to get on, like that Astor fellow."

A man in a steward's uniform spoke up. "That's all right, sir. I'm glad I made you come with me. You'll meet up with your family later."

Another woman who held a baby lifted her head. "That's fine for you, but I'm certain my husband is still on the ship. He said good-bye to us." She buried her face in her baby's blanket.

Everyone was silent.

The girl who sat beside me wore a plain gold wedding band. Did her husband stay on the ship, too, so that she and their child could be saved?

The faint notes of another song floated across the still water. No longer did the orchestra play ragtime dance tunes or relaxing waltzes. Now came the slow, somber "Nearer My God to Thee"—a song of impending death.

My heart broke for those who were still on board the ship and for the *Titanic* herself, the splendid and mighty Queen of the Ocean. Even as I shuddered in the grip of cold, the song touched my soul.

Oh, Mr. Hartley. I hear you.

CHAPTER TWENTY-NINE

Lifeboat 13, Atlantic Ocean
Monday, April 15, 1912
2:10 a.m.

While we waited, countless stars watched us from the black, moonless sky above. The fuzzy cloud of the Milky Way stretched over our heads, and the Big Dipper appeared ready to plunge into the icy water.

Only a few hours ago, I'd walked the deck of the *Titanic* and admired the magnificent starlight. Hopefully Marion saw the Dipper from her lifeboat. Did she remember how to find the North Star? *Papa, do you see it from Guntur? Are you thinking of me?*

A great deal of activity still proceeded on the ship, even as the bow was now entirely underwater. Some men attempted to free a lifeboat from above the wheelhouse. It flipped and fell into the water upside down. The men, falling or jumping, swam toward it.

The gentle notes of another waltz, "Songe d'Automne," crossed the water from atop the *Titanic*. Once more, a rocket exploded into the sky, briefly illuminating the night.

"Where are the other ships?" a woman asked, but no one responded. Surely we all had the same question on our minds.

Every light on the *Titanic* still glowed, even those from rooms below the surface. Hundreds of people ran or crawled up the Boat Deck toward the stern. Some clung to objects attached to the bulkheads, others held onto loose deck chairs and barrels.

The music ended, and we waited.

No one spoke. The oars were still. The babies slept.

Long, loud noises burst from the *Titanic* as her bow dipped lower. Everything that wasn't tied down began to tumble.

I pictured all of the beautiful dishes and vases of fresh flowers in the dining saloons crashing to the floor, library books falling through glass shelves, wicker chairs in the Veranda Café breaking through the windows to the Promenade, and the grand pianos and paintings smashing into pieces. Passengers' steamer trunks, the lovely sofas, the intricately carved tables in the lounges, the magnificent clock on the Grand Staircase ...

I gripped the damp seat of the lifeboat. Thinking of all the objects on the ship, even my beloved violin, was easier than imagining what the living, breathing souls still aboard were enduring.

The stern rose a bit higher. All of the lights dimmed and then blinked on again. Some women behind me gasped in terror as people fell or jumped from the ship into the dark Atlantic. I froze, afraid to look but at the same time unable to look away.

A deafening, crunching sound, like a medieval giant stomping through a thick forest, erupted from the front funnel closest to the *Titanic*'s bow. It broke away like a matchstick and crashed into the ocean with a mighty splash. George gave a low whistle.

Then all of the lights went out, and the entire front half of the ship dipped underwater. The stern rose high in the air, exposing three huge propellers. Waves of ocean water fell from them. Higher and higher the stern ascended, like a great sea monster rising from the depths.

The ship let out a long, thunderous growl as her stern slowly pointed to the stars. Screams and cries spread across the water, but whether they came from other lifeboats or from the *Titanic*, I couldn't tell.

"God be with them," Dr. Dodge said.

She seemed to stand on end for perhaps a minute or two, like a skyscraper set in the middle of the ocean. All along her railings, people clung desperately. Many fell into the water ... or perhaps they let go.

The great ship began to drop, slowly at first. Then it partially broke apart between the funnels with an ear-splitting crash. Finally, the "unsinkable" *Titanic*, that glorious floating city, dove … down, down, down, like an immense Hades-bound train.

I couldn't move, knowing I had only a moment to see her go.

Then she slipped away.

The slightest wave moved across the water from where she'd vanished. It reached our boat, gave it a gentle lift, and set it down again. Many passengers in my boat wept openly, but I was too stunned for tears.

With the *Titanic* gone, the night was now much darker, but I couldn't take my eyes off the spot where the ship sank. I could barely control my trembling limbs—whether from shock or cold, I didn't know. I'd walked miles, danced, slept, dined, and played my violin on board the ship for the last five days. And now, *Titanic* would rest on the ocean floor forevermore.

"Anyone have a watch?" Fred quietly asked. Darkness obscured his face, but I knew his voice by now.

Dr. Dodge fumbled beneath his coat. I caught a slight flash of gold. "Nearly two-thirty," he said. "I'd say she went down about two-twenty."

More sounds emerged from the darkness—hundreds of voices, wailing and pleading for help. The desperation grew louder, until they drowned out all other sounds and thoughts. I'd never heard anything so horrible in my life.

"We should try and help them," someone said. "Maybe we can save someone."

"Let's go back," another agreed.

"No, we aren't going back," Fred said. "We're full as it is, and we're too far away. The boats with lanterns can go."

"They'll freeze to death in this water!" Dr. Dodge said.

Fred raised his voice. "I said we're not going back."

The shapes of some lifeboats appeared to be closer to the voices. Maybe *they* would go. People were dying. They had to go back to help.

We sat in silence, unable to ignore the moaning voices. I breathed deeply and exhaled a big puff of freezing air.

How had I come to this tragic night? The journey that began in the Guntur train station had been one of thousands of miles, and faces, and so many memories. I'd hated taking it, hated being forced to leave behind all I had loved. But I'd met people at every turn, people who had reached out to my family and me with kind words and helping hands. And when all I wanted was to endure the trip, the joy of making friends had snuck up on me. Each one had offered something of themselves in their own way and had let me into their world.

My star-studded quilt lay bunched at my feet. I bent to touch the square with Sajni and me, two happy girls from another day and place. *Sajni—always the encourager, even out here.*

The blanket from my sister's berth still rested in my lap. I rubbed at the damp spots.

Leaving my home in Guntur had been awful, but I still had my family. I took some comfort in knowing Mother and my siblings were on a lifeboat ... but where? How long had it been since I got the blankets and checked the clock beside Mother's bed?

I peered at the few boats I could see. Were Mother, Marion, and Richard all right? Did the blanket I threw to them do any good?

What do I do now, trapped on a crowded lifeboat, after witnessing the greatest ocean liner ever built disappear from sight?

I'd lost my violin, but it could be replaced. Some of my fellow lifeboat passengers had lost loved ones only minutes ago, barely escaping with their own lives. Papa's words came back to me—to be brave and think of others. Sometimes he would quote a Bible verse that he'd repeated at the train station: *Be strong and courageous ...*

But I was neither, and I had no idea how I could be now.

A few women behind me whispered soulful prayers. From my heart, I prayed that I would be able to do as Papa had said.

In my right coat pocket, my fingers brushed the key to Cabin F-4. Papa's handkerchief was still there. I never dreamed I could part with it, but someone needed it more than I did now.

"Excuse me." I waved the handkerchief at George. "Here, take it for your finger."

A woman in front of me passed it to him. He reached for it with his shaking, bloody hand, but his arms and legs were white with cold.

I rose to my feet, and the lifeboat rocked side to side. "Take this blanket, too." I lifted the blanket and stretched my arms toward George. Mr. Beesley grabbed it and helped George wrap the handkerchief around his injured finger and the blanket around his body.

The other stoker, James, raised his head and mumbled something through trembling lips, and a little boy near me cried. "Mama, it's so cold."

What am I waiting for? I have something they need right here at my feet.

Sajni had spent countless hours stitching love into her quilt with every image and star. But she didn't keep it for herself. She had walked all the way to the train station and brought it to me, willingly presenting it to me as a parting gift.

Oh, the memories these images hold. I'd planned to treasure it always—but now, others were in dire need of the warmth the quilt could offer.

I stood again and asked James for the knife. After he passed it, I slit the quilt's center seam, dropped the knife, and with one hard yank, I tore Sajni's silken quilt down the middle.

The boy's mother helped me pull the two halves apart. I gave one half to her and her son, and I passed the other piece forward. "That's for you, James," I said.

Sajni would have done the same.

CHAPTER THIRTY

Lifeboat 13, Atlantic Ocean
Monday, April 15, 1912
4:00 a.m.

The girl next to me rested her head on my shoulder. Her baby slept, wrapped snug inside of her shawl.

I rubbed the girl's back. "What's your name?" When she shrugged, I pointed to my chest. "I'm Ruth."

I felt her shake under my arm. "Rachel."

"What are we supposed to do now?" someone said. "Wait here in the dark until we all freeze to death?"

No one had any answers, but Dr. Dodge said, "They had to have notified all the ships in the area on the wireless, and the ships would see the rockets. They must be on the way."

James sneered. "Eh, what makes you so sure?"

"Calm down there," Fred said. "It won't do us any good to argue."

The woman behind me was on the verge of tears. "Oh, those voices—if only they'd stop!"

"They're already quieter," her companion said. "Listen. They'll stop soon enough."

The multiple anguished cries had turned to faint moaning. "They're dying," Mr. Beesley said.

Please don't let any of those voices be Ann's.

Ann, with all her joy and faith. The sweet, eager faces of the little ones. Kind Mrs. O'Hara and good-natured Tim. Did they make it to the boats? I rocked with my arms crossed now in an effort to console myself. *Could I have done something different to help them?*

If Mother hadn't sent me back for blankets, I wouldn't have seen Ann at all. I should've gone for help and made someone open the gate. But the chaos …

"We need to stay warm," Dr. Dodge said. "Don't sit still. Keep moving however you can. Move your feet and hands, and stretch your legs if possible."

The boat jiggled and rocked as some of us tried to do as he said. A few stood and lifted their feet one at a time. I moved my toes and fingers and made circles with my feet. I made Rachel move hers too.

Were people in Mother's lifeboat kind to her, and to Marion and Richard? Would someone make them move their fingers and toes? I'd be with them, if only I hadn't gone back for blankets.

My thoughts wandered through the last five days, and my eyelids grew heavy. More passengers and crew members came to mind—the snobby girl who stood at the railing when we left Southampton. Mr. McElroy. Ann's dance partner, Jerry Hawkins. The gawky lift boy who broke the rules for me. Mr. Harper, and all the smiling faces in the lounge as I played "Spring Song" …

My head jolted, and I awoke.

"We should pray," the woman said who sat behind me.

A man led us in the Lord's Prayer. I bowed my head and whispered the prayer as others joined in. *Please let my family be all right.*

I focused on the myriad of stars and the off-and-on glow of the Northern Lights. My thoughts went in a hundred directions again, revisiting the last six weeks. *If only I had my …*

Oh, no. I'd left my journal in the cabin. All my words, all those Sky Reports, plus feelings and memories I'd poured from my soul onto the pages from the first day on the train, were now on the ocean floor, gone forever. How much more could I lose?

With no wind, faint sounds from other lifeboats reached us—quiet talking, babies crying, someone coughing. Dr. Dodge kept reminding us to move our arms, legs, fingers, and toes. Still, the cold seeped underneath my skin and clung to my bones. I longed for sleep, and everything ached. Maybe it was better than not feeling anything at all.

Beyond the sounds from those in the boats, all was still. No more voices beckoned from the water. No one mentioned it, but we all knew why.

Mothers in our boat talked softly to their children, played little finger games with them, or hummed them to sleep. A few men chatted, and George told Mr. Beesley that his shift had almost been over when he was knocked off his feet by the collision.

"I didn't like the soup they gave us for supper, and I tossed it out. Wish I had it now." He glanced my way. "But thanks to the young lady, I think I'll make it."

If only I could see someone I knew, someone who would take care of me and tell me everything would be all right. I knew Papa would hear the news about the *Titanic*. How could I get word to him that I was alive?

I'd been mad at Papa for weeks, but what he and Mother did—had to do—made sense. Besides, if he had left the mission against orders and come with us, I was sure he would've given up his seat in the lifeboat, just like Mr. Simmons did and so many others. I would have lost him.

A shooting star passed overhead, followed by another.

"Look up." The woman whose son was wrapped in half of Sajni's quilt pointed to the sky.

"I see it, Mama!"

"Make a wish, my love." She smiled through tears and kissed the top of his head.

"There's something over there." Another woman pointed toward the horizon. "I've been watching it for a while. It might be a star, but could it be a ship?"

It took a few seconds for me to locate the spot. The light seemed to match the stars in size, but it was steadier, almost like a planet. And sometimes there were two lights. *It can't be a planet—not tonight, and not this close to the horizon.*

"It could be a ship," Fred said, "but I've seen all sorts of things at sea that don't turn out to be what you think."

"Oh, God, please let it be a ship!" another woman cried out.

Mr. Beesley rested his oar and rubbed his hands together. "It's hard to tell with so many stars, but if indeed it is a ship, the lights should get bigger."

We all watched the lights in silent anticipation. After a moment, they didn't seem to change in size, and I had to keep blinking to keep my eyes open.

"Maybe we should pray aloud again," the woman said behind me. "Even if you don't believe, it'll help to keep your mind off things."

Dr. Dodge turned her way. "What is your name, madam?"

"Lucy Ridsdale," she said. "*Miss* Ridsdale."

"I appreciate your prayers, Miss Ridsdale," Dr. Dodge said. "This situation could certainly make a believer out of a person."

"I think we're all believers tonight, sir," George said.

James' teeth chattered. "You lead us then, Georgie."

George laughed a little and wrapped the blanket tighter around his knees. "All right, but I never done this sort of thing."

He bowed his head. "Lord, if you see us down here in this boat, we're asking you for help. If that's a ship out there, make 'em come and find us. Make 'em hurry too."

<hr/>

"I still see the lights," a woman soon said.

"And most of the stars have disappeared," I pointed out.

Fred cleared his throat. "I could be wrong, my friends, but I think they might belong to a ship headin' this way."

Dr. Dodge lifted his hands and laughed so loud he awoke Rachel's baby. "George, I believe your prayer has been answered."

Not long after, a bright flash followed by a loud *boom* came from the direction of the mysterious lights. We all jumped in our seats.

George popped up from where he'd been stretched out on the bottom of the boat near Fred. "That was a cannon!"

"Thirteen's going to be my lucky number from now on," Mr. Beesley said.

Some of us cheered, while others wept. "Oh, thank you, Lord," Miss Ridsdale said.

It may have just been an hour, or maybe only minutes—but sometime between watching the lights in the distance and hearing the cannon blast, the dark sky began to change. The faintest pinkish-yellow stripe now spanned the horizon to the east. It edged its way across the sky and cast a pale glow over the Atlantic Ocean.

The rough outlines of my fellow survivors became clearer, as did the shapes of a few other lifeboats that were scattered across the water.

James whistled. "Will y' look at that!"

I followed his gaze to another shape off our port bow, a large chunk of something white in the dim light of dawn. "Is that an iceberg?"

"I believe it is," Dr. Dodge answered.

Mr. Beesley shifted in his seat. "There's another." It was taller than the first and jagged across the top. As the sky turned a shade lighter, the simple shapes took on more dimensions.

The boy near me pulled Sajni's quilt away from his chin. "I see one too!" He pointed to an iceberg behind us. More soon appeared. The hint of early morning sun lit their surfaces with the softest glows of pink, yellow, and orange.

If there were mermaids in the ocean, these were their castles. How could anything so beautiful have sent the mighty *Titanic* to its grave?

~~~

The two lights on the horizon remained steady. People in nearby lifeboats yelled and waved, pointing toward the lights. Someone lit a green flare. Was it Mother's boat?

"I would say the ship's getting closer, wouldn't you, Fred?" Dr. Dodge asked.

Fred watched the lights. "I'd say so, sir."

"How long will it take to reach us?" Miss Ridsdale asked.

"Depends on the conditions where she is," Fred said. "With all these 'bergs, she might be takin' it slow."

Rachel's baby whimpered and pushed his fist out from under the shawl. She rocked him and gave him her finger to suck on.

Marion must have been half-starving by now. Even Richard would be hungry. Hopefully their boat would have the emergency food and supplies that ours lacked.

Another flare shot up from a lifeboat. "How will they find us with all these icebergs around?" a man asked. "What if the ship doesn't see the flares?"

One steward reached into the pocket of his jacket. "I have matches … I reckon they're still dry. Let's find something we can burn and wave it in the air when the ship gets closer." He and some of the other men gathered a few items—a newspaper, a straw hat, and a lace shawl.

"The other boats are rowin' toward her," Fred said. "Let's get started. Who can row?"

"I still can." Mr. Beesley moved his oar into position. "Thank God there's something to row toward."

"I'm all for rowin'," George said. "At least for a time." He gathered the blanket I'd given him, wrapped it around his waist, and moved to trade places with Dr. Dodge.

"What about your finger?" The doctor reached for George's hand to examine it. Papa's handkerchief was still tied on, now blood red instead of snowy white.

"It's all right, Doc." George patted him on the shoulder with his good hand. "I'll be fine 'til we get to the ship. Rowin' will do me good."

The two lights grew bigger. Our rowers kept a steady pace with Fred at the tiller. Still, progress was slow. I shifted from excitement one minute to exhaustion the next. My arms ached and my toes were stiff, but I did my best to keep moving them.

Finally, one of the men said, "There's the running lights."

That drew my attention to the bright green row of lights. "I see them!"

"Yes!" Miss Ridsdale clapped her hands. "Thank God."

"She's heading toward us. Northeast, I'd say," Fred said. "Let's light that hat."

The steward held the straw hat while James lit a match and set the hat on fire. He hung it on the end of Mr. Beesley's oar, clutching Sajni's half-quilt around himself with one hand and holding the oar with the other. "Over here, over here!"

Rachel's baby twisted his head away from her finger and cried out. She lifted him to her shoulder and patted his back. Her reddened, dazed eyes said everything that was in her heart.

"See the lights?" I pointed them out in the distance. "Help is coming."

~~~~

"Hand me the newspaper," James said. He got to his feet, lit the paper, and waved it over his head.

"Do you think they can see the flame?" a woman asked.

"Some of the other boats are lighting things," Fred said, "and it helps us to see 'em. Or they might see the smoke."

All night, the ocean waters had remained peaceful, hardly a ripple to disrupt the calm. Now a slight wind stirred the waves. Our lifeboat rocked like a cradle as the cold continued to pierce my skin.

"Oh, I may be getting seasick for the first time in my life," a woman said. She held a hand to her mouth.

"Keep your eyes on the horizon, Charlotte," her friend said. "We're almost to the ship."

"How long will we have to wait?" another woman said through chattering teeth.

Mr. Beesley rested his oar. "Can it see us? It might run us over, trying to find the *Titanic*."

"They'll have binoculars," Dr. Dodge said. "They're looking for us."

As the ship approached, its four masts and center red-and-black funnel were the best sight in the world. People in my boat waved and shouted.

Where had I seen it before?

Then it dawned on me—it was the exact vessel Sajni had stitched into the quilt to fill one of the last squares. She had no way of knowing it would become my rescue ship, or that the quilt would help to keep a stoker and a little boy from freezing.

"She's a beauty, she is," James said. "She's from the Cunard Line. I'd know that funnel anywhere."

Rachel's baby had stopped crying. I reached for him, and she passed him to me. He'd remember nothing from this journey, and likely would never know his father. For me, knowing that Papa was safe in Guntur again gave me solace.

"I think a coupla our boats are almost there," George said. "Let's switch rowers. The sea's gettin' rougher, and we'll have to pull hard against this wind."

Two of the stewards moved into position to row us toward the ship. They pulled at the oars with slow, uneven strokes.

Fred guided the boat with the tiller. "We're makin' progress, and I think she's stopped."

Other passengers continued to yell and wave. *Can the ship see Lifeboat 13?*

The boat that had been shooting green flares reached the ship first and pulled alongside. Another lifeboat bobbed up and down close behind. Everyone turned to watch the ship, anxious to see how those in the first lifeboat would be transferred.

As we came closer, I read the name on the ship's hull: RMS *Carpathia*. She was about half the length of the *Titanic*, but bigger than the *City of Benares*.

"Praise God for the *Carpathia*," Miss Ridsdale said.

What port had she been heading to before she changed course? Did she have passengers like us—young and old, rich and poor? Would she have room for all the *Titanic* survivors?

The lifeboats aboard the *Carpathia* hung as though ready for lowering. Two more *Titanic* lifeboats drew closer, low in the water with their heavy loads. I strained to see if Mother was aboard. Several more were still quite a distance away, too small to distinguish anyone in them.

In the pale light, crewmen appeared and disappeared on the top deck, high above the *Titanic* lifeboat closest to the ship. Our boat swung up and down with the waves, and the stewards handed the oars over to George and Mr. Beesley again.

The wind bit my cheeks. Rachel's baby had fallen asleep in my arms, so I tenderly handed him back to her. She looked with fear at the ship as she kissed her baby's forehead. I couldn't imagine how the rescue workers would get him and the other babies onto the *Carpathia*. And what about Richard and Marion?

The ship's crewmen dropped a ropy contraption down the side, and someone in the closest lifeboat below caught hold of it.

"How is anyone supposed to use that?" Charlotte asked. She bent over the side of our boat and vomited.

Her friend held her by the shoulders. "Oh, must you, Charlotte? Of all times!" Another woman beside her turned pale and covered her mouth. Nausea must be contagious. An urge to gag rose up within me, bringing with it memories from when I had food poisoning in Valletta.

Fred scratched his chin. "Looks like they're usin' a rope sling. It works something like a chair."

They began to transfer a passenger from the first lifeboat—a slender young woman wearing a dark coat. After she removed her life belt, she was helped into a sitting position in the rope sling and hoisted up the side of the ship. Three crewmen on top reached for her and pulled her aboard. Rope ladders were dropped for transferring the men.

The operation of rescuing the *Titanic* survivors had begun. *Will one be Ann O'Hara? And my family … where are they?*

CHAPTER THIRTY-ONE

Lifeboat 13, Atlantic Ocean
April 15, 1912
4:45 a.m.

George and Mr. Beesley rowed through the choppy waves and brought us close to the ship's side. Ours was the third lifeboat to reach the *Carpathia*. My stiff toes and fingers were numb, but at least I could still move them.

I'd watched every person from the other two boats ascend on the rope devices. My heart sank, because Mother was not among them, nor was Marion or Richard ... nor Ann. Would the ropes hold? It was a long way to the top deck of the ship. But besides swimming, it would be the only way I could get off the lifeboat.

Concerned faces of *Carpathia* crewmen and passengers lined the top two decks. Some of the survivors who had just been rescued watched our boat from the railing. They had to be looking for loved ones, hoping and praying they'd arrive on another boat.

"They're droppin' the bag for the babies first," Fred said. He helped James grab the canvas bag they'd used to lift babies from the first two boats.

He reached for the young mother who was close to the bow. She and Fred slipped her screaming baby into the bag, keeping his face free, and secured the straps. She clutched her hands to her mouth as the *Carpathia* crew hoisted him up and reached out for him.

Fred turned to Rachel and held his arms out for her son.

She tightened her hold on her baby. "No!"

"Ma'am, you have to," he said. "He'll be all right."

Through most of the night, Rachel had been silent, but now she cried mournful sobs as she clutched her son. A *Carpathia* crewman let the bag down for him. At the same time, the rope sling dropped, and George and Dr. Dodge held it for the first baby's mother.

"Make her hurry," a man said to me. "There's a whole boat full of people here who are cold and tired."

"Can't she hold him in the rope sling?" I asked.

"No," Dr. Dodge said. "The bag is much safer for the child."

It was apparently up to me to communicate with her, even though she didn't understand English. I held her shoulders and used my authoritative voice, the one that usually worked when I had to get Marion to cooperate.

"Rachel, I know you're afraid," I said. "But we must do this the way they say."

She looked at me intently, her lower lip quivering.

I cast a glance toward the men waiting and placed my hands beneath her baby's arms. She gently released him and slumped to the bench.

"That's the way," someone said. "Hurry now."

Her son woke and opened his eyes. I held him in place while Fred pulled the bag around him and strapped him in. Crew members on the ship watched until Fred signaled. They pulled the ropes, and up he went. Rachel held her fists to her chest and mumbled through stifled tears.

The rope sling was lowered again for Rachel, and then the other children and their mothers. Most of them left their life belts in the boat. Meanwhile, a rope ladder was dropped for the men.

Mr. Beesley and Dr. Dodge held it for George. His injured finger kept him from climbing fast, but when he reached the top deck, he let out a loud *whoop*, like he'd struck gold. The rest of us in the lifeboat applauded.

"Your turn now, miss." Fred held the rope sling for me.

A momentary flashback from a few weeks ago caught me. *With a soft thud, Michael hopped off the rope to the floor, mere inches from the edge.*

I exhaled and clambered to my feet. "Okay, can we go now?"

"Not so fast. It's your turn."

"Miss!"

I shook my head. "Okay. I'm ready." *If Michael were here now, he'd be so good at this.*

Once I was strapped in, my hands shook and were too cold to grip the ropes. I felt a strong tug from above as the *Carpathia* crewmen pulled and Fred let go. My feet left Lifeboat 13, and I rode up alongside the red and black hull and portholes of the *Carpathia*.

This is not the way to board a ship. I could only hope this ride would be uneventful, unlike my descent in the lifeboat when I left the *Titanic*.

"Are you all right, miss?" someone asked as I neared the top deck.

I had trouble getting my tongue to work. "I th-think so." *Almost there …*

Two crewmen helped me out of the sling, and my feet stood aboard a ship once again. I exhaled a long breath. I was safe now. Unable to speak, I grabbed for the railing until I could test my tingling feet.

"This way, my dear." A woman dressed in a long cape took my arm and led me through a crowd of people to a small room off the deck. Weary men and women filled several benches. A few still wore their life belts over dressing gowns and coats.

The woman guided me to an open spot on a bench. The cold and dampness had penetrated so deeply, so viscerally, that sliding onto the warm, dry bench was like falling into a friend's arms.

She handed a cup to me. "Here's some coffee. Try a few sips. I'll see what else we have ready."

Simply holding the warm cup in my ice-cold hands was enough. As I waited, I searched for anyone from Lifeboat 13 or an acquaintance from the *Titanic*, but the faces were unfamiliar.

The woman soon returned with a bowl of steaming soup and a spoon. "Here you are, dear."

I managed a "thank you" through frosted lips. I held the bowl, allowing its warmth to thaw my hands, wishing I could dip my toes in it. I lifted it to my face, and with eyes closed, I breathed in the exquisite aroma of chicken in broth.

After I finished eating, I stood in a long line with other *Titanic* passengers, waiting to use a washroom. Warm water and soap made me feel human again. I ran fingers through my tangled, damp hair but avoided looking in the mirror. *I don't care what I look like. I have more important things to think about right now.*

I wandered out to the railing to watch for my family and for Ann. As I did, a crewman approached and touched my arm. "Miss, have you given us your name?" He held a pen and a clipboard that had names inscribed onto yellow sheets of paper.

I shivered and rubbed my arms through my coat. "Ruth Becker."

He added my name to his list. "Class?"

At first, I had to think what he meant. "Second. I'm trying to find my mother, Nellie Becker. Is she on your list?"

He checked through the names. "No other Beckers aboard yet, but boats are still arriving."

No Beckers? Where are they?

"Check later in the dining rooms. Most passengers are being taken there right now." He hurried away to gather more names for his roster.

What is wrong with me? I should've asked if he had anyone named O'Hara on his list.

At the railing, I found a good spot where I could watch the boats and see each person come aboard. A few *Carpathia* passengers handed out blankets, and I took one to wrap around my head and shoulders.

The chicken soup, not to mention all the activity, had revived me enough to begin thinking more clearly. I wouldn't need to check the dining rooms. Mother would come and I'd be right there to meet her.

If Michael had been aboard, he would've swung up and down the ropes all by himself and rescued each and every passenger. The chess pawn he had given me was back in the wardrobe on the *Titanic* ... and his address was in my journal. Now they were both on the ocean floor. Hopefully, he saved my grandparents' address. *When he writes, I'll tell him I survived.*

One by one, the *Carpathia* crew hoisted exhausted and frightened survivors to the ship's upper deck. Many were too dazed or in shock to speak. Some cried tears of joy at being rescued, while others shed tears of sorrow for lost loved ones.

I could tell right away who came from *Titanic's* first-class section by their fur coats or fancy hats, and by the number of people who wanted to talk to them right away. But after all we'd been through, class no longer seemed to matter.

A familiar-looking woman who wore a dressing gown and fur stole arrived in the rope sling. She waited at the railing, shivering until someone brought her a blanket. Then, up the rope ladder came a man who'd been so kind to me—Mr. Henry Sleeper Harper. The couple embraced.

Oh, is it possible? I moved closer to watch. The canvas baby bag that was pulled aboard contained a very wiggly Sun Yat Sen. The Harpers laughed as they helped release their prize dog from the bag. Finally, someone I knew.

"Hello, Mr. Harper," I said.

Sun Yat Sen turned toward me and nearly leaped from Mr. Harper's arms. His owner stumbled back a step. "Oh, Miss Becker! Thank God you're all right." He touched his wife's arm. "Darling, remember when Miss Becker walked Sun?"

Mrs. Harper's bluish lips and straggly hair showed what kind of night she'd had in the lifeboat, but her eyes brightened. "It's so good to see you, my dear."

Maybe she isn't so bad after all. I smiled and rubbed *Titanic's* first surviving dog behind the ears. They turned to watch their servant, Hammad, climb the rope ladder. None of them had been left behind. Would the same be true for my family and for Ann's?

The Harpers were led away, and I held my post as the boats continued to arrive. Each person was carefully brought aboard until the lifeboat was empty, and then the boat was lifted onto a lower deck. I supposed the White Star Line would want them.

If only I had known the number of Mother's lifeboat. She and Marion and Richard had either not arrived yet, or I had somehow missed them. I would find them … anything else was unthinkable.

I forced myself not to cry. As soon as all of the boats were unloaded, I would check the dining rooms and any other places they might be, or find the crewman with the survivor list again. I also kept a close watch for some sign of Ann and her family.

As more survivors came aboard, more *Carpathia* passengers stepped in to help, working alongside the crew. They offered extra clothing or blankets from their cabins, served hot drinks, and consoled the grieving. Many who were lifted aboard were sent right to the makeshift hospitals in the dining rooms or were taken to various areas for hot drinks and meals.

Women lined the railings on either side of me, watching and crying for husbands, sons, or brothers. Some, like me, held out hope that maybe the next boat would bring their loved one. Others turned away, overcome with despair.

A familiar voice spoke. "Don't give up, Charlotte." I scanned the line of women who stood at the railing. Charlotte, the lady from my boat who'd been sick, gripped the railing, sobbing. Her friend draped an arm around her shoulders.

Where were Rachel and her baby? She probably knew her husband wasn't coming.

When a lifeboat arrived less than half full, my heart ached. Had the people in that boat tried to go back and save even one person?

One more boat arrived, filled to capacity. As the passengers were helped aboard, a *Carpathia* officer approached the crewmen directing the rescue efforts. He stood by until the last man, who wore a soaked and torn *Titanic* officer's uniform, was helped across the railing.

The *Carpathia* officer said a few words to him. As the man accepted a blanket, I recognized Mr. Lightoller, the officer who had questioned me the first time I took Marion and Richard up to the Boat Deck.

After Mr. Lightoller was led away, the *Carpathia* officer spent several minutes scanning the ocean with his binoculars. He turned and strode to the stairs that led to the wheelhouse.

To my right, a woman handed a blanket and steaming cup of coffee to an elderly lady. "That's Captain Rostron," I heard her say. "He's still looking for boats."

The crewmen who remained at the railing silently used their binoculars to search the waters. We stood and waited, all eyes on the white-capped seas for some sign of a boat, a flare, anything.

Finally, the crewmen went to the wheelhouse together.

"Wait!" a woman cried. "There has to be more!" She tried to follow them, but was held back by *Carpathia* passengers.

Are there no more lifeboats?

My skin was suddenly drenched in cold sweat. I pulled the blanket away from my head and stared at the ocean, searching, searching ... Somewhere far away, voices from the water begged and cried, pleading for help.

Then with eyes shut, I inhaled a deep breath of crisp ocean air and let it fill my lungs. I blew it out slowly, counting, like Mr. Liddle had taught me.

Oh God, please ... they must be here. Please let them be here.

Ten minutes passed. Then came the vibration of *Carpathia*'s engines through the deck's floorboards.

Everyone knew what that meant.

All survivors of the *Titanic* were now on board.

~⌒~

Some of the women refused to leave the railing. Others, including Charlotte, were led away, their sobs echoing across the deck.

Shaking, I wandered toward the dining rooms, my first task to find my family amid the seven hundred-plus people who were now scattered over the top decks of the ship.

Three *Carpathia* stewards directed us. "First class, this way. Second class, down the corridor on your right. Third class, last room on your right."

Some passengers spoke to one another and followed directions, but many looked too shocked or exhausted to even care. One young woman slumped against the far wall, weeping. A *Carpathia* passenger approached and helped her to a bench.

"Where is the ship taking us?" a woman asked a steward.

"The captain has ordered that we sail for New York, madam."

Many of those near me held onto each other for comfort. I didn't care where we went, as long as I found my family.

"What does it matter where we go?" another woman asked. "We've lost our husbands and everything we have with them."

Coming to the first room, I peeked inside the packed first-class "hospital." The room was quiet, considering its large number of occupants. The green draperies reminded me of the second-class dining room on the *City of Benares*. Tables were pushed together, draped in sheets and blankets, offering a place where passengers could lie down. Several crew members tended to those suffering from frostbite and other injuries.

Some passengers, including the Harpers, stood talking in groups. Dr. Dodge sat with a pretty woman and a boy—they must have been his family that boarded another boat. *Should I go to one of them and ask for help? But what could they do that I wasn't already doing?* I scanned the room for my family, just in case. Then I turned and left.

In the dining room that was set aside for second class, people rested in chairs or on top of more blanketed tables. Some sat against the wall. Another man examined the reddened ear of a young boy, and two crewmen lifted someone with bandaged feet.

I trudged around the room's perimeter. Children cried in haggard parents' arms or dozed in their laps. I checked to see if any were Marion or Richard, possibly separated from Mother. *And where are Mr. Hoffman and his little boys?*

Mrs. Simmons, Priscilla, and Peter sat close together against the far wall.

She knows Mother! Maybe she had seen her. "Hello, Mrs. Simmons," I said.

She reached for me with a shaky hand. "Ruth. Come here, dear."

"I'm trying to find my family." I swallowed tears and squatted beside her. "Have you seen them?"

Her face tensed. "You didn't get in the boats together?"

"No, we were separated. I saw them get in a lifeboat, but—"

"Then don't worry. You'll find them."

"Yes, I—I will." *How do I ask about her husband?* "Did Mr. Simmons—"

"He refused to get in the boat with us." She managed a weak smile. "He helped two ladies climb in and take his place."

I'd hoped that somehow he got in another boat, and my mind failed to fathom this news. Peter leaned closer to his mother and laid his head in her lap.

She squeezed my hand. "Go find your mother now. We'll talk later."

Dazed, I continued to pace around the room, checking every face, every person the doctor spoke with, everyone who entered or exited the washrooms.

"Miss Ruth!" A weak male voice called to me from a group of men who were seated at a table.

At first, I didn't think I knew the pale man who was bundled in a blanket. "Mr. Hardy!"

"I'm so glad to see you, Miss Ruth. Your family—are they all right?"

With another glance around the room, I gave a hesitant nod. "I think so. I'm still looking for them."

"If I see your mother, I'll tell her you're here."

Maybe he would have one of the answers I needed. "Mr. Hardy, do you know about the Hoffmans?"

"I saw them in the stairwell last night." He shook his head and pulled the blanket tighter. "I'm afraid that's all I know, Miss Ruth."

"Thank you." I turned away. Those poor little boys! If only I could find out what happened to them.

I recognized a few more people from Deck F or from the dining saloon and asked each one about my family. Only one woman recalled running into them while they were waiting for the lifeboats.

My entire body and mind ached. I returned to the corridor, fighting tears and fatigue. In an alcove, *Carpathia* stewards had set up a large table with cups of hot cocoa. I took one to sip and watched everyone as they passed. Calvin, our thoughtful waiter on the *Titanic*, had served hot cocoa to Marion and me a few times. Did he make it to a boat?

I'd been awake for at least twenty-four hours, but the hot liquid now warmed me enough to keep me going. *Just a bit more, just until I find Mother.*

My toes had thawed out, and I walked farther down to the room that was designated for third-class survivors. The room was the quietest of the three. Fewer people occupied it, and there weren't as many children compared to the other areas. But none of the children had blond hair or dimples—no O'Haras as far as I could see. Two women who looked to be third-class passengers themselves served coffee and soup, while three *Carpathia* crewmen attended to the sick and injured.

George waved to me from a corner table. He still wore Papa's blood-soaked handkerchief around his finger. James, who held two cups of coffee, took a seat beside him. Blankets draped their shoulders. The half of Sajni's quilt I'd given to James probably never made it out of the lifeboat.

A crewman passed by with a clipboard in his hand. "Sir," I said, "is that the passenger list?"

"Yes, miss. It's a partial list. Have you given us your name?"

"I gave it to someone earlier, but can you check for the name Becker?"

He reviewed the lists of names on both sides of two sheets of yellow paper. "I'm afraid I don't have any Beckers. I'm sorry."

"You don't have me either? I'm Ruth Becker."

"Your name must be on our other list. We're making sure we don't miss anyone." The crewman turned away.

This is so confusing. I hurried toward him. "Wait, please. What about O'Hara? From third class."

He checked again. "No, there's no one on this list by that name."

Not one? Shaking, I grabbed a chair. "Are you sure?"

"I'm quite certain this is the only list with the names of all the surviving steerage passengers. I'm terribly sorry."

Tears stung my eyes, and I blurted out one more name. "What about Wallace Hartley?"

The man lowered his clipboard and stepped closer. "Miss, several passengers have inquired about him and *Titanic*'s other orchestra members. I was told by a surviving crewman that they all played together until the last possible moment, and were not seen again."

Through shock and tears, I nodded my thanks. Then I turned to run from the room.

CHAPTER THIRTY-TWO

RMS Carpathia, Atlantic Ocean
Monday, April 15, 1912
9:15 a.m.

Where could I curl up and cry myself to sleep for the rest of my life?

I almost made it to the exit door when a flash of yellow and red caught my eye amid all the gray blankets. The boy from my lifeboat, seated in the corner with his mother, still held onto his half of Sajni's quilt—*my* quilt from another lifetime. Next to them, Rachel held her son. She waved me over, but I couldn't talk to one more person. I hurried from the room.

Mother, where are you? Ann! What happened to you? Tears flowed, blinding me. I wanted to collapse against the wall, but I had to get away from all the people.

I wiped my hands across my eyes and stumbled along the passageway until I reached the library, half-filled with *Titanic* crew members. Some ate or wrote telegraph messages, and others dozed on sofas. Fred sat in a corner with two other men and two women, all holding steaming cups of coffee. I had no strength left in me to scan the room for anyone else. As it was, my heart was breaking.

Behind some bookshelves, I found an empty sofa that faced a window. A place to rest and weep. With my blanket spread across the cushion, I removed my damp coat for the first time since Mr. Hardy had ordered us to the Boat Deck the night before.

In my nightgown, I lay down and covered myself with my coat. The window revealed puffy clouds and patches of pale blue sky, too lovely for such a day.

I pushed Ann and Mr. Hartley from my thoughts. *Where is my family? Why did Mother get into a boat with Marion and Richard and leave me on the ship? Could it be their lifeboat didn't make it?*

If ever I saw them again, I'd never complain about sharing or growing up or taking care of Marion and Richard. *I need them, and I need Papa!* I wanted so much to tell him everything. I sobbed into the scratchy blanket.

My mind was haunted by the sight of the *Titanic* plunging into the sea. I couldn't rid my head of the sound of the explosions, everything breaking apart, and the cries of those in the water. The number of lives lost was beyond imagining.

There must have been a thousand or more people—gone, just like that. Why had I been spared, especially if I was going to be alone?

In the lifeboat, I'd wanted to help those who had lost more than I did. At the time, I thought I still had my family, so all my losses seemed minor in comparison. Would I still have given away Sajni's quilt if I knew my family had perished?

My thoughts rambled, a jumble of terrifying scenes from the last ten or twelve hours, mixed with anguish and confusion and second-guessing my actions.

Exhausted, I clutched my coat and closed my eyes.

God, please. I can't think anymore. I'm empty and so tired. Show me what to do.

~⌒~

Ann and I danced in the third-class general room, faster and faster in a circle. Ocean water crashed into the room, and Ann screamed my name. Then, ever so slowly, she floated out into the sunshine. I tried to reach her, but the light was so bright I had to shield my eyes.

Music drifted in from somewhere beyond the light—beautiful music. It washed over me and through me. Somehow, the music spoke to my heart, proclaiming Ann was at peace.

I woke, startled. Where was I?

Glancing down at my coat and nightgown, the memories rushed back to mind, reminding me of the nightmare I was living.

The dream was still so clear—the flooding water, the light, and the music. I had no reason to question its message. In my gut, I knew Ann was safe in God's hands. Just as she had told me she would be.

My eyes no longer burned or felt heavy for lack of sleep. Although my limbs still ached, I felt refreshed, as though I'd slept for hours. I gathered my coat and blanket and wandered to the front of the bookshelves that faced the room.

A crewman stood near the library entrance. "Attention, please," he said. "A prayer service will take place shortly in the main dining room. All are welcome."

Fred and the others pushed back their chairs. I would go to the service and find someone I knew—maybe Rachel and her baby or perhaps Mrs. Simmons—and then I *would* find my family.

I stopped at the washroom and took a quick look in the mirror. My eyes were puffy from my crying spell. I splashed cold water on them, rinsed my dry mouth, and slid my arms back into my coat.

In the corridor, a gray-haired woman in a dark blue coat glanced at me as she passed. Then she turned around. "Dear, are you Ruth Becker?"

"Yes." How did she know my name?

Her eyes glistened as she grabbed my shoulders. "Your mother has been searching everywhere for you."

"Wh-what?"

"Come with me."

I followed at her heels as she led me to the bustling first dining room. We wove our way through *Titanic* and *Carpathia* passengers streaming in for the service.

I scanned the room ahead of her. *Didn't I check it well enough?*

Then I saw them. Against the farthest wall, Mother sat hunched with a blanket draped over her shoulders, Marion and Richard on either side of her.

I couldn't get to them fast enough, though they were barely visible through my tears.

Mother saw me coming and leaped to her feet. "Ruth! Oh, my Ruth!"

Marion jumped up. "Sissy!"

I fell in Mother's arms, then bent down and hugged Marion.

Richard wiggled and patted my head. "Boot!" I laughed and hugged him, too.

Mother thanked the lady who had led me to them. She wiped away tears of her own and joined another group near us.

Marion hugged me again. "Sissy, where was you?"

Tears spilled down Mother's cheeks. "Thank God! What happened to you? I was so worried!" She held me at arm's length. "I never meant to leave you. Someone pulled me toward the lifeboat, and the next thing I knew—"

I brushed her tears away, noticing her spectacles were missing. "It's all right. I've been looking for you all day. Why are you in *this* room? Why aren't your names on the list?"

She shook her head, her hair loose around her shoulders. "We were in another area at first—I'm not sure where—and I didn't know where I was supposed to go. There are so many people."

She looked to the doorway as more passengers entered. "I only added our names a few minutes ago, but the man said yours might be on the other list."

Marion tugged my coat sleeve. "Sissy, we went on a boat, and I didn't like it, but a nice lady showed me her toy pig, and I found the North Star!" She bounced up and down. "And I got to ride up in the rope swing."

My hands cupped her round cheeks. "Marion, when you learn to write, I'm going to buy you a journal." I turned to Mother. "How's Richard?"

"Much better than I am." She shuddered. "I hope and pray he doesn't take another turn for the worse."

I kissed Richard's forehead. "Can we send Papa a message?"

"Yes, of course." She smoothed my hair. "I didn't want to do anything until I found you."

A *Carpathia* officer stepped to a raised platform near the front of the room. "Ladies and gentlemen, many are still making their way here for the service. If you would kindly make room for them, we will begin as soon as we can."

I lifted Marion and set her feet on the bench. Mother settled Richard on her hip and made room for me between her and Marion.

My sister wrapped her arms around me and said, "I wanna find Catherine. And it's Cadie's birthday today."

I wasn't the only one who was missing the O'Hara family. I whispered in Marion's ear. "I have something for you."

I stuck my hand in my left coat pocket and pulled out my little carved hummingbird.

"I want you to keep this. It slept safe in my pocket all night."

As she gently lifted the bird from my hand, Marion's face lit up like a burst of sun through gray clouds. For once, she was speechless.

❧

Hundreds filled the dining room until no more seats were available. Some of the temporary table "beds" were separated to make extra room. *Carpathia* crew members lined the walls. *Titanic* passengers, sullen and worn, carried children, blankets, or both.

Dull eyes and sloped shoulders marked the surviving members of *Titanic's* crew as they entered the room. They formed several lines near the back and around the sides. Some gave up their seats or made room on the floor for those who were too weak or injured to stand. I looked for Calvin. As soon as we sent Papa a telegram, I would try to find out about him.

Soon, it seemed that every man, woman, and child on the *Carpathia* was present. A damp, sour odor filled the air from those who'd escaped death and endured so much. Unlike the smell on the stuffy, crowded train to Cochin, it was somehow a soothing proof of life. We'd come through a disaster that we would carry with us the rest of our lives.

Captain Rostron stepped to the platform, and people quieted the children in their arms. Others coughed or sniffed, but the room gradually fell silent.

"Let us bow our heads as we open with prayer," he began. "Oh, Lord, we come to Thee with heavy hearts for the many souls who have gone to their rest in this catastrophe. We give Thee our deepest thanks for sparing the lives of those gathered here today."

He paused, cleared his throat, and spoke with reverence. "We remember the many passengers, officers, and crew members of the *Titanic* who so selflessly gave their lives in order that others could be saved, including Captain Edward J. Smith."

Richard pulled my coat sleeve until I opened my eyes and reached for him. He stretched his little body toward mine and settled his head on my shoulder.

"We of the *Carpathia* thank Thee for guiding our ship through the icebergs in order to rescue those in the lifeboats ..."

With my head bowed against Richard's, I reflected on the past six weeks. My own ideas and plans might not have matched up with God's, but as Ann had said, there still seemed to be a plan for me, nonetheless. As with my violin, I would treasure the past but also find a way to let go and look beyond what I could see to all that lay ahead.

What Papa had told me in his office was true—putting others first was better than thinking about oneself all the time. It had a funny way of bringing about the most joy.

The Great Frank and Son were naturals at it. Ann had lived it every minute, even to the last. Mr. Hartley and his orchestra knew it, giving everything they had to help encourage those who were in the clutches of death.

Music was a gift, as Mr. Liddle had said. Ann was right—it truly was powerful.

On this long and twisted expedition, countless people had crossed my path to show me what it meant to live for others and to love them. One after another, they taught me what I might have never learned had I stayed in India. As I recalled each face, each smile, they seemed to tell me to keep going, to keep living.

As Captain Rostron led us in a hymn, I lifted my gaze to the windows that faced *Carpathia*'s stern. Rays of sunlight fanned out from behind the clouds, and the ship's wake was the only disturbance on the placid ocean's surface. Every passing minute, we added more miles between us and the RMS *Titanic*. But the love that connected us with those who now rested in the arms of God would never die.

I would always remember them. But I was alive, and I would embrace my future. It had been quite a journey since I left Guntur. But sometimes, we have to go a long way to find out who we are.

Good-bye for now, Ann. Thank you for showing me how to keep playing the music.

I promise I will.

RMS Carpathia, Atlantic Ocean
Monday, April 15, 1912
9:00 p.m.
Sky Report: A kind steward from the Carpathia has given me a few sheets of paper to begin a new journal. We head west under clear skies and starlight.

My journey continues.

THE END

EPILOGUE

Ruth Elizabeth Becker
1899-1990

Following their arrival in New York City aboard the *Carpathia*, Ruth and her family traveled by train to Benton Harbor, Michigan, where Ruth's grandparents welcomed them. Nellie refused to discuss the *Titanic* and told Ruth to never tell anyone she had been aboard the ship. Eight months later, Reverend Becker left the orphanage in Guntur and joined them. The family later moved to Wooster, Ohio.

Ruth graduated from Wooster College and became a teacher. She married Daniel Blanchard, a former classmate who shared her love for music. They moved to Kansas, where Ruth taught high school and raised two sons and a daughter.

As a young adult, Ruth never spoke of the *Titanic*, but after her retirement and a move to California, she attended reunions of *Titanic* survivors and granted interviews. A member of the Titanic Historical Society states that Ruth made delicious chocolate-chip cookies and always gave tins of them to society members when they visited.

At age ninety, Ruth took a cruise to Mexico, her first voyage since the *Titanic*. She died four months later. At her request, her ashes were scattered over the site where *Titanic* sank.

～

Marion Becker moved to San Francisco when she finished school and was quite independent. She died of tuberculosis at age thirty-six. She never married.

Richard Becker recovered from his childhood illness, thought to be a serious case of viral meningitis. He became a nightclub singer and, later, a social welfare worker. He married and had three children, and died of kidney disease at age sixty-five.

Nellie, Ruth, Richard, and Marion Becker. Taken in 1912,
shortly after the family arrived in Michigan.

DISCUSSION QUESTIONS

1. If you made a quilt like Sajni's, what symbols would you include that are unique to your family and/or culture?

2. What are some of the current events and developments Ruth discovers throughout her journey?

3. Ruth is angry with Reverend Becker for much of the journey, and yet she sees the stars and the Sky Report as a connection to him. Why do you think this is?

4. What fears is Ruth forced to face along her journey?

5. What kind of changes does Ruth undergo, and what causes those changes? Did you notice any correlation with the rocking ship, the slow drift along the Suez, or the speed of the *Titanic*?

6. Name the best qualities and the flaws found in the following characters: Michael Frank, Nellie Becker, Mr. Clayton, Ann O'Hara, and Ruth Becker.

7. If you were a passenger on *Titanic*, what would you have enjoyed the most prior to the sinking? The least?

8. What are your thoughts regarding the varied treatment of *Titanic's* passengers based on their class?

9. Why do you think so many of the passengers and crew willingly sacrificed their lives in effort to save others? If a similar disaster occurred today, do you think people would behave differently?

10. If you were in a lifeboat with strangers, how do you think you would react? What do you think of Ruth's actions, given her age and the fact that her family's safety was uncertain?

11. How does Ruth see the relationship between music, the stars, and her future?

12. How does Ruth's faith play a pivotal role in her eventual change of heart concerning her move to America?

13. Can you identify the significance of the hummingbird gift Ruth gave to Marion?

14. What does Ruth mean when she says, *Sometimes we have to go a long way to find out who we are?*

AUTHOR'S NOTE

The idea for this novel began in 2012, the 100th anniversary of the sinking of the *Titanic*. While reading through a list of survivors, the Becker family's story caught my attention. They had been on their way from India to Michigan, my home state. Ruth was separated from her mother and siblings as they boarded the lifeboats, yet she helped a sailor with a cut finger, shared her blankets, and comforted those who were with her.

What was Ruth like? How could a frightened twelve-year-old girl, alone in a boat full of strangers, act so heroically? How had she felt about leaving India? And what might have happened along the way to influence her actions in the lifeboat that terrifying night?

As I considered these questions, *The Stars in April* took shape. The book is based on true events, including the family's missionary work in India, Richard's illness, their departure by train, and the week in London prior to boarding the *Titanic*.

Facts related to the *Titanic* were carefully researched, including the ship's design, the meals, and the experience of the sinking. The story brings in additional factual details, such as life and culture in India, current world events, how the real Reverend Becker—Ruth's father—always wore white shoes, and a tea party that was truly taken over by monkeys!

As I wrote, I empathized with Ruth and how she must have felt about leaving her father and the mixed emotions that may have been involved. I pictured her watching the stars along her journey as she imagined him doing the same. A mutual love for stargazing between her and Papa became a connection across the miles, and the "Sky Report" came into being.

Bandleader Wallace Hartley's story also touched my heart, so I gave him and the rest of the *Titanic* orchestra members a key role by adding Ruth's dream of playing violin for an orchestra. The real Ruth also loved music, but she played piano rather than the violin.

In my story, Ruth meets others who were indeed aboard the *Titanic*, such as Henry Sleeper Harper, Mr. Hardy, and Dr. Dodge, but her interactions with them are fictionalized. Ann O'Hara is a fictional character, although several large Irish families were on board, and most of them perished.

The Beckers did travel to Southampton aboard the *City of Benares*, although all of the characters that were on board in the story, including The Great Frank and Son, are fictional.

Nellie, Marion, and Richard were in Lifeboat 11. Fashion buyer Edith Russell brought her musical pig into the same lifeboat and entertained the children aboard, including Richard and Marion. The couple with the baby who climbed into Boat 13 at the last minute were missionaries Albert and Sylvia Caldwell, who were returning to America from Siam, and their son, Alden.

On *Titanic*, Mr. Hoffman and his sons did in fact occupy the cabin across from the Becker family, and Ruth played with the real-life Michel Jr. and Edmond. The boys' last name was Navratil, but their father assumed the name Hoffman for the voyage. He died in the sinking, after putting his sons in the care of a woman who was boarding a lifeboat. The boys were known as the "*Titanic* orphans," until their mother, in France, recognized them from a newspaper photo.

During my research, I learned an amazing story while corresponding with Floyd Andrick, a member of the Titanic Historical Society. Ruth had always believed the *Titanic* orphans did not survive. But in 1987, while attending a *Titanic* anniversary convention, she was reunited with Michel Navratil—seventy-five years after they had last seen each other.

I hope this story provides a true sense of what the *Titanic* passengers and crew experienced. But more than that, I hope it portrays Ruth Becker's bravery and fighting spirit as she faced major life changes, an incredible voyage she would never forget, and embraced the God-given strength to move forward into an uncertain future.

CONSTELLATIONS OF THE NORTHERN HEMISPHERE

Constellations are clusters of bright stars that form shapes in the sky, depending on your point of view from Earth. Ancient societies saw patterns among the stars and associated them with stories. The first references date back 6,000 years. Later civilizations considered the stars themselves to be divine.

The Greek astronomer Ptolemy identified forty-eight constellations in the second century. In 1920, the International Astronomical Union (IAU) compiled and officially designated eighty-eight constellations. Read more at www.iau.org.

While Ruth was in India and during her journey, she and her father would have seen many constellations of the northern hemisphere, such as these listed here and others she describes in the story. They would have seen circumpolar constellations, which circle the North and South Poles and never rise or set—and seasonal constellations, which can be seen at different times as the earth rotates and makes its year-long orbit around the sun.

To learn more amazing star facts, visit Windows to the Universe: www.windows2universe.org.

Aquila (the eagle): Aquila, the celestial eagle, is one of the three constellations that have bright stars forming the Summer Triangle. When you look in the sky and see the three stars that form a triangle with perfectly straight lines, that triangle symbolizes part of Aquila's wings. To the ancient Greeks, Aquila was the servant of Zeus, keeper of his thunderbolts, and he had the power to bring rain. Aquila may also be the great eagle that devoured Prometheus' liver as punishment for giving fire to humans. The eagle was rewarded a place in the sky.

Argo Navis (the ship): The Argo was a ship that was a gift from Athena, whose captain was named Jason. Its maidenhead had the power of speech and assisted Jason during his adventures, and it was placed in the stars as a memorial of the constellation Argo.

Bootes (the herdsman): Bootes rides through the sky during late spring and early summer, and modern star-gazers identify this constellation by its kite shape and the red, supergiant star Arcturus at the "kite's tail." The brightness of Arcturus is more than 100 times our sun, and it is the fourth brightest object in the sky. Arcturus is thirty-six light years away (close for a star). To ancient Romans, Bootes represented a shepherd, and the seven stars that make up this constellation are the same stars within the Big Dipper, which was considered to be the herdsman's plow.

Leo (the lion): Leo is one of the oldest recognized constellations and contains several bright stars. Hercules was said to have killed the lion with his bare hands when it terrorized the land. The brightest star in the constellation is Regulus, sometimes called the Lion's Heart.

Ursa Major (the great bear): According to mythology, the god Zeus turned the maiden Callisto and his son Arcas into bears and hurled them into the sky to protect them from his wife Hera. Ursa Major is the third largest constellation, and its brightest stars form the Big Dipper. The handle of the Dipper is the bear's tail.

Virgo (the young maiden): The young maiden is Demeter (also known as Ceres), goddess of crops, vegetation, fertility, and harvest. Her daughter, Persephone, was kidnapped by Hades while picking flowers. After a failed attempt to rescue Persephone, Zeus stepped in and ordered that Persephone stay with Hades for three months of the year. During the three months with Hades, Demeter suspended the growth of plants which is now called winter. The appearance of the constellation signals the return of Persephone to Demeter.

PHOTOS

Ruth Becker posing for her photograph at age fifteen.

Ruth is missing from this photograph of a hospital groundbreaking ceremony in July 1911. Nellie and Allen Becker (far right) attend with Marion and Richard at ages four and one.

Missionary families in Guntur, India. Ruth Becker sits in the front row, third child from the right. In the back row, Rev. Allen Becker stands on the far left. Nellie Becker is third from the left.

RMS *Titanic* ready to depart from Southampton, England, on April 10, 1912.

Titanic Captain Edward J. Smith, shown here aboard the *Olympic* in 1911.

Wallace Hartley, *Titanic* violinist and orchestra leader.

Drawing of *Titanic's* Grand Staircase from the White Star Line 1912 promotional booklet.

The First-Class Dining Saloon.

A lifeboat carries *Titanic* survivors.

Titanic **survivors recovering aboard the *Carpathia*.**

The "*Titanic* Orphans," Michel Navratil (age 4) and Edmond Navratil (age 2). Photo taken before they were identified. Their father assumed the name Louis Hoffman when boarding the ship and used their nicknames, Lolo and Mamon. He died in the sinking.

Titanic survivors at 75th anniversary event, April 10, 1987, Wilmington Radisson Hotel, Wilmington, Delaware. (Reunion of Ruth Becker [front row holding white shawl] and Michel Navratil [back row, far right].)

**Ruth Becker Blanchard with Titanic Historical Society member
Floyd Andrick, September 9, 1984, Santa Barbara, CA.**

Ruth was once asked, "Do you have any advice or suggestions on how to live a successful and full life?" To which she answered:

"Keep busy. Tackle things that are worthwhile in life. Keep believing in yourself. Meet any problem full of confidence so that you have the courage and the strength and the know-how to face it. If you think success you will be a success. Make a commitment and stick to it. Stay healthy and have a sense of humor. Don't take life too seriously. Spread your love and you will be loved back."

~Ruth Becker Blanchard

BIBLIOGRAPHY AND RESOURCES

Allen, Charles. *Raj: A Scrapbook of British India, 1877-1947*. St. Martin's Press, New York, 1978.

Brewster, Hugh and Coulter, Laurie. *882 and ½ Amazing Answers to Your Questions About the Titanic*. Madison Press Books, Aurora, Ontario, 1998.

Lynch, Don. *Titanic: An Illustrated History*. Hyperion Press, New York, 1992.

Tibballs, Geoff, editor. *Voices from the Titanic*. Skyhorse Publishing, New York, 2012.

Chrisp, Peter. *Explore Titanic*. Carlton Books, New York, 2011.

Beesley, Lawrence. *The Loss of the SS Titanic* (kindle edition). Harper Perennial Publishing, 2012. Originally published in 1912.

Geller, Judith. *Titanic: Women and Children First*. W. W. Norton, New York, 1998.

Gracie, Archibald. *Titanic: A Survivor's Story* (kindle edition). The History Press, 2011. Originally published in 1913.

Lord, Walter. *A Night to Remember* (kindle edition). Open Road Media, 2012. Originally published in 1958.

Robertson, Morgan. *Futility, or the Wreck of the Titan* (kindle edition). Amazon Digital Services. Originally published in 1898.

Exhibits:

Titanic: The Exhibition at Henry Ford Museum, Dearborn, MI, 2012. http://www.rmstitanic.net/exhibitions.html

Titanic Experience, Orlando, Florida, 2016.

Titanic: The Exhibition at Sloan Museum, Flint, MI, 2017.

Articles:

British Slang Words. http://www.essortment.com/british-slang-words-40442.html. 7/8/2013.

Children of the Titanic. http://www.freewebs.com/titanic-children/ruthbecker.html. 4/25/2012.

Circus Talk. http://www.pbs.org/opb/circus/circus-life/talking-circus/

Edwardian Slang. http://www.edwardianpromenade.com/resources/a-glossary-of-slang/

Exclusive: The India-born family aboard the Titanic. http://www.rediff.com/news/slide-show/slide-show-1-titanic-has-an-india-connection/20120412.html. 7/11/2012.

Guntur, India. http://www.aboutguntur.com/

Languages spoken in Guntur. http://www.mapsofindia.com/andhra-pradesh/languages.html

Passenger lists leaving UK 1890-1960. http://www.genesreunited.co.uk/

Popular Words and Phrases from 1912. http://quotidianiceman.wordpress.com/2013/09/23/popular-words-and-phrases-from-1912. 7/8/2013.

Ruth Elizabeth Becker. http://www.encyclopedia-titanica.org/titanic-survivor/ruth-elizabeth-becker.html 4/25/2012.

South Indian Food. http://www.food-india.com/region/southIndian.html. 6/6/2012.

Typical Food of India. http://traveltips.usatoday.com/typical-food-india-11306.html. 6/6/2012.

Twelve-Year-Old Ruth Becker's Courage and Faith Helped Her Survive the Sinking of the Titanic. http://voices.yahoo.com/twelve-year-old-ruth-beckers-courage-faith-helped-10810705.html. 6/8/2012.

Victorian Slang Terms. http://mentalfloss.com/article/53529/56-delightful-victorian-slang-terms-you-should-be-using.

Viral Meningitis http://www.meningitis.org/disease-info/types-causes/viral-meningitis. 7/14/2012.

Photographs:

Please see my blog at www.peggywirgau.com for stories and more photographs of the *Titanic* and her passengers and crew.

Luci (Small) Goodman, "Marion Louise Becker Image Two," 1912, photo, Titanic Project, WikiTree.com. https://www.wikitree.com/photo/jpg/Becker-2202-1

"Ruth Becker," photo. Reprinted from Wikimedia Commons. Public domain in the United States. https://commons.wikimedia.org/wiki/File:Ruth_Becker.jpg#/ media/File:Ruth_Becker.jpg.

"Groundbreaking Ceremony," July 1911, photo, Archives Collection, Evangelical Lutheran Church of America, Illinois. ELCA.org. Used by permission.

"Missionary families," photo, Archives Collection, Evangelical Lutheran Church of America, Illinois. ELCA.org. Used by permission.

"Titanic at the docks of Southampton," 1912, photo. Reprinted from Wikimedia Commons. No known copyright restrictions. https://commons.wikimedia.org/wiki/File:Titanic_in_ Southampton_(cropped).jpg.

"Captain Edward J. Smith, Aboard the *Olympic*, 1911," photo. Reprinted from Wikimedia Commons. No known copyright restrictions. https://commons.wikimedia.org/wiki/File:EJ_ Smith2.jpg.

"Wallace Henry Hartley, Band Leader on the RMS *Titanic*," photo. Reprinted from Wikimedia Commons. Public Domain in the United States. https://commons.wikimedia.org/wiki/ File:Wallace_Henry_Hartley.jpg.

White Star Line, "Grand Staircase of the RMS *Titanic*," 1911, drawing, *White Star Line Triple Screw Steamers Booklet*. Reprinted from Wikimedia Commons. Public domain in the United States. https://commons.wikimedia.org/wiki/ File:Drawing_of_the_Grand_Staircase_onboard_the_RMS_ Titanic_from_the_1912_promotional_booklet.jpg.

"Photograph of the main dining room on the salon deck of the ill-fated White Star Liner 'Titanic,'" 1912, photo. Reprinted from Wikimedia Commons. No known copyright restrictions. https://upload.wikimedia.org/wikipedia/commons/a/a6/ Photograph_of_the_main_dining_room_on_the_salon_ deck_of_the_ill-fated_White_Star_Liner_%22Titanic%22_..._ LCCN96503966.jpg.

"Titanic-lifeboat.gif," 1912, photo. Reprinted from Wikimedia Commons. Public domain in the United States. https://upload. wikimedia.org/wikipedia/commons/ thumb/0/0c/Titanic-lifeboat.gif/1280px-Titanic-lifeboat.gif.

"Titanic survivors aboard the *Carpathia*," 1912, photo. Reprinted from Wikimedia Commons. Public domain in the United States. https://upload.wikimedia.org/ wikipedia/commons/5/5a/Titanic_survivors_on_the_ Carpathia%2C_1912.jpg.

"Louis & Lola?—TITANIC survivors," 1912, photo, George Grantham Bain Collection, Library of Congress, flickr.com. No known copyright restrictions. https://www.flickr.com/ photos/library_of_congress/2535973345/ or https://commons. wikimedia.org/w/index.php?curid=53642899

Floyd Andrick, "Ruth Becker at Titanic Survivors 75th Anniversary Event," 1987, photo, Floyd Andrick personal collection. Used by permission.

Floyd Andrick, "Floyd Andrick with Ruth Becker," 1984, photo, Floyd Andrick personal collection. Used by permission.

Illustration:

"The Journey of Ruth Becker, March-April 1912," Illustration, Laurel Childress, 2021.

Recording:

Mendelssohn, Felix. *Spring Song*. https://www.youtube.com/ watch?v=8mz5Rtx-Eu0.

Songs:

Sarah Flower Adams, *Nearer, My God, to Thee*, 1841.

Sabine Baring-Gould, *Onward, Christian Soldiers*, 1871.

Irving Berlin, *Alexander's Ragtime Band*, 1911.

Irving Berlin, *After the Honeymoon*, 1907.

Irving Berlin, *Angels*, 1907.

Seymour Brown, *Oh, You Beautiful Doll*, 1911.

Frederic Chopin, *Nocturnes*, 1827-1846.

W. A. Fletcher, *Farther Along*, 1911.

Wallie Herzer, *Everybody Two-Step*, 1912.

Archibald Joyce, *Songe d'Automne*, 1908.

Richard Leveridge, *The Roast Beef of Old England*, n.d.

Lowell Mason, *Mary Had a Little Lamb*, n.d.

Oley Speaks, *On the Road to Mandalay*, 1907.

William Whiting, *Eternal Father, Strong to Save*, 1860.

Websites:

Encyclopedia Titanica. http://www.encyclopedia-titanica.org/

International Astronomy Union. http://www.iau.org;
    http://www.iau.org/news/pressreleases/detail/iau1603/

P&O Heritage. http://www.poheritage.com/

Titanic Historical Society. http://www.titanic1.org/

Titanic Pages. http://www.titanicpages.com/

Vintage Victorian. http://www.vintagevictorian.com/
    costume_1912.html